David Bacon

MANIFEST

AUSTIN MACAULEY PUBLISHERS
LONDON * CAMBRIDGE * NEW YORK * SHARJAH

Copyright © David Bacon 2024

The right of David Bacon to be identified as author of this work has been asserted by the author in accordance with sections 77 and 78 of the Copyright, Designs and Patents Act 1988.

All rights reserved. No part of this publication may be reproduced, stored in a retrieval system, or transmitted in any form or by any means, electronic, mechanical, photocopying, recording, or otherwise, without the prior permission of the publishers.

Any person who commits any unauthorised act in relation to this publication may be liable to criminal prosecution and civil claims for damages.

This is a work of fiction. Names, characters, businesses, places, events, locales, and incidents are either the products of the author's imagination or used in a fictitious manner. Any resemblance to actual persons, living or dead, or actual events is purely coincidental.

A CIP catalogue record for this title is available from the British Library.

ISBN 9781035866786 (Paperback)
ISBN 9781035866793 (ePub e-book)

www.austinmacauley.com

First Published 2024
Austin Macauley Publishers Ltd®
1 Canada Square
Canary Wharf
London
E14 5AA

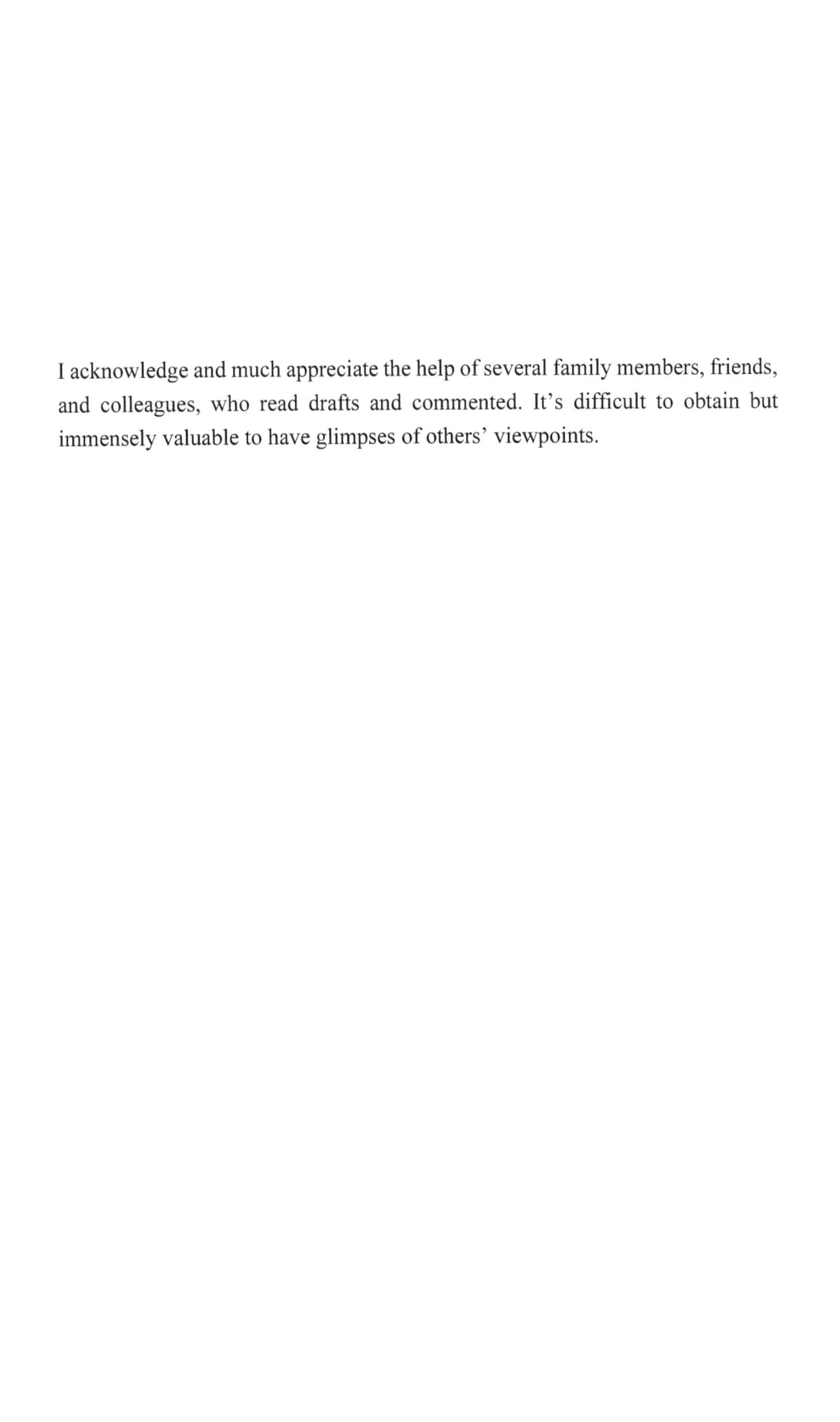

I acknowledge and much appreciate the help of several family members, friends, and colleagues, who read drafts and commented. It's difficult to obtain but immensely valuable to have glimpses of others' viewpoints.

Table of Contents

My Story: How It Started	7
What Had Been Happening: Will	22
What Had Been Happening: Guy	55
What Had Been Happening: Sid	103
What Had Been Happening: Francis	142
My Story: How It Finished	165

My Story: How It Started

The fleshy face with dead eyes and droopy moustache reminded me of that Kitchener poster. At least he wasn't jabbing a gloved finger at me over the table between us. "Tell me everything that happened."

"I don't *know* everything that happened."

He leant back in his chair with a professional police air of disbelief. "Ah, you're an expert in evidence law, are you?"

The other man stirred, seated sideways to us. Had introduced himself as detective superintendent someone. Up to then, he had been looking at me. Now, he shifted his gaze.

Both men were large. Kitchener did it mainly vertically. Super concentrated more on the horizontal. Kitchener took the hint and suppressed his incredulity. He sat forward again with, aggressively, "OK, then tell me what you *witnessed*."

Presumably Super is senior. Kitchener was just a sergeant.

"I was with Roger Ainsworth and Bill Johnson, fitting out the 120-foot walkway. Guy was with the other three, building the legs up above us. That is, Mr Beardsley. He came down to my level to announce the midday break. He must have jumped down from the leg strut. I heard him land on the walkway behind me. So far, it hasn't been worth rigging ladders any higher. We're still climbing the leg struts above the walkway. But we have temporary ladders rigged up to 120 foot. Guy reminded us to make everything safe before coming down. I said sure thing, or words to that effect, and turned back to finish what I was doing.

"He had this trick, getting down from a shift quickly, of sliding down a rope. He wrapped an arm and leg round it, slid down fast to begin with, and then braked just as he reached the ground. Once we were above a certain height, he would keep a rope fixed for this purpose. He wouldn't allow anyone else to use it. But then none of us wanted to."

"Did this trick of his comply with regulations for builders?"

"Probably not. We all thought it was a stupid bit of showing off. But he was our boss. Everyone in the company knew he did it, but no one stopped him. Another thing, word got round when we were on a job. I've seen people gather towards the end of a shift just to watch him. Perhaps to see him get killed." That was a stupid thing to say, but it didn't seem to bother Kitchener.

"You mean you do this dangerous work without any official regulations?"

"I don't know if there are legally enforced requirements. Our company doesn't let anyone climb until they fully understand the techniques we use, both manufacture and construction. The boss of each team is responsible for making sure everyone works safely. And no one is forced to do it. There's plenty of work in the company without having to climb. We on the erection teams do it willingly. In fact, we enjoy it."

"OK then. He said this thing about making everything safe, and you turned back to what you were doing?"

What Guy had said was routine for him. It was unlikely we'd leave something behind which could cause an accident. We were professional steel erectors and we checked things as we went along. We were protecting our own safety. No one else has any business up one of our constructions until it is finished, and all the safety features are in place. Just in case something happened, however, Guy could always say he had reminded us. There is nothing wrong in reminding people about safety, however ironic this now seemed in his case.

"Yes, I had just turned round again and was getting down to work on the flooring when there was a loud scream. By the time I got to the handrail and looked over, Guy had hit the ground."

"What did you do then?"

Perhaps it was natural he didn't want me to expand on the scream. Like most people, I suppose, he probably viewed a scream as just a scream. But this one wasn't. I have never heard anything like it. It was a savage animal outpouring of rage and hate. The scream of someone who has lost and can't do anything about it. A curse thrown at an enemy. A cry to the heavens against an unjust fate, the despair of unfulfilled revenge. Guy took liberties with our feelings as it suited him, but he wasn't basically a shouter. He was outspoken and had a rough voice with an abrasive edge. But he didn't need to raise it, except to shout up or down steelwork. It surprised me he could make such a sound. Of course, he had no need to protect his vocal cords at that point.

But Kitchener didn't know about that and didn't ask. After all, he only told me to say what I had *witnessed*. Do you witness a scream? I was the last to be questioned. Had any of the others tried to describe that scream?

"We were shook up. Rog and Bill were just clutching the rail and looking down. I looked up to the others. Al and John had started down the leg. One of them said 'Blimey what happened?' I can't remember who. Sid had just come down from the gin pole. He seemed frozen. I noted that Guy's rope was still in place. I—"

"Hold it there. What's a gin pole?"

Yes, of course. This guy's never put together anything more daring than a case. "It's sort of a temporary crane. Our kind of steel construction is usually built up with pre-assembled sections. Ten feet or so. Our gin pole on this job is a section of lighter-weight mast. You clamp or lash it to the top of where you've got to, so it sticks out above you. It has a pulley at its top. It's strong enough to hoist the next section and get it clamped in place. Then you move the gin pole to the top of that section and keep going."

Kitchener's brow darkened. Probably practises in a mirror. "That sounds dodgy. Is it what you're supposed to? Why not use a proper crane?"

"A crane that can lift sections from the ground to the final height of this tower, 280 feet, would be very expensive. And you might not be able to get it onto the site. Gin-poling is a well-established method. It's widely used."

"And what's this business of Mr Beardsley sliding down a rope? If he started off fast, and then slowed himself, wouldn't the friction burn his hands?"

"It's a steel-wire rope, not the normal sort made of manila or sisal or whatever. It's kept a bit greasy to prevent rust, so there's less friction. Guy would wrap a rag around his forearm but didn't bother about his legs. Our dungarees tend to be messy anyway."

I noticed for the first time that Super was jotting in what looked like a journalist's notebook. Moreover, from the way his hand moved he was taking it down in shorthand. Our office manager does shorthand. She can take dictation as fast as anyone is likely to talk, at least when trying to compose a sensible letter. She demonstrated it to me once, just for interest. It's based on what the words sound like. You work out the spelling later. Funny for the senior man to be taking the notes. Perhaps he'd been a journalist before joining the force. So, anything I say may be taken down and used in evidence against me. But no one said I was under arrest.

"OK. You were a bit shook up, and someone said blimey. What happened next?"

The crew had in fact been somewhat more eloquent. Roger had observed, 'I just knew that would happen one day', although he had never, in my hearing at least, mentioned this belief earlier. Bill expressed the opinion that it served the stupid bugger right. When Al got down to the walkway, he maintained his normal breezy manner with a cheerful 'Ha! He won't do that again' and John maintained his reputation for thoughtfulness with, 'That seems a safe assumption'. But how much of all this would be relevant? and should I be expected to remember it all, word for word? For some reason, I did remember it, quite clearly.

"I told everyone to carry on down, reminding them to have only one man at a time on each ladder."

"Why?"

"Why go down?"

"No, why one at a time?"

"Oh. The ladders are strong enough to take more, but they flex with your weight. You get used to how it flexes for you, but someone else's flexing can be upsetting."

Yes, we do have our own private rules, and break them occasionally if there is a reason and it can be done safely, but it hadn't then been a good time to take liberties. Another point was by that time there had been institute staff looking up at us.

"And you were the boss once Mr Beardsley was dead?"

"I was his deputy, yes." In fact, the very first thing I remember after the scream was from Roger. He had looked carefully down at Guy's corpse and then asked me, 'Are you going to be our boss now?'

"So, they all went down. You were the last man down?"

"The first thing I did was go up the leg and check the anchoring of Guy's rope. It was clamped up tight, as I expected. I also wondered whether it could have snagged on something and then shaken loose when his weight came on it, but there was nothing to make that happen."

"Could one of the men up the leg have loosened the knot such that the rope slipped down a bit and then tightened again?"

"This is a *steel* rope. It is made from many thin strands of wire. You can't tie a knot in it. Guy's rope was bent round a thimble and clamped back, and the thimble shackled to a strut."

"OK, but someone could still have loosened it, couldn't they?"

"No. The rope is far too stiff to slip without completely removing the clamps, and that means a spanner on two nuts on each clamp. I think there are three clamps. The shackle bolt had its safety wire in place. That would be a pliers and spanner job. There simply was no time for anyone to arrange the rope to look OK until Guy got on it and then slip. And the rope would then have fallen with Guy. To get it back in place would mean hoisting the end with our pulley system. Nothing like this could have taken place in the time available, and we would all have seen it."

The tone of this interrogation was starting to rattle me. We were building a specialised mast in the grounds of a government research institute. Something to do with meteorology. It was obviously an accident. Guy had run this stunt of his just too long. Could old Kich here think we were all in on plot to fake an accident, even the scientists? Some of them had rushed outside when they heard the scream, and some of those went straight back inside when they saw what was on the ground.

"But unlike the other men you sent down, you went up to check the rope. Didn't you think to go down and see if there was anything to be done to help Mr Beardsley?"

"He was dead."

"Ah, so you're a doctor too, are you?" The super stirred again, but Sergeant Kitchener would not be put off now. "Qualified to pronounce a person dead? From 120 feet?"

I looked at him carefully. Yes, about my age. But in 1914 he had been a policeman, a reserved occupation. No white feather to be feared. An important and respected uniform. For that matter, why hadn't I thought of that? For all the news and comments flying around about the arms race and continental politics, many of us just hadn't believed it would come to war. Not a big one, anyway. I spoke slowly and clearly.

"In the trenches, our heads were the part of us most exposed to shell fragments or snipers. We did not even get helmets until late 1915." He wasn't staring into my face now but looking down at the table. He understood the point I was making, but I continued even slower and clearer: "*I know what brains look like when they have been bashed out.*"

He was still looking down. "How do I know you didn't go up the leg to fix the rope properly, with no one to watch what you were doing, and no one timing how long you took up there, apparently?"

This made me angry. It might not be sensible, but hang it. "I doubt whether I could ever understand how *you* know anything."

Super broke in for the first time. "How do *I* know you didn't?"

I took a deep breath. Is this routine after an accident? What's got into them?

"Go up and look how the rope is anchored. To arrange it to slip with Guy's weight you would have to remove the clamps and partially bend it out of the thimble. I'd have had to do that before anyone else got there to see what I was doing. In fact, Guy and the other three went straight up to where they were working at the beginning of our day. *And,* as I've said, with Guy's weight the rope would have fallen to the ground. I would then have had to get the ground crew to hoist it back up so I could anchor it again. Perhaps 15 minutes if all went well, probably longer, *and* watched by the whole crew and several people from the institute."

Sergeant took it up again. "You didn't like him, did you?"

They said at the beginning they just wanted to get the facts straight. '*Just what happened, please.*' They now seemed to want to pin murder on me. Perhaps they've tried it on each of the others. Wonder how they got on. I thought for a bit, because I didn't greatly like Guy, but that wasn't the whole story.

"He was a good gang foreman. He knew how to put steel up. He was allowed to choose his men, he understood our strengths and weaknesses, and distributed work accordingly. Look, there was competition to get on his team, because we got the good jobs, finished them on time, and they paid us well. But he was personally unpleasant. He led a good team, we did well on it, but he verbally abused us in the process. Mainly sarcasm, snide remarks, innuendoes. Sometimes crudities, although he wasn't normally vulgar. I don't think any of us liked him, but we worked under him since we did all right from it. We just put up with his manners."

"You were his deputy. Right? Second-in-command. Yes?"

"The recognised stand-in when Guy was not there. By no means, his automatic successor. That's up to the company."

Super spoke for a second time. "Thank you, Mr Butcher, that will be all for now."

"What do you mean 'for now'? Will you want to do more of this questioning? How on earth could it have been anything except an accident?"

"We may need your cooperation later. Please just continue as you would have done."

It was about 4:30 of a summer's afternoon. The others were waiting for me outside. I was the last to be questioned and thought they might have gone by now. John was looking more thoughtful than normal. "Tone, Stephen said he was coming here to see us, didn't he? No one's turned up."

They call me 'Tone' to avoid confusion with Tony Baker, the general manager at WIS. I call him 'Anthony' to hint they could then call me 'Tony'.

But Stephen disappearing like that made me think. He knew the country all around these parts. I had used the institute's telephone to report to the company immediately after the accident, about four hours ago. Stephen would have driven here in no more than an hour. "And no one else has been in touch from Wiz?"

"No."

Super had been behind me, listening. "Is 'wiz' your company?"

"It's William Ingalls Steel, but that's how we say it."

"And this is Stephen Adams who hasn't turned up? At around midday, he said he would drive here to check things out and hasn't arrived yet. Is that it?"

I didn't know how he had got Stephen's name, but the police could have been speaking to WIS, or even gone there. "Yes, apparently."

"You're all staying in the village, are you? Will you be back in the morning?"

"We've had no instructions from the company. Are we free to continue working on the site, if that's what they want us to do? Do you need any more inspection of the scene? You haven't sent anyone up to look at the anchoring of Mr Beardsley's rope yet, have you?" with a slightly malicious tone.

"Er, no." He might just have run into a shortage of bobbies willing to climb up there. "I will need to talk to colleagues before you go back to work. You would be cooperating with the police if you were all back here in the morning but stay on the ground until we get word to you, please."

The institute let me use their telephone again, and I got through to Anthony Baker. I told him we hadn't seen any sign of Stephen.

"You've finished with the police, have you?"

"I'd say they seem to have finished with us, at least for now. They were rather pointed in their questioning." I hoped the Super-man *was* listening. "What should we do now?"

There was a pause before Anthony replied. He did a long 'Hmm' to let me know he was still on the line and thinking about it. Then, "Please go back to your lodgings for the night, return to the site in the morning, but stay on the ground until I arrive. If the work can continue, I'll bring reinforcements. If not, I'll bring you all back."

"That's sort of what the police said."

"Well, I hope you have a good night. This is all very difficult, and we appreciate the position you're in. Hope it's not too bad for you. I'll try to find out what's happened to Stephen."

He's a decent bloke, Anthony. He could understand we were skewered. We said goodbye until the morning and hung up.

As we gathered to leave, Kitchener and Super were also making for their car. The sergeant turned to me and gestured for us to step away from the rest for a quiet word. I was intrigued. Was he going to give me a clue why their interrogation was so probing? Not exactly. We stopped and he circled a finger at me as though just remembering something. He spoke calmly and conversationally. "You know, you remind me of a Kraut I met once. He shot my mate. With a dum-dum." He did not imitate the clear-slow delivery I had adopted earlier so that the dimmest intellect would understand. He did not even parody it. As though it was the most ordinary recollection there could be: "I stuck my bayonet right in his guts, I did."

I believed him. What he said had the ring of authenticity. He treated it as part of life, the part called 'war'. People had been shoving sharp things into their enemies for thousands of years. Just a normal part of war, which is a normal part of life, from time to time.

I had misjudged him. We stared at each other. I wasn't going to apologise, but I acknowledged him with a shallow nod, and turned back to what was now, at least temporarily, my squad.

It was a strange evening. Although we were spread around the village between the two pubs and a couple of lodgings, we all had dinner in the Dog and Duck, which had the best kitchen. The staff had a lot of questions. Mainly sympathetic, but some wanted to know why Guy had been allowed to slide down his rope. While he had been doing it without anything untoward, it had been an unofficial feature of the company. Something to tell other people about. It might even have increased our sales a little. Now that the performance had killed its impresario it reflected badly on the company. I'd heard somewhere that a few opportunists were setting themselves up as professional advisors on how a company's activities will affect public opinion. Apparently, they charge remarkably high fees. There are no recognised qualifications in the subject, so they just claim expertise. I wondered what they would have said about Guy's behaviour. That is, *before* his fall.

We had a quiet dinner. We were all in various ways upset. It was bad enough to have had a fatal accident, but with Guy gone we were unsure of our future as the company's top construction team. What's more, all of us had been questioned more aggressively than seemed appropriate. And then Stephen appeared to have got lost somewhere. He'd been to the institute several times. He wouldn't lose his way. And the car was with the AA. If he'd had a breakdown, he would have been rescued by now. Maybe it was a long walk to the nearest AA telephone box, but it couldn't have been that far. We compared notes. Our interrogations had been similar, but they were harder on the men up the leg at the time, but then most so with me, who wasn't. The consensus was that something had gone wrong somewhere. Not a difficult conclusion to reach. There were a few attempts at enforced jollity, but they died out quickly. It wasn't an occasion for dark humour.

It took a long time to get to sleep that night. I couldn't stop running through the interrogation in my head. Had I been wrong to gloss over the various minor details? Particularly just who said what. Would my bit of petulance come back to bite me in some later police procedure? I tried to tell myself they were indeed only insignificant details. They couldn't matter. Guy had been dancing too near the edge of a cliff for too long and had at last slipped over. Then I started worrying about WIS. Would the company be subject to an investigation? What would my position be as Guy's deputy? Some days later it depressed me to reflect that while waiting for sleep my mind never turned to what the day's events would mean for Deidre and her children.

Next morning, we turned up at the institute at our normal time. We hung around for a while, until it was noticed that we were one short. "Hey, where's Sailor?" someone asked. That reminded John, who said before going to sleep he thought he'd heard Sid's motorbike growling off somewhere with its normal clatter. Good old Sailor. If he saw no point in obeying an instruction, right, he would go his own way.

Sailor Sid was both proud of his bike and very fond of it. As far as we knew it was the only love in his life. It was an ex-W.D. Triumph, thousands of which, he claimed, had been known as 'Trusty' in France for the model's reliability. It was advanced, with a proper gearbox and free-engine clutch. The latest thing, in 1915. We were now in 1922, but he still loved it.

Roger had asked him once what makes it so advanced. 'Don't cars have gearboxes and clutches?' Roger knew about cars but couldn't afford one.

Sid put him right. "The previous model the year before simply had a belt from the crankshaft to the rear wheel. When the engine was stopped the bike was stopped. When the engine was going round, then the bike was going along. Simple and reliable, but, well, a bit inconvenient."

"But how on earth did you start and stop?"

"I asked them at the place selling them. They were a good deal cheaper than the later model. You can start various ways. One is to put it up on its rear stand and use the pedals to get the engine turning over, and then release the exhaust-valve lifter. If it fires, push it off the stand and off you go, all rather sudden like. But in France that was a feature. It worked well in mud, since the back wheel slipped and then got a grip. And from what people say there was a lot of mud in France. Or you could hold the exhaust-valve open, pedal like mad, and then release it when you've got up a bit of speed. Or you could remove the push-bike pedals and chain if you don't like them, and just push and run beside it to get up speed and then jump aboard. I tried all of these, but in the end I paid extra for the later model. It takes a lot of ingenuity to fit a gearbox and clutch into a motorbike frame, but it's worth it. And you get a kick-start, and that's right handy. Well, footy, I suppose. Oh, the best way to stop the old model was just switch off the magneto. That helps the braking, too."

"How many gears does yours have?"

"Three. Obviously, there isn't a reverse. And there are four horses."

"Really? Not all cars have much more than that. It must be exciting."

"That's why I like it."

Interestingly, under the circumstances, it was Guy who had tipped Sid off that they were selling them cheap in Nottingham when Sid was getting demobbed. The big advantage of having a motorbike to Sid was independence. The rest of us serfs accepted company transport to where we had to work, and grateful for it. But Sid just set sail after his own fashion.

It was amazing how little harm his somewhat mutinous attitude caused. I think he had enough sense to know how far he could go and get away with it. We didn't think his absence would matter right now. He had no reason to run away from anything. However, we sheep, obedient to our instructions, were back at the institute, remaining on the ground, and awaiting whatever would next befall us.

During which, we had some entertainment. A young police constable turned up on a pedal-cycle, with a rope over his shoulder. He greeted us politely but briefly, giving the impression that he wasn't sure whether he should speak to us, as characters under suspicion. Then he went over to the foot of the tower and looked up. The rope looked brand-new. Presumably it was intended as a climbing aid. He shuffled it in his hands for a while, and then tried to uncoil it, resulting in a major tangle. It was obvious he couldn't see how to use it. In the end, he overcame his scruples and asked for help. He had been sent to inspect Guy's steel rope. What do we normally do about safety?

Under the circumstances, it was a faintly ridiculous question. As gently as possible I explained our technique: climb carefully and hold on tight. Our colleague had his accident because he had neglected these rules. "Take my advice, that rope will only get in your way. You would have to carry it up, and you would spend most of the time tying knots and then untying them, and probably getting tangled up in it. Just be careful. Everything up there can take your weight."

He seemed reassured by this. He dropped the tangled rope and set off up the first ladder. This was the longest, a single heavy-duty bolted-up length. It stretched through what always seemed a lot of empty space up to the 80-foot walkway. If you weren't used to it, the amount of flexing around halfway could be alarming. His ascent slowed considerably during this middle region. I quietly asked everyone not to call up to him, nor make fun in any way. He obviously wasn't used to climbing this sort of structure, and yet was bravely doing what he saw as his duty. Or maybe foolishly following inappropriate instructions. We approved. After all, any of us might be frightened if asked to disarm a dangerous criminal. It took him a while, but he reached the 80-foot level without freezing, as some newcomers do, and then with more confidence climbed the shorter ladder to the incomplete 120-foot walkway.

He rested there, looked above him to where Guy's rope was anchored, and then tackled the climb up the steelwork, standing on the diagonal struts. He'd got into the swing of it now. He was far enough above the ground for it to be beneath his attention, and the leg was much more rigid than any ladder. You didn't feel it flex at all. Fortunately, there was little wind. That can be the other disturbing influence until you get used to it. On a windy day, you must always be prepared for a sudden gust. When he finally reached the shackle holding Guy's rope, he did something I was half expecting. Instead of staring at the anchoring arrangements, he looked around at the view.

He'd arrived. He was up a tall, if incomplete, lattice tower, and the landscape looked so different. He twisted his neck, and to some extent his whole stance, to take it all in. I noted that he had one elbow round an upright. That's normal. In fact, I think it's an instinct. If you don't have the right instincts, it's better not to do this sort of climbing. Stick to hills. Down on the ground we were all now highly impressed. There were a few quiet commendatory observations.

I could imagine something of what he felt. He had climbed above his fear. It wasn't that he was superior to those below him on the ground. He was just higher than they were. He could see further. His horizons were more distant. And he'd got there by climbing, unaided. I guessed that he would never be quite the same again. Some real climbing does wonders for a person's confidence.

Finally, the copper in him pulled him back to duty. He inspected how Guy's rope was fixed. It didn't take him long. Then he started down. If you're going to have a slip, it's normally during descent. Our lad did it all slowly, and he had a bit of a struggle trusting his weight onto that last long section of ladder down from the 80-foot level, but in the end he came safely back to the ground. I had the impression his legs were a little wobbly by that stage. He smiled at us, weakly, but we could see he was a happy man. There was a round of sincere applause. We congratulated him and made sure he didn't think we were making fun. We weren't. And, interestingly, neither he nor we mentioned how Guy's rope was fixed. "Have you done anything like that before?" He shook his head. "Do you climb anything else, like mountains?" Around Normanton isn't exactly mountain country. Again, a shake of the head. "Well done, Mate. If you get tired of the police, just apply to us."

He then picked up his rope and noticed we'd hanked it for him.

During this performance, Anthony turned up in a WIS lorry, with the driver, two men to join the construction crew, and more sections of the tower.

We explained to Anthony about Sid. He was no more surprised than we had been, but he went into the institute's office to use their telephone and came back with news that Sid was at the WIS works. No one had expected Sid to do a runner.

We unloaded the lorry, but Anthony wasn't sure whether we were free to carry on building. To postpone the decision, we agreed it was time for a morning cup of something, so adjourned to the institute's mess-room. By now, we were regular contributors to its kitty. We even persuaded our favourite copper to join us. He must have been new since he seemed unsure whether he should accept hospitality when on duty. Was it bribery? Sort of perverting the course of justice? Most coppers I've known over the years were well beyond such scruples.

Ours didn't hold out for long. But while enjoying his mug of tea he was called to the telephone. He was soon back, and asked if Mr Baker would speak to the Nottingham police. This took much longer. Anthony returned with a frown. He looked around to see who else was in the room. It was just us WIS people and our bobby. "They want to take you into custody. They have asked me to take you all to the central Nottingham police station."

The stunned silence didn't last long. "They're bonkers!"; "What are we guilty of?"; "Shouldn't someone read us our warning?" No one mentioned Sid.

Anthony answered carefully, "Wiz insists on being a responsible part of society. We will always cooperate with the civic authorities, and that includes the police." He paused. "However, I have no power of arrest. If any of you refuse, then you don't have to come with me to Nottingham. I will have to report your refusal, of course."

We looked at each other. Someone had an idea. "Can't our constable here do the arrest? Do you know how to read the warning, Mate?"

Our copper was not a strong conversationalist, but on this occasion, he readily achieved speech. "I'm not from the Nottingham police." Good for him. He could think on his feet. Well, he was sitting down. But he could collect his thoughts. I reflected from what we'd seen of him that this lad might go far.

It was a new situation for me, as no doubt for all of us. We probably weren't collecting our thoughts at all well. But I was sure we had some rights. "We can each ring someone, can't we?"

"Yes, I'm pretty sure you can, but I think it can wait 'til we get to Nottingham. We've made enough use of the telephone here. Oh, I should have mentioned. Superintendent Girling has stressed this is simply precautionary. Some things have happened which make it necessary. He's sure your detention won't last long. And secondly, Wiz will appoint our company solicitor to represent all of you if there is any legal action. Unless you want to engage your own lawyers, of course."

Ha, ha, we all thought. We said goodbye to our bobby, wishing him well with his career, and trying to seduce him again. "If the police aren't exciting enough, you would fit in fine with us. We're in Beeston. Just ask for Wiz."

As we went off in the back of the lorry towards Nottingham, I was getting worried that the air of jollity which had started to come over us again was not only unseemly but might be inadvisable. Quite apart from the respect we ought to show Guy's memory, probably more real for some than others, the tone of our interrogations suggested the police might read something into any cheerfulness after his accident. We ought to arrive at the police station suitably abashed. I tried to suggest these points during the journey. It calmed us down a little, but we were obviously affected by the weirdness of it all.

It was a strange way to get arrested. My experience of the process is limited, but it was more friendly than one might assume is normal. At the station, we were invited into their canteen, where another young policeman was appointed to keep an eye on us. No one read anything we should be cautious about. Coppers came and went. I suppose being a policeman accustoms you to the vagaries of life. No one seemed very interested in a bunch of ne'er-do-wells in their mess-room. I was not convinced we were properly under arrest. They just wanted to know where we were, for some reason. I wondered what they were doing about Sid. Had they telephoned WIS and asked someone to keep an eye on him there? Who would do that?

We tried to be sombre but couldn't help cheering up when given a snack a bit after midday. Lunch was, apparently, railway sandwiches plus over-sweet tea. We had about finished with that, not entirely ungratefully, when there was a familiar rattle and growl outside, ending with the characteristic phut-phut-clank.

"That sounds like Sailor coming alongside."

"Giving himself up!"

Outright levity breaking out again. Our brush with the police had been unpleasant to begin with but was growing increasingly farcical. I didn't know what to do. Then Sid pushed such thoughts to the back of my mind by walking in with something close to a smile, by his standards.

"Hi yer Sid!"

"We've left you a bit of lunch."

"Want a dry crust?"

Sid took a superior tone to such mundane considerations. "I bring good news. You are pardoned. You are going to be set free."

"This is getting barmy! Tony Baker arrests us 'cos the bobbies can't be bothered, and now they send you to release us?"

"No, actually. They told me to come and hand myself in. But the sergeant on the desk said you're being let out anyway. Maybe you've got time off for good behaviour."

Sid making jokes? What on earth had been happening?

What Had Been Happening: Will

William Ingalls considered himself third-generation English. Rather more than a century earlier his family had been smallish landowners in Ireland. Along with numerous relatives they were, or considered themselves to be, true historic Irish, not the resented Anglo-Irish. Together they claimed title to several small farms generally between Limerick and Galway. The soil was less suitable for agriculture than towards the east, but they could make it work for grazing and drought was rarely a problem. Grass grew well and they specialised in breeding horses. With some extra effort at market-gardening and small-scale farming, they were by no means wealthy, but sufficiently above the widespread poverty to be nervous about increasing opposition to British rule. Despite the so-called Irish Parliament, the country was essentially under London's thumb, and not getting a fair deal. They would prefer to be ruled properly from Dublin, but the cooler heads in the tribe thought violent rebellion was more likely to make things worse.

Towards the end of the 18th century the Levellers started to be a serious nuisance. Several attacks had been made on their holdings. Fences needed to be replaced, and horses rounded up, those that weren't stolen. The Ingalls and their relatives were deeply resentful of being subjected to such treatment. They were Catholics, if not very ardently. In no way did they represent the Anglican Ascendancy, nor any of the other oppressive segments of society.

Then the failed attempt in 1796 to land a French invasion at Bantry Bay in support of another group, the United Irishmen, opened their eyes to just how serious things were getting. 'Mary and all the Saints, our patriotic brothers really need *French* help?'

If it was bad then, the situation became a lot worse after the outbreak of armed rebellion in 1798. It launched several years of open conflict and guerrilla warfare, conducted with extreme violence on both sides, including atrocities which were mainly but not exclusively committed by the English and their loyalist allies. Ireland transitioned from the 18th to the 19th century bordering on civil war.

The Ingalls and related families hated the blatant advantages given to those with English or protestant connections. But they could equally see that the independence movement was not strong enough to win. Even with French help. But it was dangerous, in their position, to appear unpatriotic. For this reason, they didn't discourage, at least not very strongly, their wilder and generally younger members from joining armed groups. These young heroes were probably unstoppable anyway.

In the event, French help didn't amount to much. After an unfortunate delay, they did manage to get ashore, in County Mayo, and helped set up a small Republic. It lasted 12 days and was then defeated.

The Act of Union, when finally passed, was not going to settle the question. It was the opposite of what the rebels wanted. Largely as a result, William's forebears finally concluded they would be better off and more secure if they could get established in England. Not all the wider family approved. 'Isn't it treachery, man?' Well, it could be viewed that way, but at a practical level there were advantages. A base in England would improve trading prospects for all of them. *'Well, sure now, that's something to think about.'*

With not entirely enthusiastic help from family and some distant connections in England, and after several decades of negotiations and dealings, William's wing of the family became small landholders in Derbyshire.

With enough fit young men for horse-breeding and agriculture, and renting and in time buying several farms, the Ingalls started to be profitable again. They could start paying off debts. They not only worked hard, but skilfully. Few English studs had their experience with Irish thoroughbreds, and they found it easier to sell for racing than they had back home. They also started to appreciate some of the English heavy-horse breeds.

The more thoughtful among the Ingalls were not entirely free of guilt as to whether they had let their old country down, but by 1850, with vastly better economic conditions in which to trade, and learning in horror about the famine in Ireland, they had reason to think they'd made a good move.

That was the year William was born. He had three elder brothers who seemed to both desire and be destined to continue in horse-breeding and farming. His childhood home was the main family stud near Belper. He grew up on familiar terms with horses in general, and greatly attached to a well-behaved animal he was encouraged to consider his own, by which his parents meant: 'You do the work of looking after her'. By the time William reached his tenth birthday, he was an expert rider and a fair judge of horses, but it was clear to all that his main attachment was to things mechanical. He was more interested in the recent invention of spring-steel piston rings for steam engines than what the possibilities might be from their latest stallion.

William read Boy's Own and similar magazines during his childhood, partly for the adventure stories, more for the occasional item about science or engineering. These didn't adequately satisfy his curiosity, but his father knew a member of the local Mechanics Institute. With a spot of conniving, he could smuggle the young William into lectures likely to be of interest and within his understanding, usually judging it correctly on both counts. As he grew through his teen years, William became fascinated by the new Bessemer process for making steel. It was one of the topics he pestered his schoolteachers to investigate and then explain to him. On this occasion, one of them did. By the time he was twenty, William was convinced that steel was the material of the future. Not just iron. Steel. Moreover, by now the family was wealthy enough to consider serious diversification.

At age thirty, with family money, Will had become the majority owner of a small company. It was a family-owned business, part of what they were starting to think of, privately, as the Ingalls English Empire.

They had bought a small operation, not much more than a village blacksmith, on the edge of Beeston, a village near Nottingham. The attraction to William was the site included a good-sized field round the back. It was largely covered with rusty abandoned ironwork, but the key element was room for expansion. He had ideas about expansion.

William outlined his plans to the others. It was a family occasion. Steel was already a well-established material in precision engineering, such as engines and guns. They could not compete with the large companies doing that kind of work, nor in the construction of skyscrapers, large bridges, or ships. The investment needed was too great. The big boys were too well established for a new outfit to muscle-in easily. However, now that the Bessemer process made steel so much cheaper, it had advantages over wood for such things as agricultural and commercial buildings. By that time, William knew it also had advantages over cast or wrought iron in many situations, on which topics the other directors were happy to trust his judgement.

A steel-frame building could have all its components made in their workshop, and then be assembled on the customer's site, much quicker than timber and not requiring skilled carpenters. They would need different kinds of skill, but the steel parts would just be bolted together. With a frame strong enough for the whole building, the weather could be kept out by whatever was convenient for roof and walls, such as tiles, boarding, corrugated iron, or whatever. Anything suitable and available. The integrity lay in the frame, so you had a wide choice for the rest of the building. And a steel frame takes up much less space inside.

And so 'William Ingalls Steel' was born, WIS for short, pronounced 'wiz'. William became Chairman of the Board of Directors. His brothers, and one of his several sisters, were the other directors. They supported his plan, wished him luck, and attended no further meetings unless legally necessary.

William himself had no intention of picking up so much as a hacksaw. He regarded himself as a good judge of people, with a clear-sighted view of the future, and to a large extent he was right. Construction in steel proved to be a growth area, and Will found the right kind of people to run his firm, including a graduate from the first intake to an engineering course at the new University College in Nottingham. They started by making sure they could do simple things like wrought-iron railings. They confirmed that without much difficulty, and then graduated to steel-frame structures.

By the dawn of the 20th century, the WIS site contained office and workshop facilities, including a proper design section with engineers and draftsmen. Moreover, they'd finished clearing out the rusty iron round the back, and now had a (steel-framed) materials store occupying a small fraction of the generous space available for further developments. They also ran increasingly experienced construction crews. A customer could explain what was wanted. The design staff made drawings to get the details agreed. WIS would quote a price, and once that was accepted, the parts were made in their workshops, usually with partial assembly, and then the construction men would put it up at the required premises. They developed a reputation for delivering what they said they would, on time, and with no extras on the price. It went down well with their clients.

Fire escapes on the outsides of tall buildings started to be one of their specialities. With increasing numbers of multi-floor commercial buildings and the ever-present danger of fire, the supply of external open-frame steel stairs became a growth area. These sometimes had to fit awkward spaces, which allowed their experts to exercise ingenuity. Calculations were needed for each special design to ensure safety without excessively heavy construction. The WIS brainy types enjoyed putting their education to practical use.

They had to learn quite a bit about paint for external steel, and in this area worded their guarantees rather carefully until they had amassed enough experience. And with that experience they continued to word them carefully.

If a customer really wanted it, particularly a valued customer, they were still willing to supply simple work, such as railings and the like, but it wasn't what they wanted to do. The previous blacksmith had done that, but wrought iron was an old technique. Will much preferred structures where the light-weight strength of steel could be used to advantage. They started to get work in supplying steel-frame buildings, or sometimes just steel roofs. Will was feeling his way to some extent, but the future looked bright.

However, WIS maintained the horse-shoeing service provided by the previous blacksmith. In fact, they asked him to stay on for a few years to teach them, particularly to reassure established customers. The old gaffer stressed how important it was that the horse had confidence in the farrier, and that can only happen if the farrier is confident in the first place, which only comes with experience. Will had been using his family's expertise for his own horses, but switched to WIS once they had a few staff competent in the smithy requirements of equine management. The WIS farriers appreciated the implied compliment. The village appreciated the continuity of service.

All these promising commercial developments gave Will great satisfaction, but they took up only part of his life. The company largely ran itself. This left him time for social activities. He quickly found that getting to know prominent people in and around Nottingham was both enjoyable and good for business. And that led to discovering the London clubs. He soon surmised that the investment needed to join a few carefully selected establishments would pay for itself before long. In this way, he started to meet men who were prominent at a national level.

On his rail journeys between Nottingham and London Will would look up and admire the metal frames of the vast station roofs, mostly made of cast iron. He was in the habit of saying to himself: 'Beyond our scope as yet, but one day we will do better'. That thought was underlined when the Nottingham Evening Post reported that a train collision at the station had thrown a milk-wagon off the track and into one of the cast-iron columns, breaking it and bringing down part of the roof. Will was not an engineer, but by this time he was certain a steel frame would have bent, perhaps, but not break. A milk-wagon, for goodness sake! Bringing down a railway station roof!

Will took no pleasure in such an accident. There had been some casualties at the station. But the fact it happened told him WIS was working along the right lines. There are many places where steel can do a better job than iron, especially cast iron. It frustrated him at times that so many people carried on with old methods simply because, in effect, they *were* old. They felt safe with something known to have worked in the past. But that wasn't how to make progress. He reckoned he could analyse matters objectively. He felt a bit special in this respect, despite having no scientific qualification. Basically, he was happy. He had recognised the potential of steel and had a good team to exploit it.

Meanwhile, his social activities around Nottingham took some unexpected turns. He was a large man, with a breezy and amiable manner. He had always been comfortable in rural surroundings. A village fair, a race meeting, or a livestock auction, these seemed his natural habitats. When they weren't too far away, he would turn up on horse-back. As an increasingly prominent businessman he discovered he had expertise, so people seemed to think, in such things as farm animals, pets, homemade cake or jam, flower arrangements, brass bands, maypole dancing, or pretty much anything else likely to be on competitive display. Without deliberate, or at least too obvious, self-promotion, he found himself a favourite judge, a presenter of prizes, a cutter of ribbons, or whatever else needed a local dignitary with a loud clear voice. He wasn't expert in anything except horses, steel and as a judge of people. But that didn't matter. What he soon learnt *did* matter was that judging competitions, and thus who gets the prize, was socially the most dangerous thing he did. He survived well enough in his cheerful way by keeping an ear to the ground and steering a creditable balance between competing expectations.

During this development of his business and social life Will also fitted in a family. He married Val, who came from an established local farming family. Everyone was pleased with the match, and they were set up in an old farmhouse conveniently close to Beeston. In time, they had a daughter and two sons.

Val came to consider herself the long-suffering partner in this arrangement. Will was neither cruel nor inconsiderate, and she rather liked having such a widely known and respected husband. She was also aware that she was comfortably settled. They were not short of money. In time, she and Will were better off than her parents in cash-flow terms. Most of her relatives had toiled through much of their waking hours to make farming pay. Will seemed to generate an income just by existing, although he obviously gave a lot of attention to his company. That was really the issue. In a contest between her and WIS, she was far from confident Will would make the right choice.

For his part, Will probably considered that he had chosen a wife well, just as he would choose a horse or a business. He was pleased Val understood the country, rode well, enjoyed the events they often both went to, and seemed happy looking after the farmhouse and running her own activities. And Val did run things. It seemed to rub off from Will that she was the obvious person to organise a social occasion or chair a ladies' committee. That she never claimed expenses may have helped.

As the 19th century was left behind, Will began to take a serious interest in the new science of wireless transmission. Initially he was just fascinated to read in the papers about what Mr Marconi was doing in Chelmsford. Sending messages, apparently, just through the air with no wires. It should be impossible, but it seemed he was doing it. Will wasn't a scientist. He had little more than basic arithmetic in his head. But this sort of development gripped him with something close to excitement. The impossible becoming possible! It was a new century, and it was going to be a new world! This was where the businessman in Will took over. If Mr Marconi really could make it work, telegraphing messages without the need to lay wires was going to be big. Apparently, wireless telegraphy *did* need wires. They just had to be held up in the air at each end, and somehow the messages got through without wires in between. As a result, these wireless wires needed supporting structures. He would probably never understand it, but it might be a new business opportunity. *'Can't just spend our lives making fire escapes.'*

He took a trip to Chelmsford. An assistant at WIS studied Bradshaw's for him, and then actually did the journey as a reconnaissance to check out hotels and make bookings. Will did things properly and liked advance planning. He travelled in short stages to be kind on his heart. *'It's not kind to me, blast it.'*

At the Wireless Telegraph and Signal Company, he was introduced to Mr Marconi, who by Will's standards was a rather a slight figure. He was also friendly, charming, and somewhat to his surprise, equipped with perfect English. On being congratulating on this point, Marconi mentioned that his mother was Irish. This could have formed a link between them had there been time for it to develop. In the event, Marconi took a keen interest in Will's suggestions about support structures, but, after a short further conversation about the prospects for wireless communication, explained that he had many investigations in progress, and passed him over to two assistants.

Will received the impression that Mr Marconi had formed an instant appreciation of what WIS could offer for supporting aerials, but when it became apparent that Will knew nothing else about wireless the inventor had better things to do.

The meeting with the assistants took longer. They had a useful discussion on various details to do with aerials and how they should be supported. The essential feature is copper wire held up in the air. The wires must be the right length and at the right height. They might need wires connected in special configurations. The wires usually needed insulators at their ends. There was immediate interest in Will's description of slender optimally designed lattice-steel masts. While Will was privately thinking that they would probably need another clever lad or two from the college, Mr Marconi's assistants had some discussions between themselves. If slender steel masts were held up by steel ropes, they said, then those stays might have to be sub-divided by insulators. Marconi's would specify the exact lengths. Will managed not to drool. This was exactly the kind of development where WIS could shine. Relatively light steelwork, but with specialised requirements which suited the company's expertise. *'We'd be a wiz at it,'* was his private joke.

No, Marconi's did not see the need for any commercial agreement at that time, but it took note of Mr Ingall's interest and the capability of his company. They would bear it in mind.

Will was realistic enough not to expect more. In the event, his visit paid for itself many times over. In due course, WIS was contacted for a small but increasing number of aerial installations. He was intrigued to note reports in the papers from time to time of Marconi and his various experiments, including claims which were sometimes controversial. Will also discovered that Marconi was an Italian marquis, something which had not been mentioned in Chelmsford.

On his way home from Chelmsford, Will stayed in London where he had arranged to be invited to a dinner at the National Liberal Club. It was hosted by a somewhat younger man, a certain David Lloyd George, an MP for somewhere in Wales. The dinner was to welcome into the Liberal Party another even younger MP, Mr Churchill, who had defected from the Conservatives. Will had heard of Churchill before, but not Lloyd George. What he had read about Churchill did not inspire him, and the evening did nothing to change that view. But this Lloyd

George fellow seemed much more promising. Moreover, he was an earl, so he simply had to be a good contact. William had no politics, but he sensed that this George fellow was someone like himself, viewing life as something to enjoy. Try not to spoil it for other people, of course, but the big thing is not to waste its opportunities. The not-quite-English and rather sedate businessman on one hand, and the Welsh firebrand on the other, had a friendly chat. They got on well. Will gathered that the roguish glint in George's eyes (he hadn't established whether the MP was 'George' or 'Lloyd George') was mainly reserved for the ladies. William was more conservative in this area, but enjoyed being on chatting terms in a London club with an MP who was also an earl.

Like other industrialists he knew, Will considered himself superior to politicians. Although he accepted that a democracy needed them to make laws, and of course avoid too much power in the hands of any one person, politicians mainly just talked. That's all they seemed to do. What's more, often in near-total ignorance of what they were talking about. By contrast, Will, and men like him, *did* things. Useful things which provided jobs and improved people's lives. And when they talked, it was about something they understood.

However, the useful thing about politicians is they're influential. He should get to know the more important ones. He kept in touch with Lloyd George. They would fret about the increasingly belligerent noises in some quarters about a coming war. Why should anyone want a war? They're expensive. And yet it became progressively clearer that war was likely. Some said it was certain. With the money Germany was spending trying to catch up with Britain in dreadnoughts, France lusting for revenge on Germany for 1871, and the instability of the Austro-Hungarian Empire, a major conflict did seem in prospect. Italy yearning to be a major power didn't help. And to the east of them all was an inscrutable monster. Some wit had described Russia as an absolute autocracy tempered by assassination. It seemed appropriate. The vast country had often been expansionist in the past. Whatever ambitions they had now were not on display.

Such was Europe. Something was bound to go wrong.

There was much public comment about these things. Will departed widely from the view that, with modern weapons, any outbreak of fighting would soon be over. Really? Hiram Maxim's gun could fire five or more bullets per *second*, and the Vickers company was reputedly improving on it. There was talk of the gun firing 10,000 rounds in an hour. You would then have to change the barrel, but that could be done in the field in two minutes. What would a weapon like that do to war?

The obvious answer was to make it a stalemate. Opposing forces would have to be entrenched or within fortifications. That doesn't make for battles of manoeuvre, the supreme skill of military commanders, or at least, what they thought was their genius. The concept of brave men walking forward into a hail of lead, such as at Gettysburg, simply could not be entertained. Even the numbskull brass hats who seemed to run the British army weren't going to ask men to attack over open ground against fast-firing guns. Surely not? These weren't muzzle-loading muskets or single-shot rifles. So how would a war work out? More importantly, how could such a war be won? Will thought about it.

Accurate and long-range artillery would be available to both sides, but to bombard an enemy fortification would churn the ground up and make attacking even more difficult. It can rain at any time in Europe, and much of its land can become a quagmire. Horses? They could get troops there quicker, but they were a larger target than just a man and needed a great deal of feeding and looking after. Also, Will frankly had a soft spot for the creatures. Surely not even the cavalry generals would so much as consider it. No, the best way would be a surprise attack with a limited objective. Get into the enemy's trench or fortification, deal with the opposition, and be prepared to defend it against a counterattack. Winning ground on that basis was going to take a long time. It would also be expensive. Will knew enough military history to appreciate that attack, however much it suited the generals' love of dash and daring, usually suffered more losses than defence.

Of course, better weapons are always being developed. What could be available if a war started in the next few years? Self-propelled armoured vehicles? Possibly. Dreadnoughts fighting on land. But with churned-up muddy terrain, and potentially against artillery, not until major engineering developments are available. If ever. However, he stored the thought away. After all, it would need a lot of steel.

The air? Airships must be far too vulnerable over a battlefield. Heavier-than-air flight was now possible, and small targets high in the sky would be difficult to hit, but what could they do? Scout, mainly, Will guessed. And spot for the guns. Well, yes, that could be useful. But wouldn't high-angle artillery be developed to fire at aeroplanes? That could be effective with shrapnel.

What about shrapnel timed to burst above enemy trenches? That doesn't seem too difficult to arrange. But what one side could do, so could the other. What effect would that have? Trenches with roofs. No obvious route to a rapid advance.

Will began to think that the war would depend on each side's ability to continue fighting. That includes all the materials needed to keep troops effective in what would probably end up as a vast system of trenches. What nation has the right psychology in its men? Was raw courage or dogged persistence going to be the more important? And how would the economies of the warring countries hold up? Britain seemed particularly well placed to maintain supplies. It had the Empire and a large commerce fleet, plus a navy to protect them. Germany might be working along the right lines by competing in naval power, but they were coming from a long way back, and they had less access to the world's oceans. On this basis, the prospect of war did not seem too daunting, but he had no doubt it would to be a long, heavy slog. No doubt at all.

He discussed the issue with his horse-breeding brothers. They were less interested in his thoughts about weapons and strategy. Their attention was on expanding their business, and war would provide market opportunities. They went for quality where they could, but there was going to be a seller's market for almost any type of healthy horse. They intended to be ready for it.

"But do you think horses will play such a large part, against machine guns?"

"The age of the glorious cavalry charge may, or may not, be over, but four legs are going to play a large part in transport for a long time to come."

"In fact, we're looking into mules. You might laugh, Will, but they have a reputation for being sturdy *and* intelligent. Brighter than horses, and less easily spooked, is what we've gathered from people with experience of them. Some say they are brainier than a lot of people. Brighter than soldiers, anyroad."

It was encouraging to know the rest of his family were still business minded. So how best can Will prepare for the possibility of war? Obvious, really. In 1908, he joined the army. Not actually the British army as such, but the Territorial Force established the previous year.

It happened because he met a lieutenant of the South Nottinghamshire Hussars, one Chasewell-Phipps. He was in civvies at the time, if you can call a monocle, bow tie, plus-fours, and spats civvies. He urged Will to join as well. "I say, old man, yes! I mean, welcome you with open arms. It's super, old chap, y'know. Best club in the county, what!"

Will's immediate impression was that he had discovered a specimen of a species previously thought to be extinct. However, he liked to think he was broad-minded, and you couldn't hold weak eyesight against a person. What sounded like a weak brain was perhaps more serious, but maybe it was an act. *C. phippsulus*, as the naturalist in Will liked to think of this creature, was from an old army family. Probably back to Hastings. With severe short-sight and a squint, he was probably safe from being sent anywhere near fighting. It would make his brothers-in-arms safer, too, to keep him away from firearms.

Nevertheless, Will was attracted to Phipps' regiment, particularly the uniform. And there was an argument that to show early willingness to serve his country in its hour of need might put him in a favourable position for whatever role he might subsequently be required to play. In this respect, he was placed somewhat similarly to *C. phippsulus*. One of Will's carefully preserved possessions was a letter from his school doctor:

'To whom it may concern, William Fitzgerald Ingalls, date of birth 24 June 1850, has a dangerous heart condition such that he should not be required by any employment to engage in energetic activity. As a prudent guide, he should not exert himself to the extent that his breathing becomes rapid. It should be noted that this is a severe limitation on what he can do. Labouring, climbing, energetic walking, and any form of military activity, must be excluded. Climbing stairs should be done only slowly, with a rest between floors.'

"As it happens, I might be in rather the same situation as you as far as active service is concerned. I have a dickey ticker. It's serious. I have to limit exertion to very small amounts. The fact is, I may have done rather well to get this far. Does it really make sense to join with such a condition?"

"Fwah, fwah, me boy. Nonsense. You see, Yeomanry Force is Home Defence. Hardly come to fighting in England, what? Things get really sticky, some units might go abroad. Nobody can be forced to, y'know. Now, volunteers, they might, what? There's talk of having first and second lines if there is war. I'd be in the second line. You too, what? People like us can do plenty here at home. I say, you're a born organiser. Must know hundreds around here. Hundreds know you. Probably thousands, what? Make a fine recruiter, you know. Organise camps. Training. That sort of thing."

As an afterthought, demonstrating that some serious activity did occur in his head, he added, "Of course, if we did get invaded, I mean, they'd throw even wrecks like us into it. Nothing to lose then, what?"

The significance of that last comment took a while to register with Will. 'Nothing to lose then, what?' wasn't an insignificant verbal decoration like much of Phipps' normal speech. It revealed his attitude towards the possibility of defeat. Some people might decide that if we were clearly beaten, the enemy having crossed our best defence, to wit the English Channel, and was now established on our soil, then the only sensible course is to accept the inevitable and seek terms. Will not only knew there were many in Britain who would think like that, he knew who some of them were. But not his favourite dinosaur. He might be a dim-witted fop, but in the event of a German army winning against them in England Phipps just assumed and accepted that the likes of he and Will would die in the hopeless last fighting. It might be utterly unrealistic, stupid, in fact, but Will thought the same. Surrender wasn't in the thinking of these two wrecks.

Yet why did Will think like this? He had never approved of Irish violence to gain Irish independence, even though London's rule had been highly repressive. Why was that? Was he being inconsistent? Will fully appreciated the motivation of the republicans but didn't think their cause justified violence. He would fight to the finish against foreign invasion, but not for secession. Was this a rational position? He just didn't know.

On the topic of Will joining the S. Notts Hussars, *C. phippsulus* might also have added that the successful businessman had plenty of money, which could be useful to the regiment.

The regiment was indeed welcoming. The colonel was particularly genial. He suspected there would be a great need to recruit if it came to war. A businessman as well-known as Will seemed ideal. He'd seen Will judging competitions and presenting prizes at village fairs. He could see Will knew how to enliven a crowd. Nevertheless, the regiment did want to see his letter. This made it quite clear that there was no question of him ever serving in a trench, with or without a roof. Excellent. An organiser and no doubt an effective recruiter. We'll keep him here. Make him a figurehead. In fact, after some discussion amongst the senior officers, it was decided to make Will an honorary captain. He was asked to read up on some basic formalities in case he was asked questions he couldn't otherwise answer. This seemed sufficient to fit him for the proposed recruitment role despite his otherwise total lack of any military experience.

In this manner Will Ingalls, a 3rd generation Englishman, joined the South Nottinghamshire Hussars, second line. He was flattered by his uniform, which he paid for himself, of course. He started wearing it to events, and found he was increasingly asked to make the main speech. He began to refer to the serious times in which we all live, and the obligation to be ready for whatever the country needs from us. It was well received.

Rather to his surprise, Will grew quite fond of *C. phippsulus*, rather in the way you get attached to a pet, despite inconvenient side-effects. Phipps had no instinct as to what was socially acceptable behaviour. Will could occasionally nudge him away from the more serious type of *faux pas*. Poor Phipps really did seem to have little brain, just enough to pursue his own whims. Possibly this was why he joined up.

And Phipps had been right. The S. Notts was indeed a good club. Despite not being quite a genuine officer, Will socialised readily with those who were. Some seemed a bit stand-offish, but he was such a convivial man that he was generally popular.

Despite his lack of army experience, Will had taken an interest in military history. He couldn't help wondering about anecdotes in circulation at that time about a senior officer who had no hesitation in holding forth on the undesirability of brains in the army. It was said that he once bestowed an accolade on a valued subordinate along the lines of 'Now, you Sir! You're a fine officer! I have great confidence in you! It is obvious that you have no brains at all!' It sounded like a story which may have improved in the telling. On the other hand, the kind of blunders which had been made during the Boer War suggested that, perhaps, it really could be true. Not even an exaggeration. One thing Will was quite certain about was that *he* had a brain. Quite a good one, in some ways. Even if the whole British army didn't fully appreciate it.

He was, of course, fully aware that in the heat of battle an army needs a disciplined body of men who unhesitatingly obey orders. You can't hold a committee meeting when the enemy is charging at you. But in running WIS he had soon learnt that his most valuable staff were those who could see what needed to be done and got on with it. Early on he had suffered a manager who insisted on blind obedience from his workers. His department found they could disguise sabotage as exact compliance with his instructions. The unpopular man was unable to get the work done he was supposed to manage but couldn't fault his subordinates. They found him obnoxious and were too clever for him. Will didn't suffer him for long. It was the first and only time he had sacked someone senior in the organisation.

Will preferred to make sure that everyone in WIS realised their pay depended on the performance of the whole company. He laid down his general requirements and expected them to be followed. After that, he wanted everyone to take any sensible initiative to make it work. It had worked. He had found it necessary to step in a few times, but in the main he was delighted with how well people who were trusted could use their own judgement in a responsible manner.

Would it work in an army? Surely it would be beneficial for some degree of responsibility to be encouraged at all levels, even down to privates? Most conversations between officers in the yeomanry getting anywhere near such concepts tended to be based more on the premise that privates should correspond to cogs in a machine. Perhaps a living fossil like *C. phippsulus* really was the ideal kind of officer. For some reason, Will never got round to discussing the finer points of this philosophy with Phipps himself.

In general, however, Will was content with his new identity as a soldier. His main disappointment, in the years before the war, was not being in the regiment's detachment to the King's coronation. He was somewhat mollified when he learnt that it would be in dismount review dress, that is, they would be on foot. More importantly, when the detachment returned and reported how strenuous it had been, lining different routes on two consecutive days, and marching to and from their camp, he realised it was just as well he wasn't part of it all. It might have been fatal. His heart could be a nuisance at times, as well as a pain.

However acutely he had analysed how modern conflict might evolve, Will had neither foreseen nor planned what WIS would be doing during a war. They had been supplying increasing numbers of fire escapes, but presumably the army wouldn't need many of those. They had recently designed and put up a couple of wireless-telegraphy masts for a naval shore station. Will was tickled to be told not to tell anyone about it. He wondered how the Royal Navy would keep two 100-ft high masts secret. His not to reason why.

Initially the level of work decreased. At the very start of the war, the yeomanry regiments assumed they should immediately be busy with recruitment. Will did a bit of preparation, mainly on speeches. In the event, there wasn't the slightest need. The forces, and the army in particular, were swamped with more volunteers than they could handle. They army most definitely didn't need part-time soldiers to help process them. Men, and even boys, rushed to join up. It was difficult to cope with them all.

But it quickly became apparent that a large proportion of the volunteers were not fit enough to accept. Moreover, the early fighting did not lead to immediate victory, and as it became entrenched, with mounting losses, the flow of volunteers decreased. Discouraging news also came back from recruits at training camps, where conditions were dire that autumn. In many cases, they did not have weapons to train with, nor uniforms to wear. As the early flood of recruits abated, Will started to be an effective speaker, encouraging the reluctant to embrace arduous service for their country. Some of the regular army recruiting sergeants were effective as well, generally on a less high-minded basis.

Will was pleased he had a good general manager running WIS. Anthony Baker was efficient and sensible. Will himself had been wise to stay above routine details. He was an ideas and policy man, above the fray, and it now allowed him to do his bit for the war. He followed the news from the front as closely as the available information allowed, and it was plain well before the end of the year that he had been right. This war was not going to be anywhere near over by Christmas.

What *did* happen over the winter was an increasing public outcry at the lack of shells for the artillery. Early in 1915 Will visited London and arranged a short meeting with Lloyd George. At the Houses of Parliament, what's more. Could WIS help by manufacturing shells? The MP seemed well informed on what was needed. "You're too small to make shells, but there is a shortage of small-arms ammunition as well. The public don't realise what a shambles we are in, and the liberals just haven't got a grip. I think there will be large changes soon. I'll make sure you are not overlooked."

Just before the war Will had a telephone installed. Not at WIS, but at the farm. This became possible, after much asking, when the Post Office started taking over the various telephone companies. He probably would not have got one after the war started. Government departments needed a lot of them as soon as possible and had priority. Will took a somewhat smug pleasure in giving the MP his home telephone number and noting that Lloyd George seemed suitably impressed.

The government did not fall until May, but only a few days later an official in London got through to Will's telephone. "Lloyd George, the new Minister for

Munitions, thanks you for your offer. You will soon be visited by officials to advise on conversion to ammunition manufacturing. Please keep yourself available and be ready to drop all other work." By this time, their work had largely dropped itself, and the WIS staff were down to well under half. Many had volunteered during the first few months.

The conversion was not as immediate or rapid as the first telephone conversation suggested. To meet the first requirements WIS had to surround its site with a tall steel fence designed to be difficult to climb over, and fit strong lockable gates. 'That shouldn't be difficult for you', he was told. Moreover, they weren't paid for doing these preliminaries. Will never found out whether he would have been eligible for reimbursement. Later, secure storage within the site was specified. There were then delays in getting the necessary machinery. Meanwhile they should recruit women who can work in shifts. 'There's no point in employing men because we're going to need most of them in France' was the ominous prediction. At one point, the minister himself was on Will's telephone, fortunately catching him at home. That made Will feel proud, but he realised that the WIS premises needed a telephone as well. He resolved to canvas for a new line, at least as soon as the war was over.

By summer, production had at last started. Deliveries of the necessary materials were carefully recorded. A retired armourer was on the staff, and an indoor range set up for testing. A telephone was installed without asking.

There were teething troubles, but by autumn production was running flat-out. Meanwhile Will's recruitment speeches were not patriotic extras at village fairs, most of which no longer took place, but the central point of street meetings, typically outside recruitment offices. With the casualty rates, which couldn't be hidden, he didn't feel so proud of his efforts to send even more into the slaughter. Volunteers were far fewer, and there was talk of conscription. No one knew then how much worse it would get. The general theme of Will's speeches had developed from 'This is a glorious opportunity to show what we can do' in the early days to something more like: 'We need men with courage and grit in this hour of need'. He strongly resisted the temptation to paint sacrifice for your country as glorious. No artefact of wording could disguise what the sacrifice might be.

It was amongst the crowd one afternoon following his speech that things started to go wrong.

"Holy Mother of God! If it isn't William Ingalls! My, how grand you look in that uniform! You're a sight to behold, bless you. Is it happy you are about all these lads you're sending to the trenches?"

Will looked where this was coming from. He had to look down as well as around, the speaker being rather more than a head shorter. "I don't think we've been introduced, have we? Who am I—"

"Jesus and all the Saints! You're a real English, look you now? 'Haven't been introduced' he says!"

"Please tell me who you are." Will had already understood this man wanted to be known as an Irish republican. Will had a trained ear in this area. The sarcastic oaf was from an Irish family and had spent at least his early years in England. He would normally speak fluent English, with whatever regional accent he had picked up, but could put on a fairly convincing Irish voice when needed. "More importantly, what are you getting at?"

Will was not surprised when he reverted to Midlands. "Look, man, I've lived in England all my life, as you have. But we're both from old Irish families, aren't we now? Don't you feel any loyalty to our real country? You must know how the English impoverished us. If you hadn't been able to afford moving over, and were still living in the Emerald Isle, wouldn't you want to be free of British rule?"

"I admit that British treatment of Ireland has been disgraceful. It's the normal problem of a less-wealthy region of a country. But I don't think it would be a good move for Ireland to become independent, and I think Home Rule is a generous offer. But even if I did want independence, I wouldn't murder people to get it."

"But you're murdering people by encouraging young men to join the army and go into the trenches, isn't it?"

"And thousands of Irish have gone to the war voluntarily, including republicans. They fight well, too, I'm told, irrespective of their politics."

"To be sure man, that's what we're good at. But look, don't let's argue about politics. Let's go in and have a quiet pint. I've a suggestion for you."

It was chilly, it was past opening time, and the nearby pub was where he had been going. Will allowed himself to be accompanied by the man into the public bar. Each with a pint in hand they found a corner. A bench ran around a bay window looking into the garden at the back. It was just being vacated by a couple sliding out from behind a table. Will and the man took their places. They sat side by side, looking into the room, over the sizeable table. Two other men with pints came from the bar and sat on the bench at the far side of the table with their backs to it. The room was starting to get crowded and noisy.

Will felt resentful. This meeting was a setup, although not something to fear. Several of his military colleagues were also in the room. The fact was he did feel queasy recruiting for a British war with so many Irish volunteering. On the other hand, his perception that the Irish automatically resorted to violence as the best solution to any problem jarred with him, even though he knew it was an unfair generalisation. As a private fantasy he wondered whether their lads were volunteering for the war on the grounds it would get them into a better fight than available locally. No, that was stupid, but it fitted his general impression.

The man spoke with a broad smile, wholly dissonant with his proposal. "Our brothers need ammunition. You're making it. We don't need much, but we can't just land stuff onto beaches like we used to."

The two men on the bench the other side of the table, looking away from them, might just be within earshot. This did not seem to bother the man. No one else in the room could conceivably hear their conversation. Could anyone in the crowd lip-read? No one was looking at them. Why should they? They looked as normal as anyone else. Several other men were in yeomanry or regular army uniforms.

To keep up appearances, Will smiled back at the man. He wondered whether he minded if the Irish shot at each other, guessing that's why they wanted ammunition. He wished he could have simpler sentiments about his family's origins.

The man continued, "We're not asking much. What do you say? We let you know when, your watchman forgets about locking, and can't keep awake. Just one night. No one gets hurt. No one would miss a box, would they now?"

This was wildly beyond anything Will could tolerate. WIS was his creation, his baby. Its good reputation was most definitely not going to be besmirched. "Oh yes, they would. Goods-in and goods-out are all carefully recorded, and our security has to be total or we'd be shut down. Cooperating with you like that just couldn't be hidden. You send your thugs anywhere around our place and I'll blow you. I'll give your description to the authorities, and that wouldn't just be the police. You'd have to kill me to stop me, and that wouldn't help your cause now, would it?" Will didn't realise he was so brave. But there was a pain in his chest, and he could feel his heart thumping. Bit like a rat in a cage, he thought, something he knew about. He was uncomfortably aware that he hadn't refused this brazen man outright.

The man in question wasn't fazed. He looked serious, forgetting they were supposed to be having a cheery conversation. He then stroked his chin with a smirk as though thinking of something improper, which he was. "You say that records are kept of everything?"

"Yes, of course they are."

"And when you deliver ammunition, what happens? The army sends a lorry?"

"With an armed guard."

"...and there is paperwork showing how many boxes are loaded onto the lorry? A bill of lading, like?"

"A manifest lists everything in each consignment, with the date, destination, quantities, and all details. Everything is checked against the manifest as the goods go onto the lorry, it's then signed, and given to the guard. I'm told everything is checked against the manifest again as it comes off at the other end. It's a vital part of their security, as well as ours."

"And this manifest is produced in your office?"

Why was he confirming all this to the man? "It's typed in our office, usually on the day the lorry arrives since we never know when that will be, and it needs to be accurate and up to date. And we keep a carbon copy."

The man paused, and then placed his hand briefly on Will's shoulder with a warm smile, the picture of old friends parting. "Thanks, Will. It's been good to see you. That's been useful. I think we can work something out. I'll let you know. Keep up the good work with your army now, won't you?"

And he was gone, moving smoothly around the furniture to the door of the bar, without looking back. His beer was less than half drunk. Shortly after, the other two men followed him.

Will felt terrible. The commotion in his chest, he realised, was dangerous. The pain was severe. He was angry and frightened, and above all horribly divided between what he thought was duty to Britain and any responsibility he might have towards Ireland. He determined first to sit where he was until his heart settled down, which could be a long time. He had finished his own beer. He looked at the man's. Pity to waste it. But he shouldn't drink more. Probably bad for me. No, calm me down. He turned the glass round to avoid the man's spit and was about to take a sip.

"I say, Old Man. Friend of yours?" It was *C. phippsulus*. He sat down beside Will without invitation.

"Not exactly. We're both from old Irish families, and he recognised me. I don't even know his name." Will was surprised how smoothly he improvised a reply, but then realised it was true.

"They do well in the trenches, what?" referring to the Irish volunteers.

"Yes, they do. You could argue they're a violent lot in the first place. But I'm only three generations from real Irish and I don't feel any need to shoot people. And I've nothing against Germans. They're good engineers, and the country's an industrial powerhouse."

"They do, I mean, yes, those dreadnoughts. They make them pretty well, don't you know? Seems so. Lucky we've still many more than them, eh! what?"

Will felt himself calming down. This was the sort of conversation he was used to. It was a difficult time for the country, but there was a sense of security in the underlying strength of Britain and her Empire. He fully understood that her most important strength was industry, plus trade with her far-flung dominions.

"I say, finish your drink. Let's take a walk around. I mean, chaps we should talk to."

"Sorry, I'm going to have to rest a bit longer. You know I've got a heart problem? It's been acting up. I'll be alright in a while."

Phipps stood up to leave but looked thoughtfully at him for a while. Then with a pat on Will's shoulder, eerily like the man's only a few minutes earlier: "Look after yourself, Ingalls, we need you," and he too went off between the tables. He had recruited Will, and despite being junior in rank, if Will's honorary status is recognised, in a pub with their helmets off they could talk like that.

Will was disturbed. The lingering pain was quite enough to disturb him, but he had been forced to face the question as to where he really belonged. Despite viewing Phipps as a dinosaur, he knew he was closer to him than the unnamed man. He had probably refrained from giving a name knowing Will wouldn't have believed him. Anyroad, Will thought, let's hope that's the last I've seen of him.

Will didn't see him again, but about a week later received a letter. It was typed, short, very much to the point, and there was no signature:

When we want some we'll send you a letter with an address. The letter will tell you which item we are interested in, like 'item 1' or 'item 2'. This will be for the most recent delivery. Whatever item we mention, reduce its quantity by one. Leave the signatures blank. Post it to the address without folding it and with a piece of cardboard to keep it flat. And do it immediately.

Will was in a bind. He was certain that the mild obfuscation in the wording wouldn't protect him if it came to light. But what the letter required of him did keep the action away from WIS premises. He could type a duplicate manifest himself, at home. It would have to match the original in all respects but one, but he could easily get the same model of typewriter, an Imperial, as used in the WIS office. Typing can't be difficult. He could do it really slowly and carefully. That man was right, the Irish have been treated badly by the British government, and yet many of them are willingly serving in the trenches. But do I want to take this risk? Will had a sense of the inevitable.

Without making any final decision, he prepared his ground. He spoke to their office manager and secretary, Lilly Loeillet. In his unconventional way, Will liked the company to run on first-name terms. The younger ones didn't dare call him 'William', but the more senior staff got used to 'Will' in the end, except for a few of the older men for whom it just didn't show proper respect. In Lilly's case, she preferred to be addressed as 'Lilly' because no one could pronounce her surname properly, and she was averse to being known as 'Mrs Lolly'.

Will explained that he found himself making arrangements about deliveries to and from the company over the telephone to London in evenings and at weekends. "The shortages are getting so severe they are shifting priorities around, particularly cutting back on ammunition for training to send as much as possible to the front."

"Surely that's not a good policy, is it, Sir?" Lilly, despite her personal preference for how to be addressed, was still a traditionalist. "If the new men are insufficiently trained at shooting, will they not get killed sooner once they are involved in fighting?"

Not for the first time, Will wished people like Lilly ran the country, or at least the army, not just his office. "You're right, but I'm afraid it's what's happening. And I need to be better armed with facts at home." Was that a sensible metaphor? He had a feeling it could be what people call a Freudian slip. "Could you please firstly give me a summary of all the goods-in and goods-out records involved in ammunition since we started making it, and then a carbon of each manifest from now on. Can you manage an extra carbon?"

"We can give you the summaries now. Young Susan registers all deliveries to us with two carbons. I type the manifests for our deliveries to the War Department, with two carbons of those as well. You can have all the first carbons now. When you are typing something important, it is always sensible to make copies as you go along. Retyped copies so often contain mistakes."

Val and Lilly were friends. Val shared Will's appreciation of Lilly. Val only saw the obvious activities going on in WIS, and she did not have occasion to speak much with other staff. But she could see that the entire WIS operation was comprehended in Lilly's prim head.

Will had already explained to Val that should his heart give out one day she would inherit his controlling interest in WIS. "Just discuss everything with Lilly. You'll get on fine." Val had half a suspicion that Will pretended, or at least exaggerated, his heart condition. Mainly just to avoid physical effort. She did not give the thought of running the company much attention.

The Easter Uprising shook Will badly. He had been lulled by the readiness of so many Irish men to go to the war. Hadn't the republican movements declared they would cease operations for the duration? He guessed they hadn't been completely inactive, but this was on a different scale. It required a contingent of the British army, including artillery, five days to defeat it. It was like a side-show to the main war.

By this time, he had received several demands for falsified manifests, and had duly produced and posted them. The first had set his tidy mind at rest on a point in the first letter containing his instructions. It required the modified manifest to be *for the most recent delivery*. This had worried him. It was quite common for deliveries to be made on consecutive days, and sometimes more than one on the same day. Unless they watched the WIS works and hand-delivered each letter, he might easily generate a false manifest for the wrong delivery. The last thing Will wanted was a muddle requiring several further letters to sort it out. As it was, each letter requesting a duplicate manifest arrived through the post and consisted of just three items: an address, a small number which he interpreted as the item, and a longer number he recognised as a WIS manifest reference.

Until Easter 1916 Will had vaguely thought the smuggled ammunition was needed so Irish factions could shoot at each other when they had nothing better to do. It was a fuzzy mental picture, perhaps to justify his repeated cooperation with them. But he was being naive. Perhaps WIS rounds had been fired in

Dublin. Had WIS bullets flown in *both* directions during the uprising? It seemed a symbol of his confused thinking.

He pondered refusing any further requests. Perhaps simply not responding. But in addition to being disturbingly unclear what he thought about the Irish question, he suspected that not complying could be dangerous. The uprising had shown just how far these men were prepared to go. All they had to do was shop him to the police or the War Office. Will had no doubt about the outcome. It was ammunition smuggling during war. He would hang.

In the event, there were only five further requests for false manifests. Will complied with each.

But quite apart from the Easter Uprising and his treachery, because he didn't pretend anything else to himself, Will became increasingly depressed by the war. Through the yeomanry he received slightly fuller news than was in the papers. In addition to the enormous losses, it seemed clear that generals who took the sensible view that frontal attacks were wasteful and ineffective were sacked, whereas those who bull-headedly insisted on continuing with them were loaded with decorations, promoted, and praised, at least publicly.

It was encouraging that his early thoughts about armoured vehicles had come true. They had been deployed too early, before adequate testing and development, but they had been used, and with some degree of success. Will approved of mechanisation.

Even so, it was an enormous relief when 11th November 1918 arrived, as it was to everyone. Ammunition manufacturing at WIS had stopped some time earlier, which insulated Will from the fear of any further smuggling.

After the war-end celebrations, grim reality settled over the country. Economic recession was accompanied by serious levels of unemployment, with special resentment over the lack of work for ex-servicemen.

At WIS, work picked up slowly. Not all their men came back. Some were no longer alive. Some wanted their jobs back but had disabilities due to war wounds. Where possible these were found suitable posts, but it wasn't always practicable. Most of the ammunition girls left, but some stayed on. They had developed a taste for wage packets at the end of a week, and the old gaffers had to admit it was surprising what some of them could do. There were tensions, but as work and thus recruitment picked up the company was able eventually to get back into something like its pre-war happy stride.

One major area of business growth was wireless. Will's earlier visit to Marconi's had given them a head start in aerial support structures. He experienced a warm glow of satisfaction that he'd spotted the opening so early. Steel masts and towers for wireless stations began to be routine work. It pleased Will that considerations of economy and safety demanded more critical design, and sometimes specialised construction methods.

As life in England returned to a new normal, Will was able to get back to attending rural events, although he did so now in civilian clothes. Although he really preferred being just 'Will', he couldn't deny that being addressed or referred to as 'Captain Ingalls' was flattering. His dark feelings about the war began to be replaced by his previous sunny approach to life. He started to feel better and had less trouble with his old ticker.

What turned his contentment to delight was the investiture. The knighthood was genuinely unexpected. He had considered himself fortunate to get through the war without his secret becoming known, followed by disgrace. He was now 'Sir William'. His staff also liked it, since the honour reflected credit on them too. They called him, and addressed him, as 'Sir Will'. He discouraged no one from adding the honorific.

For Val, it was the crowning glory. For the first time since her wedding, she took a serious interest in what she would wear. She was, after all, a country lass. It involved taking advice and spending a lot of money. She did not have very good advice, but it did not matter. She loved every moment, mainly because she was deaf to the several minor snobberies which came her way at the Palace. The great point was that she had been to the Palace. She had been presented to the King. She did not ask for more.

It did not compensate for what the war had cost their family. Each of their three children had played their part. Their eldest son had lost a hand but was managing without it. The other boy's eyes had been damaged by gas. He could still see, although not as well as he would like. The great loss was their daughter. She had been driving an ambulance in France when it took a direct hit from a shell. Everyone on it was killed outright. The fact that she was driving an ambulance in France was sufficient testimonial to the kind of young lady she had become. Will was immensely proud of Louise, but quite unclear as to how Val thought of her memory. Did she think Louise had been noble to volunteer for the Red Cross, or just foolish? Her loss was grievous to them both, but somehow, they just didn't seem able to discuss the subject.

Will also wondered at times how Val thought about his knighthood. She professed to be pleased and impressed. But he could see that the boys' service to Britain had been much braver than his. They had their medals, but it was he who was Knight of the Realm. Louise, however, had given her life, with no public recognition at all. Will could see the unfairness in this, and knew it was typical of the entire system, from top to bottom of the pecking order.

He did, in fact, make a start at trying to get recognition for Louise, but immediately met a brick wall. "Genuinely sorry, Sir William, there are thousands of such cases. It must be someone who really stands out."

What made this worse was when he caught wind of some story which had been put about that he had paid Lloyd George for his knighthood. He had indeed heard it suggested that the PM was susceptible in such matters, but in his case the rumour was totally false. He had done no such thing, and the knighthood had been a total surprise. He then heard a whisper that a certain Chasewell-Phipps had something to do with the slander. This greatly depressed Will. Why do people have to be like this? Fearing his own heart, which was a strange situation to be in, Will resolved to despise and ignore the whole business. He was reasonably successful in this, although of course there was no question of forgetting it.

Overall, however, Will considered himself to have been fortunate. At least, he did until the horror started again.

It was at a motor-race meeting. There had been a notice about it in the newspaper. The racing circuit and a hotel were near a railway station. He was able to book a room by telephone. It was only an hour or so on the train, but in his normal relaxed style he avoided both journeys on the same day. He liked a night at a hotel.

He was expecting a proper racing circuit with permanent facilities, as it would be for horses. The actual event was a much more casual affair on a private estate. And strictly it wasn't racing but timed trials, but it was called racing and Will found it an exciting event at which to be a spectator.

The cars were fascinating. Unlike ordinary passenger vehicles, they were low-slung, with no roof, typically only two seats, and were described as 'sports' or 'tourer' models. Sunbeam and Vauxhall were well represented. He'd seen such cars on the roads, but not so close. They looked rather fun. At this meeting, they were more competitive in appearance, with some equipment removed, presumably to make them lighter. This seemed to include the silencers since they were horribly noisy. Will was impressed by how fast they went but thought the spectators should be better protected from them. He enjoyed looking round the machines when stationary. He had some interesting chats with drivers and mechanics.

Unusually, he'd had to negotiate with Val for permission to take this trip. Ridiculously, in his opinion, the difficulty centred around it being his birthday. A couple of weeks back it had been quite decent weather. To Val the only possible way to celebrate such an auspicious milestone as her husband's birthday would be a family get-together at the farm, in fact a garden party, as a surprise for him. For his part, Will was unimpressed by anniversaries of anyone's birth, and genuinely preferred his own to pass unremarked. He had arranged to make use of this first opportunity to watch car racing, forgetting what the date was and not thinking to mention his plan to Val. When the dust had settled following discovery of this imbroglio, they settled for a smaller gathering on the Sunday afternoon. He would be travelling back that morning, and would be tired, but he wouldn't have to play musical chairs or hide-and-seek. He wouldn't make a speech, either.

On the day of the racing, the weather was cool, windy, and rainy. Will was an all-weather man, and appropriately dressed to enjoy the event. It certainly wouldn't have been a good day for a garden party, and it was unlikely to be much different tomorrow. The smaller group could be comfortably accommodated in the farmhouse. He wondered, not with complete conviction, whether this might to some extent justify his attendance at the racing.

Will was no longer a soldier. He had resigned when the Territorial Force became, in effect, the new Territorial Army. He kept his courtesy rank but stopped wearing uniform. He was not at these races in any capacity. He did not see anyone he recognised. He assumed that no one there knew him. He was just a person in the crowd. It made a change, and he quite liked it.

As it turned out, someone did know who he was. "Top of the morning to you, Sir William. Congratulations on your elevation. I'm pleased to see you."

He was taller than the previous man. Slim, smartly dressed. Spoke with a moderate southern Irish accent. He wasn't being sardonic. Seemed genuinely pleased. Will just looked at him, carefully, saying nothing.

"You haven't forgotten your brethren over the water, now, have you? We still have the struggle going on."

Will was perfectly aware that the Anglo-Irish Agreement had not satisfied the hard-case republicans. To them the so-called Free State within the British Empire was an insult.

"And it's not so easy getting supplies."

Will spoke for the first time. "I've done my bit for you. My company has gone back to its proper work."

"Ah, but, you know, your army has quite a number of commitments, here and there. We think they are going to need your help again. You were good at it. The government appreciated it."

"There are manufacturers doing it on a much larger scale than we could. There is no prospect of us being asked again."

"Don't be so sure. You have your friends in London. We have ours."

Will didn't like that. He could feel his heart reacting, but he stuck to a pre-existing resolution. "In any case, I shall refuse."

The stranger tilted his head and laid a finger across puckered lips, as though considering a conundrum. "It isn't Beardsley you're worried about, is it? We can take care of him for you."

This hit Will hard. How did they know about Guy? He unfolded his shooting stick and found he had to spread his legs wide to sit on it without falling sideways. His chest was hurting.

The stranger was sympathetic. "You take a rest, Sir William, and don't you worry. To be sure, man, we'll look after you." And with that he wandered off.

Their conversation had taken place at the edge of the crowd. People were strolling about, selecting new positions from which to watch the next event, visiting refreshments and other facilities. They had attracted no attention, and no incriminating words had been spoken. But there had been no doubt as to what had been said. Irish republicans thought they could influence the authorities to ask his company to make ammunition again, in peace-time. There was no national justification for this that Will could imagine. Lloyd George's coalition government was crumbling, and his power as prime minister was in decline. What could these Irish firebrands do?

"We'll look after you." What did that mean? Then Will remembered that only two days earlier a British field marshal had been assassinated in broad daylight outside his home in London. He was shot dead by two men, widely assumed to be Irish republicans. Sir Henry was a controversial military leader, suspected of much intrigue on behalf of both his politics and career, but it seemed likely that the IRA killed him for his support of Unionist politics.

It illustrated how ruthless these dissidents were prepared to be. And how dedicated. The two assassins had given themselves little chance of escape. Apparently, after the shooting they were surrounded by a crowd and arrested by the police. There were numerous witnesses, and their guilt was clear. It was expected they would hang. These were the type of men he could be up against. And they would 'look after him'. Look after Beardsley too, apparently.

How on earth could they have known about Guy? Will did not regard Guy as a threat. Sure, the lad had rumbled him over the smuggling. Will knew he had been blackmailed into giving Guy his plum job. Despite the potential risk, Will trusted his judgement that Guy would stick to their bargain. He had so far, happy just to leading his gang, as he called it. And bless me they really do good work. Easily our best construction crew. But someone else must have known about what Will had assumed was a secret between the two of them. Was Guy in touch with these Irish people? Or were they just observing him? It was deeply unsettling.

Will had a quiet evening at the hotel. After dinner, he found a comfortable armchair in the lounge, and with a G&T to help concentrate (yes, he knew he shouldn't), tried to work it out.

How did the IRA learn about Guy? The man at the race implied Will might regard Guy as a threat. That means they must have a good idea of the situation. Will found it difficult to believe Guy was cooperating with them. Yes, he was a bit of a rogue, and Will knew the way Guy spoke to his men, but Will was certain that Guy was basically honest. In some ways, Will thought, a bit like Lloyd George. He was reminded of a poem he had memorised once about a pirate. He couldn't remember much now, but the ending had stuck in his mind. It was something like:

And so must we scan life's horizon
For all that we can clap our eyes on.

Try not to make too many enemies in the process, of course.

He felt better in the morning and took the earlier of the two trains he had selected from the timetable. Arriving late for the afternoon party wouldn't readily be forgiven.

Almost as soon as he was settled in the train and it was moving off, however, another question flashed up in his mind. It should have been obvious at the time, although not something to inquire about. How did that man know he would be at yesterday's event? Surely the IRA wouldn't keep him under constant surveillance? He couldn't be important enough. It would take a great deal of manpower. So how did they know? It worried him greatly. He hadn't discussed the motor racing with anyone in WIS. He brooded on it with something close to rising panic until the light dawned. It had to be family or friends who Val had invited to his birthday party, which should have been yesterday. When he dug his heels in about going to the motor event, she would have sent postponement and cancellation notes to set up the smaller gathering this afternoon. He could imagine Val's wording: '*He insists on going to some car racing do.*' She would have done that about a week ago, ample time for whoever it was to find the venue. There weren't so many motor-race meetings going on.

It meant someone in their circle of relatives and friends was at least a republican sympathiser, perhaps full-blown IRA. Will guessed it was likely some hothead on his side of the family, perhaps one of numerous nephews. He was pleased to have worked this out. It reduced the sense of panic. But it was depressing. The picture of a fly on a spider's web came to mind. It rather looked like his original ambivalence about loyalty, back during the war, now had him trapped.

As planned, he got home in time for lunch, and was thus dutifully at the delayed party. He apologised for the postponement, explaining his trip had been most enjoyable but had tired him, and did they mind if he was mainly sedentary during the proceedings? In fact, he didn't feel well at all, and was glad not to mingle much. Val was clearly less than pleased about it all, but she bravely played the perfect hostess, at which she was so accomplished in her homely way, and the relatively short celebrations had to be considered a success.

Rather than socialise, Will observed all the guests as closely as possible without it being conspicuous. He failed to detect anyone letting slip pleasure that something tiresome must have happened at his race meeting. He spitefully hoped the guilty party was miserably squashed by being on the cancellation list. They would get to hear that the elite of the family attended a select and most enjoyable occasion.

On Monday morning, he stayed at the farm and gave his situation some serious thought. He kept it all in his head. It didn't seem sensible to make notes.

He tried to be logical. He always did. He made some progress, but this meant facing some unpalatable possibilities.

What is the worst that can happen? Well, one outcome is I refuse to cooperate with any further smuggling, and they top me too. I don't think I'm important enough. I'm not a symbol like Henry Wilson was. But these people can no doubt be vindictive as well as calculating.

Another possibility is that the republicans take some action which exposes my smuggling during the war. I would probably spend the rest of my life in prison, which might not be long if a noose is involved, which it still could be.

And then, of course, I'm 72. The ticker has been getting more and more sensitive, even when I just worry about something. It may well not last much longer. I've got to face up to that.

Accepting he probably didn't have much more life in front of him, Will found it easier to assess what he most valued. The family, especially Val, and the company he had created, were the most important. He wondered whether, to be honest, the company trumped dear old Val. WIS reflected his worth. He wanted it to continue. With the initials 'W.I.S.' remaining as his memorial. He loved Val sincerely, and their boys. He wanted to protect them from hurt. But the company could be shut down, as a worst outcome, and then be forgotten. He must leave evidence to ensure that, if the balloon went up in one way or another, it would be clear that he was the only person in WIS involved in the smuggling. Was that true? He decided that he believed it was true, and so would plan on that basis.

Will felt much better having reached this point. Late in the morning he rode over to the works to check everything was humming along with no hitches. It was. He chatted a while with Anthony, called in on Lilly, and then went round to the nearby pub for lunch. It had just been brought to his table when Anthony caught up with him.

"Sir Will, I'm dreadfully sorry. There has been an accident."

"What's happened?"

"Guy's had a fall. I'm afraid he is dead."

He could not help clutching his chest. He had never been shot in the heart, but it couldn't be much worse. Anthony had to support him, or he would have fallen from his chair.

"Oh my God, I'm sorry." Anthony had forgotten about the heart problem. Will made no secret of his disability, but he normally managed it unobtrusively. Anthony helped Will to an armchair propped with some cushions and asked the girl behind the bar to stay with him. "I'll get the car and we'll get you back to the farm."

He was back in a few minutes. "The car's in use. Stephen has left to get over to Normanton to see what happened." Strictly, Stephen should have checked with Anthony before taking the company car, but it was an emergency.

Anthony viewed it as two emergencies, Will's health, and Guy's accident. The publican had his own car, and helped Anthony get Will home. Back at the works, Anthony delighted one of the younger lads by asking him to ride Sir Will's horse gently back to its stable at the Ingalls' farm. It was the highlight of the lad's career so far. He knew Sir Will loved his horses like his children. He rode the docile animal more carefully than necessary. In fact, all he had to do was sit on her. She knew the way.

Will recovered enough at home to fabricate an explanation for his extreme reaction to the news. He admitted to Val that he could be guilty of negligence by not banning Guy from his stunt of sliding down a rope at the end of a shift.

"But is there any legislation against it, Dear?" Val was a very practical person.

"I don't know. I probably should know. Probably not something like 'Steel construction workers should not descend by sliding down a rope'. But there might be something more general that could be interpreted to catch such goings on. I'll have to rest now."

"Yes, of course, Dear." Val was worried, as well as upset. She had known Guy and quite liked him, even though aware of his rougher side. It was worrying that the accident might have consequences for the company. But Will was right. Better for him to get over the shock first. She wanted to fetch their doctor, but Will insisted he only needed rest.

The following morning, Val checked that Will was well enough for her to go out for her normal Tuesday morning excursion. Will had in fact come to a decision after going to bed, and a strange peace had enveloped him. He had lain awake for much of the night reflecting on so many things, but his mind did not change. In the end, he slept. "I feel much better now, Dear, thank you. Yes, yes, you do your normal. My greetings to the gang." His reference was to those she would meet for coffee and a good natter in the village, under the flag of each taking their dog for a walk, or whatever other suitable cover. She would then do some shopping on the way back.

Will reviewed his decision. Whoever they were, they had the contacts to know about Guy. Perhaps Guy had been in cahoots with them. Possibly Guy was working for another Irish faction. Maybe Guy's blackmail to lead an elite construction crew had been just a perk on the side. And whoever wanted to remove whatever threat Guy represented had the reach to arrange an accidental death for him between Saturday afternoon and Monday morning. There was no doubt about it, events had reached a crisis.

He decided he didn't need breakfast. He made some careful preparations. He checked the horses and told their stable lad he could take the rest of the day off. It took him a while to decide how to start the note, but then it came quite readily. He checked that his study was as he wanted it, pocketed his revolver with one round in it, and left Val's note on the hall floor where she couldn't miss it. No one should come in before her.

In the stable yard, he chose what to sit against. He sat a while and started to get frightened. Then his resolution, which had never deserted him in life, but which tended to be under-used, went into action. Check the round. Yes, that's the right position. Muzzle in his mouth, pointed upwards. He had never been a brilliant shot, but he isn't going to miss this time. He remembers the refrain that you don't *pull* the trigger, you *squeeze* it. It had never seemed necessary to him. Obviously, all your other fingers should be holding the gun firmly, except for the trigger finger, which should be loose, and just slide the trigger back to take up the slack, check the aim again, and loose off. That was how he got his smallest groups. And here he is now, holding the butt the wrong way round, and just pushing the trigger away with his thumb. It was his last thought.

What Had Been Happening: Guy

Guy did not have the accolade of being the naughtiest in the school but was generally acknowledged as an exemplar of adventurous boyhood.

Even the teachers recognised this. His school gang had been the only one anyone could remember keeping its identity from school year to school year, as he worked his way through the classes. It wasn't easy to join, they enjoyed all sorts of pranks, quite ingenious, some of them, yet they managed to cause little harm, and only minor injuries. They largely stayed out of trouble, mainly because Guy had a good feel for what they could get away with. Moreover, he maintained control over them. Some of the teachers envied him on this point.

Most of the gang's activities consisted of boisterous but organised games in the fields and woods around Beeston. Hiding, seeking, chasing, mock battles, competitions involving stealth and manoeuvre. Also, ropes strung between trees, fallen trees as bridges, insect-ridden shelters amongst trees.

The gang was only for boys, and it was not easy to join because the initiation ceremony included being caned. That kept the cowards out. No one outside the gang knew how severe the caning was, and members were sworn to divulge nothing. They didn't, either, because they saw the point. "We're brave and tough. We don't want sissies." In fact, what they got on joining was much less than what the school could give them, if they were rash or careless enough. But applicants didn't know that.

Deidre longed to join Guy's gang. The trouble was, she was a girl. It wasn't that she wanted to be a boy. She was a girl, she went to the girls' end of the school, and one day she would be a woman and probably a mum. That was alright. She thought that women had a good deal, compared to the work some men had to do, like going down the pits, but she had observed that boys, and especially Guy's lot, had more fun than the girls.

She had also decided that children generally enjoy life more than adults. Although she did not know the word at that age, she had reached this conclusion on purely empirical grounds. She noted that, when released from parental or scholastic supervision, children generally whooped it up and larked about. Boys and girls did this in essentially different ways, but they enjoyed themselves.

Grown-ups didn't seem to. The adults in Deidre's life were serious most of the time. Men could get enthusiastic when watching football or a darts match, but, for instance, they didn't charge away from a factory at the end of the day in quite the same way as children spreading out from school gates. You would get frequent bursts of laughter from gossiping women, occasionally from groups of men, but somehow it didn't sound carefree.

Thus, liking to play with words, and based on her observation of old and young around her, other than in pubs, Deidre had assembled and polished her philosophy on this topic into a quatrain:

Now when you are young
You want to have fun,
Since later in life
There's trouble and strife.

This was just in her head. She had never written it down. She couldn't find a way to get the first rhyme perfect but had decided 'young' and 'fun' were close enough. She would have preferred to replace the first word in the last line with 'Must be', since it reflected the logic of her conclusion, but she couldn't re-jig it to get the syllables right. As it stood, the scanning was nicely regular, and that pleased her in a way she could feel but not describe. She had numerous other such scraps in her head, which is where she kept them.

Both girls and boys have fun, of course, but the kind of fun boys had was more to her taste than the girls' variety. Naturally enough, therefore, she wanted to join in with the boys. Like everyone else, she understood that joining Guy's gang was a risky business. It might be even worse if a girl tried to join. But if she wanted real fun, she would have to take risks.

She had caught wind that a new boy had applied to join, and she already knew where the gang's meeting place was, in one of thickest parts of a wood outside the village. She would lie in wait and see what happens.

The wait was long and tedious that Saturday morning, but in the end the gang gathered, noisily and in straggles. *How on earth do they keep secrets?* she wondered, deep inside undergrowth and behind several trees.

The candidate for admission was the only boy not looking happy. Guy was right beside him, but not holding him. He came willingly. Having got the membership in a half-circle around one side of a fallen tree, Guy commanded attention. "Right, you worms. This is serious. We have someone who wants to join."

This was Guy's style. He wasn't a bully, and he wasn't cruel, but he led by making it completely clear that they were the lowest form of life compared to him. It was their privilege to be in his gang. They had so much fun that his way of speaking was a sort of badge they all wore, with pride. "Does this miserable looking earwig want to join us?" looking hard at the person concerned.

The earwig, looking less happy but with grim determination, managed to state that yes, he did want to join. Guy turned to the circle of boys who had all been through this. "If he passes the test, can he join?"

"Yes, yes," on all sides. If they objected at this stage, there would be no spectacle to enjoy. Finally, back to the applicant. "If you pass the initiation test, do you swear to keep secret and never tell anyone about the organisation and activities of this gang, for as long as you live?"

With somewhat more difficulty, the earwig managed to produce an audible, "Yes, I swear." He was then told to take off his trousers.

The procedure for the new member was to lie face down over the fallen tree trunk. On the far side, the land fell towards their river, as they termed it. It didn't really qualify as more than a ditch, but it was nice to think of their meeting place as by a river. The upper half of the slope was covered in stinging nettles.

Guy explained the initiation requirements to the candidate, "You must keep your hands over the trunk. The nettles are far enough down not to bother you. You'll get six strokes of the cane. You must not cry out, get up or bring your hands back to protect yourself. There will be a longer pause after stroke three to change the lookouts, so everyone sees at least part of the test."

Lookouts! Deidre hadn't thought about them. She couldn't see any. They must be behind her, further away from the centre of things. Was she hidden from all directions of view? And talking of direction of view, she couldn't see the victim's bottom very clearly, particularly what she was most curious about. Just after the third stroke, against every sensible tactical principle, she attempted to move her position, and was spotted by a lookout on his way in.

"Hey, there's someone here!"

"It's a girl!"

"It's Deidre!" Most of the boys knew her. She was a good sport. But she was a girl. She was brought to Guy, held in various ways by several of the boys. Guy stood between her and the current victim and told them to let her go. Deidre came straight out with 'I want to join'.

"OK," said Guy, "turn around and face away while we finish this test, then we'll discuss it."

The current initiate passed his test. He remained motionless and silent, except trying to look around, most unhappily, when he heard about Deidre, and even worse, heard her voice. There are limits. But, like most, he was surprised how light the caning had been. Guy never did it himself, but kept a firm check on how it was done.

When the latest member was decent again, Deidre was turned around to face Guy. "I want to join. I'll take the cane."

"Rabble, this is a boys' gang. Do we let Deidre join?"

The rabble was in no doubt. Merry cries came from all sides. "Yes! Yes!"

"She must be caned!"

"Her drawers must come down!"

"Can I do it?"

"No, me!"

"Shut up, you slime. We can't cane her. It would be more difficult for a girl to hide the marks. If they were discovered, there'd be trouble." Guy had four younger sisters, and he knew about these things. In practice, the marks wouldn't amount to much, but Guy believed in being careful. There was a general cooling. Several of those present, including Deidre, could see why Guy was the leader.

"Anyway, first things first. Assuming she passes some sort of test, are we quite sure Deidre can join?"

"Yes, yes," with no hesitation, except where a more thoughtful hand went up.

"Just to be sure. We are voting only to let Deidre join? If she passes a test and she joins, that doesn't mean any other girl who comes along is allowed to take a test?"

"That's correct. Deidre is a special case. This is a boys' gang, and we are not going to let any old girl join." Guy had already marked this younger boy as his successor when he left school, which would be as soon as he was allowed to.

Guy liked the idea of having Deidre along. He could already see ways in which she could be useful. Guy administered the oath and explained the test. He'd only just thought of it, but it seemed about right.

Deidre had to wear stockings for school, but when she went out to play, her mother allowed her to leave them off, otherwise they would just come back shredded.

"Deidre, to join this gang you must stand on the tree trunk and jump down into those nettles. You must then go down the bank to get out of them. Don't climb back on the tree. You'll be stung badly, but you must not scream or call out. Meanwhile, a few of you Slugs"—addressing the gang—"go and look for dock leaves. There must be some around here."

This presented a choice to the Slugs. Some wanted to stay right there are see how Deidre coped with her ordeal. Others were willing to forgo that immediate thrill for the future prospect of being allowed to rub Deidre's legs with dock leaves. Guy liked to think that he could size people up, and the group split on roughly the lines he expected, except for one lad who tried to do both, walking away but looking over his shoulder, straight into some nettles. In short trousers.

Deidre showed no hesitation. She was straight up onto the trunk, immediately jumped down into the nettles, and then waded very rapidly indeed out of them onto the ditch-side grass, where she threw herself to the ground, writhing with her mouth wide open, taking violent rasping breaths and making a frantic mewing sound. Guy was worried. That must have been far worse than their canings. Was Deidre really hurt? Would she need hospital? Her legs were already covered in red blotches. He stopped the first Slug back with dock leaves, who surrendered them most reluctantly, but was then mollified when Guy passed them to Deidre with good advice. "Rub these on your legs. They'll reduce the pain, and it will distract you." It worked. Having something to do made it easier, as well as the effect of the leaves. After a few minutes, she recovered enough to stand and breath normally again. Well, more-or-less normally. But there was no hiding the discolorations on her legs. "Say you slipped off a tree trunk into some nettles." After all, it was true.

The Slugs gathered around her with warm congratulations. Guy had a feeling that somehow the gang had grown up a bit. But he could also see that Deidre simply must be an exception, or the whole nature of the outfit would be spoiled.

Her parents generally accepted her explanation. Mum harboured suspicions but kept them to herself.

Deidre turned out to be a valuable gang member. She didn't expect to do everything the boys did, but there was a great deal she could join in with, and she was a good organiser. She occasionally helped with minor injuries, sometimes wondering if they really were accidental, and she made an effective lookout until everyone around the district realised how she stood with the gang.

One activity she didn't participate in was their speciality of climbing trees. She wasn't bothered who saw her legs. It was just that heights made her dizzy.

Guy made it an important activity on the basis that every boy should be good at climbing. He even gave instruction on the subject, since some of them didn't approach it correctly. He never pressed the few who simply had no head for heights, but some of the others needed to be shown key points, such as go slowly, spread your weight between two or three branches where necessary, and, most importantly, recognise dead branches which can snap without warning.

The pinnacle of success in Guy's arboreal academy was to get one's head above the highest part of the tree you're climbing. Many a lad found just how difficult this is. You must choose the right kind of tree, and you may need to pull several branches together to support your weight at the very top.

Guy closely supervised all attempts to reach this ambitious pinnacle. He keenly appreciated that one serious injury would shut his gang down. Both the aspirant and tree had to be approved, and the latter must have a high enough density of branches such that anyone falling would be slowed down by them and have a good chance of grabbing one. Despite the competition for the pre-nominal 'tree-head', nobody ever did fall. Not properly, anyway. A few slips and panicky grabs. Quite a few grazes.

Guy particularly appreciated the view afforded to the tree-head, looking out over the top of a tree's canopy. There was nothing like it. It made one feel special. Other boys who had achieved the same status agreed, which acted as a spur to others.

An entertaining experience for the tree-head could be the reaction of birds who were not expecting their domain to be so invaded. There was an example the first time Guy finally got his head above the highest leaf. He was gazing in awe at the extraordinary scene when a fat wood pigeon landed neatly almost within arm's length. After contentedly getting its wings comfortably stowed, it looked around and only then identified the unusual object for what it was. The wings were redeployed on an emergency basis, and it shot off with an alarmed squawk. Guy feared his laughter would make him let go.

Another skill Guy liked to promote was knots. Both how to tie the important ones and choosing the right knot for a particular job. A much-used gang knot was the highwayman's hitch, necessary for one of their versions of release-o.

Each team took a hostage to their base and tied him between two trees. A rope went from each wrist to a tree where it was hitched with the loose end hanging down. The hostage couldn't bring his hands together to untie his wrists, nor either hand to a hitch to release it. He might well try to shake a hitch loose. If he succeeded, then the other side deserved to lose since it hadn't been tightened properly. The game was to release your hostage. The types and degree of violence allowed to stop the other side releasing theirs were adjusted with experience and according to participants.

Deirdre loved knots. She was good at them. She even assisted in providing tuition. To her disappointment, however, Guy banned her from release-o. Too disruptive. She would be the only person attacked. She was normally the umpire.

Another application of knots was to make a rope bridge between two trees. Not being all that well off in rope, they normal made the bridge from just two, one to stand on and the other to hold. The difficult part was getting them secured around fat trunks. Some of the more reckless wanted to install them at serious heights, citing the ease of tying them to something smaller. Guy banned anything above a safe height to fall. Between two trees a falling boy doesn't bounce from branch to branch. It's straight down to the ground. And if someone froze halfway across, Guy couldn't see a way to rescue them if the ropes were too high. They could help a boy down from being stuck up a tree at any height, but not from ropes strung between trees unless low enough to reach from the ground.

A useful lesson they learnt from bridges was how much stronger a rope needs to be if you stretch it tight and then stand on it, compared to one hanging down for swinging on. They soon stopped trying to make the bridges very tight. You can still cross ropes which sag a bit, and the one you are standing on is less likely to break.

It was while the gang were concentrating on rope and what can be done with it that Guy's teacher decided to include knots, briefly, in his syllabus. Guy was generally sceptical as to the value of what the school tried to teach him, so he initially viewed this as an encouraging development. How to tie a reef knot was demonstrated, but no explanation was given as to the right and wrong places to use it. Guy was wondering whether to raise the question of appropriate application, or possibly ask about the difference between a reef and a thief knot, when the master forged straight on by warning them about always tying a knot carefully to get it right, otherwise it might prove to be a slipknot. "And that's no use to anyone, is it?"

Guy raised his hand and started to frame a question on what seemed to him a serious misinterpretation when the class comedian jumped in first. "Please Sir, slipknots can be useful for some things, can't they?" The teacher unwisely asked for an example. "Well Sir, if you wanted to hang someone!"

The class exploited the well-established principle that a hearty laugh can take a minute off any lesson. Two minutes if it's the teacher's joke. The teacher in this case realised he had been caught in a trap, but also looked less confident. Had he got slipknots wrong?

To Guy this was serious, but he was prepared to consider the alternative interpretation. The teacher seemed to think 'slipknot' meant a badly tied one which slips apart when it comes under tension. Guy's concept was a knot which is intended to slide and thus tighten around something, such as a bunch of fallen tree branches to carry over the shoulder to where a den was to be built. And, of course, not to be used around your body to support you. You might not be able to breathe. Yes, he had met this specific warning in a magazine. It must be the proper meaning.

It was only a little episode in school one day. It wasn't repeated, and their teacher never went back to knots. But it confirmed to Guy how little use his education was proving to be. Sure, they had taught him to read and write. He knew enough arithmetic to see him through life. But what else had he learnt at school that would be useful? What help was it to know the date of the Battle of Hastings? Would he really need to know who wrote 'Oliver Twist'? He had thus been disappointed when a teacher addressed a useful subject for once, and then turned out to be ignorant about it. It confirmed his attitude to school for the rest of his life.

The following summer Guy managed to leave school. Dad had insisted he did a year beyond the minimum leaving age of 14. Guy's father was a butcher in Beeston, in fact *the* butcher in Beeston. He had long hoped that his only son would join him in the business and in due course take it over. But although the teenage lad helped willingly enough at times, it plainly wasn't what he wanted as a regular job.

Guy knew he was a leader. Spending his life as a butcher meant being polite to customers, and for that matter not moving around much. A few visits to farms, abattoirs, trade markets; that's about it. Otherwise behind the counter, being polite. Not at all what he wanted. It wasn't that he wanted to be rude. He wanted to lead, and his style of leading omitted courtesies.

There was a factory on the outskirts of the village doing steel construction. On a visit to Nottingham, he had seen them putting up a fire escape. He'd been able to chat briefly with one of the workmen. It looked like something he would enjoy. A good career, too. And it was close to home. Guy just walked there, went in, and asked for a job. The general manager liked his frank and open expression, and took him to see the Workshop Foreman, who noted his robust-looking build. Steel bashing can be hard work.

Business was going well. Mr Ingalls gave them a moderately free hand over employment. They offered him a trial period. There were a few formalities, and before long he was putting in regular days in the fabrication shop. A week later they started paying him. That really made a difference to his outlook. He was living at home, so he decided that half of his pay would go to Mother. He'd keep the other half. Mother and Father considered this to be proper, but were still impressed. "Maybe we did something right with him, Love."

That same summer Deidre also left school. She had a realistic view of her prospects in life and had already decided that the best she could do is get a capable and considerate husband, a home of their own, however small, and children. She had spent a year as an official, if irregular, member of Guy's gang, and this had confirmed her earlier impression that he was something special. She needn't look any further. She intended to nab Guy before any unprincipled siren got their claws into him. She never, then nor later, stopped to think she should have cast her net wider.

They became a recognised couple. Guy's work kept him too busy from Monday to Friday to do much in the evenings, and sometimes there was work on Saturdays. But they had time together at weekends. Both families were happy with the arrangement. Deidre's siblings were impressed that she could bag a guy like Guy, as the joke went. Some of the cruder minded of her old school friends suggested her actual wish was better described by prefixing a pair of letters to 'bag'. Guy's sisters approved of Deidre. In their view, Guy might be the best lad around but he would need to be kept in line, and they reckoned Deidre had what it took. So both families were content, and a certain amount of socialising and cooperation became normal.

Although Mr Beardsley was disappointed that his only son didn't want to take over the butcher's shop, he accepted that the boy had the right to decide for himself. And in a way he was proud that his son had the initiative to get work at a well-known and prosperous local firm without any help from him. He'd brought him up right, to stand on his own feet and find his way in the world.

But it was worrying. He couldn't see any of his four daughters continuing the business, and he really thought that, with its loyal local clientele, it was well worthwhile to keep it going. For one thing, it was his main hope of a pension.

He already approved of Guy's choice of girlfriend, but this changed to positive enthusiasm when she proved not only happy to help in the shop but was strong and reliable enough. She rapidly developed an almost alarming facility with the various tools of butchery and had no reluctance about dismantling a carcase. She got on well with the customers, too. It became her regular occupation. Guy earned a decent wage packet at WIS, and Deidre helped her prospective father-in-law in his shop.

Up to the time he left school Guy had mainly thought about girls as sillier and weaker versions of boys, Deidre being the outstanding exception. Spending more time in her company, sometimes in discretely selected locations, his thoughts rapidly swung in the normal direction. In this area, although she reciprocated his spoken feelings, she proved much the stronger of the two. There was no shifting her: marriage, home, children, in that order. And as fond of all their parents as she was, 'home' meant a place of their own, not shared with anyone. It was just as well they could discuss these practicalities openly, and Deidre wasn't entirely ungenerous, but she maintained a firm line beyond which she wouldn't go. For that matter, beyond which he wasn't allowed to go.

Mum, who still did Guy's laundry, began to understand the situation, and discussed it with Dad. He was embarrassed by such talk, but they reached an agreement. Guy and Deidre were obviously serious about each other and a suitable match. The sooner they got married the better, as young as they were.

The immediate outcome was financial. Guy had received two pay increases under Chairman Will's enlightened employment policies. Only small, but useful and encouraging, the sort of thing you can base plans on. Moreover, he now had his own savings account with the Nottingham Building Society. Left to himself, Guy would have continued giving half his pay to Mum. That was changed. His parents could manage without it, and they wanted to see the youngsters set up. From then on, Guy kept all his weekly wage, and Dad even started paying Deidre a small amount for her work in the shop. Also, she could take time off when they weren't busy to look for somewhere to live.

Around the time Guy left school, copies of *Scouting for Boys* had begun to appear. A weekly magazine, *The Scout*, started to sell well. Guy had mixed feelings. He considered himself the inventor of boys larking around out of doors in a semi-organised fashion and took the view that this Baden-Powell chap had pinched his ideas. But his old gang could never have competed with the scale and scope of this new movement.

The Brownsea Island camp attracted widespread interest. Guy's gang had often thought of spending a night sleeping in the woods during the summer holidays, but the cooler heads were worried about shameful defectors retreating home around midnight, especially if it rained. The disgrace could never have been expunged. Nor could they ever have afforded tents. In the event, although often discussed, no serious attempt was made to obtain permission from enough parents to make it worthwhile.

And now the Scouts made it all look easy. Obviously, they were an organisation with money. While they initially looked attractive to Guy, some of the scouting objectives seemed too civilised, even goody-goody, for his taste. Later, as he became more involved in work at WIS, and started to think increasingly like an adult, he was attracted to being part of the movement. Perhaps he could be a leader in one of the 'packs' being formed around the district. There had always been the Boys' Brigade in Beeston, at least as far as he could remember, but they were church-based and that didn't suit him. In practice, what with work and spending time with Deidre, there never was the time to inquire about scouting, and then other events took over.

To start with at WIS he was mostly involved in keeping workshop and store areas clean and tidy. Dad had perceptively warned him about this. "If they can't trust you to do the simplest job, m'boy, they won't try you out on more difficult things, will they?" Guy quite understood the point. WIS an exciting place, particularly the workshops, and he could see that there was much to learn, stuff that had never come up at school.

He'd originally wanted to go straight into a construction crew. That was squashed immediately. "No one does construction 'til he knows metal work."

When he had proved his willingness to do menial tasks, his education with tools began. He was expecting it to be something larger than a file, but he soon found that he needed to learn how to use even this simple tool properly, even if it did come readily. He hadn't heard of a 'safe edge' before but could immediately see how important it was when working in a corner. And he quickly discovered just how versatile a selection of files could be for all sorts of shaping tasks.

The hacksaw, which came next, was not so easy. "You're pressing too hard, son. See? The blade is twisting." The old gaffer in the workshop was right, it was twisting. But why not make the blade stiffer? This was all new. He thought he knew how to use a saw.

Guy had helped in Dad's shop on occasions, including sawing through bones. But no one had previously asked him to cut like this. The gaffer had scratched a thin line across an offcut of steel angle using a try-square and a special hard-pointed tool called a 'scriber'. He was now expected to cut the steel right beside this line using a narrow flexible blade which was only kept straight by being held taught in a frame.

"Put your left hand on the far end. That's it. Now, slow long strokes the whole length of the blade, and only enough pressure to hold it firmly down. No more. Watch the blade and watch where it's cutting. That's it, much better."

It did start to get better, but he had to restart a few times with a new scribed line, the lump of steel getting progressively shorter. Another member of the workshop, passing by, stopped when he heard the gaffer telling Guy that his cut should just touch the line. "He's making it easy for you, Guy. Just to start with. You actually have to cut away *half* the width of that line, leaving the other half in place to show where it is."

Guy looked at the gaffer, who gave nothing away. '*Ok,*' thought Guy, '*they're joshing. At least, I hope they are.*'

Just as he was making progress aligning with the scratch, it turned out that there was another angle, literally.

"OK, son. You've got the blade running in a groove within sight of my line, but it's not going straight down. It's sloping when you look at it the other way. That's why I scribed a line on the front here as well. You've got to watch both directions. Oh, and lift the blade on the return stroke. That way you push the swarf away from you. So it don't clog the blade."

This was the first time Guy had faced something he wanted to do but couldn't just pick up easily. Some inner voice said to him, '*OK, boy, you're in a man's world now.*' It was frustrating, but he had a feeling he was where he wanted to be.

He also, in the end, got an explanation as to why the blade wasn't stiffer. "Have you ever used a tenon saw? The sort used by carpenters. That blade is stiff, so you can make accurate straight cuts. But you can't steer it hardly at all once you get going. You've got to get it right pretty much from the start, or you're in dead trouble. The hacksaw blade can be steered easily, which, once you get the knack, you can use to keep it just beside the line. In fact, removing half the scratch is the ideal, but asking rather a lot.

"And, you're cutting steel, which is hard work. If the blade was thicker, you'd be cutting out more steel, and that would be even harder work. Another thing, if you want to know, the blade is made from special hard steel, or you'd never cut mild steel with it, and that means it's made from expensive steel. And the teeth must be very small so you're only removing a small bit of metal with each. So, what with the tiny teeth and the hardness, it's not worth trying to sharpen the blade. Instead, it's made with as little steel as possible to keep it cheap, and when it's blunt you throw it away and fit a another one." He chuckled. "Does that answer your question, son?"

Guy didn't like being called 'son', but he appreciated the explanation.

Apart from being an acknowledged success with his gang, Guy had performed less than average at school. He saw the point of simple arithmetic. Obviously, you must be able to count things, work out prices, and check your change. But most school subjects seemed invented just to give teachers something to teach. Take fractions, for instance. They're supposed to be another way of writing division. But why not just divide? And what use is all the business about common denominators, or whatever they are?

At WIS he met, for the first time, an engineer's rule marked in inches with fractions from half to sixty-fourths. It looked intended to confuse to start with. But when he had to work out the mid-point of a steel bar six and five-eighths long it suddenly made sense. After a bit more of a struggle, he could do it for *seven* and five-eighths inches.

And take angles. At school, they were just a provocation. Now he needed to lay out where a diagonal brace would go, and the difference between 45 and 60 degrees became significant. He even learnt the difference between a sine and a tangent, and how to use the angle scales on a slide rule to find them.

His world expanded rapidly. WIS was the only company for some way around to have installed one of the new blueprint machines. It had paid for itself almost immediately since they no longer had to all work from the same drawing, or get a draughtsman to trace it, which took extra time and could produce mistakes. Guy learnt to read those diagrams. In time, he was qualified on most of the workshop equipment and could be trusted to make the simpler types of part as specified by the drawing office.

Meanwhile, Deidre had also been busy. Guy needed to be close to his work, which limited her search area, but at last she found two upstairs rooms to rent from an elderly widow who lived downstairs in a terraced house on the edge of the adjacent village of Chilwell. It was just over a mile from WIS. Guy could walk that. She would have a dual gas ring for cooking, a tub for washing, and they would share the toilet outside in the back yard. It wasn't luxury, but they would manage.

She was pleased with her arrangements, and she knew Mum had been quietly assembling a modest trousseau for her. She also relished the sense of continuity in wearing Mum's old wedding dress, carefully preserved, and needing only minor adjustments. This pleasant anticipation turned into panic when she spotted a serious gap in her preparations. Good old mum, she had seen it coming, and a crash course in cooking the day before the wedding was enough to see her through her first few days.

It was the summer of 1913. A rather grey day. It wasn't a lavish occasion. But the simple ceremony was charming. It was well attended, since they both had wide circles of family and friends. Quite a few of Guy's old gang were there. St John's, a thoroughly traditional parish church, was just right, and the vicar knew what to say.

As they walked back through the nave together, Guy was not entirely comfortable. He was delighted to be married to Deidre, and he sincerely admired her. But he liked to be the active leader, not at the focus of events over which he could exercise little influence. On the other hand, the beam on Deidre's face would have challenged any sunbeam outside, had there been any. A whispered exchange near the back was probably heard by more than intended.

"Is there something of the angling competition here? You know, holding up the largest fish?"

"Oh, don't be so horrid! Hmm. Tee-hee."

For the reception, they adjourned to the Crown. It didn't matter whether you were invited. The pub was legally open.

The honeymoon was the following Sunday and Monday, much of which were taken up by moving selected possessions, including some presents, into their new home and getting it organised. It was all very new to Guy. Deidre had planned most of it, and seemed pleased with how it went. It was only as he was setting out for work on Tuesday morning, feeling a somewhat different man, that he realised he hadn't formally proposed to her, as far as he could remember. Should he do it sort of retrospectively? In the end he decided to let it go. Etiquette was low on his list of priorities, and Deirdre seemed happy enough.

His first experience of steel construction came when illness laid a man off from one of their crews, briefly but unexpectedly. Guy was sent to make up numbers but worked only on the ground. It was a medium-sized fire escape in West Bridgford. Parts were delivered by cart from Beeston. Guy helped with attaching the hoisting rope and sending them up in the required order.

Guy already had his own ideas about knots. He and his gang had been experts at swinging around in trees with old bits of rope. None of their knots ever came undone. They knew how to tie them. The crew had quite different ideas, and quickly made Guy understand what they wanted. A figure-of-eight and a shackle. That's how we do it. Don't argue. If a section falls off a hoist, we're the people underneath. See? Once that was settled, he fitted in fine.

The man in charge of the ground crew had a schedule of parts and blueprints of the design. He, and the foreman working aloft, discussed and decided the hoisting order. Guy could see how important it was to get it right. Each section hoisted needed to be fixed in place when it got there, before the next one went up. Some of the assemblies were handed. Do we need the left-hand or right-hand one for this next corner? For that matter, how do we know which is which? You must be able to visualise it after it has been hoisted and swung into position.

He enjoyed helping with that fire escape. It reawakened his original wish to do construction. The trouble was by this time he considered himself an important member of the workshop staff. Guy rarely suffered from self-doubt. Developments in powered tools were being considered. He was looking forward to seeing it happen. And was a move into construction even open to him? Would the company allow it? Anyroad, which did he want?

This conundrum was solved for him in August 1914. He knew that many people thought a war was coming, particularly with the threat of this upstart Germany trying to challenge Britain's naval supremacy. And then there had been an assassination in Europe, which apparently was causing international problems. Guy had been too occupied to pay it much attention. He enjoyed his work, and at home there was now their 4-month-old son Tom, on whom Guy doted. Deidre's first pregnancy had gone well, and Tom was a robust and generally cheerful baby with distinct signs of ginger hair. Guy reckoned he was a good prospective gang member. When he's a bit older, of course.

"Do you have any ginger relatives, Love?"

Guy didn't know. "I'm not certain, but you do, don't you?"

"Yes, but I believe there has to be someone on both sides."

"Really?"

"Yes, they told us about it in biology. It was discovered by a Swiss monk experimenting with peas, but I can't remember how it works."

"It does make you wonder what peas have to do with it. This was something they taught you in school, you say?" It sounded like further confirmation of Guy's views on education.

And then Britain was at war. There was a wild outbreak of enthusiasm. Thousands of lads were volunteering, worried it might be over before they had a chance to show what they could do. Guy was divided in his mind. He was a family man now. Was it right for him to leave them to do what he saw as his obvious duty? And have a grown-up adventure, of course.

Deidre brought it up. She could see what Guy was thinking. "You want to go, don't you?"

It took him by surprise. "I feel I ought to."

"You're married. You're not expected to."

"No, but other married men have signed up. I hate the idea people might think I was using it as an excuse. Or worse, that I'm a coward."

"No one thinks you're a coward. But look, Love, I know what you're like. If you want to get into it before it's all over, then off you go. I can do my bit. I'll look after Tom for you."

The ground shifted perceptibly under Guy's feet. Perhaps he was no longer the most important member of this family. He was unhappy with indecision for a few days. Then he discovered that Deidre had already made the arrangements. They would stop renting their rooms in Chilwell, and she and Tom would move in with the senior Beardleys. It would be far too crowded with her own parents, and staying with Guy's would be handy for helping in the shop. It was all settled and agreed with both sets of parents, apparently.

Guy couldn't remember it being discussed and agreed with him, but it made it easier for him to make up his mind.

He still waited a few weeks. By now, he identified with WIS. It was a large part of who he was. He didn't want to leave his job to join up, but then the war fizzle out and he couldn't get his job back, even though he was pretty certain he would. Then the question was settled by the war itself. It didn't fizzle out. It looked like being a real war, and not a short one. Once that had become clear, Guy was decided. He would have found it difficult to say, but he was a loyal Englishman. If his country needed soldiers, he was ready. Also, it sounded dangerous and great fun, an attractive combination. Guy was not a deep thinker, not in the philosophical sense. He volunteered.

He had no trouble getting in. He not only *was* over 18, he looked it as well. It upset him to find that he had to take all his clothes off for the medical. His eyes were fine. He hadn't thought they weren't. The solemn promise he had to make struck him as unnecessary, although later he found it had moved him a bit. On the other hand, he was disappointed about the King's Shilling. He'd somehow picked up the impression he would get this useful tip on joining the army. He must have misunderstood. Perhaps His Majesty couldn't spare the change.

Most of the basic infantry training was tedious. It was also conducted under gruesome conditions. As autumn turned into winter their life in the increasingly crowded training camp became hideous. It was cold and muddy. Petty requirements and bullying sergeants seemed intent on making everything as tough as it could be for the once-eager recruits. They hauled railway sleepers through water-filled holes and endured endless route marches with bricks in their packs. And stupid things like how to hold a lump of wood pretending it was a rifle. Some of the lads were still fretting that the war would be over before they got their chance. They had yet to find out that there would be plenty of war left for them when they got there. What's more, their training turned out to be an excellent preparation for what they had let themselves in for.

Guy didn't complain. He considered himself tough, and doggedly put up with the nonsense and chaos without making a fuss. He was determined to be a good soldier, as well as a brave one.

He was not impressed by some of his fellow-recruits. He might be able to turn a few of them into a good gang if he got the chance. But he didn't, and wisely didn't try.

He thought the drill training barmy. "Surely we're not expected to march in straight lines when attacking the enemy?" he asked. His drill sergeant had recognised the natural soldier in Guy, and in private was sympathetic. "No, of course we don't," hoping to Gawd he was right. The sergeant had more insight into the mental processes of senior officers than Guy. "But you might 'ave to parade for the King, and you will certainly 'ave to parade for the colonel. And drill does 'elp a body of men to get used to movin' together. So just stick with it, lad."

On the firing range things were much better, except there wasn't enough of it. Ammunition was not only strictly controlled but highly rationed. Guy understood the Lee Enfield rifle almost immediately. Once he knew the striker hitting the back of the cartridge fired it off, and he didn't need to know how that worked, the rest just fell into place. The range scale on the rear sight was obvious. He hit the target with his first shot, and with a few more was correcting for recoil and wind. He qualified as marksman unusually quickly. There wasn't enough ammunition to cover all distances and firing positions, as well as fast and slow. He was obviously good at it. In his case, they were justified in cutting some corners. To Guy, it didn't seem to need much skill. Estimating range was tricky at first, but it was important and only needed practice. Otherwise, calm attention and firm steady hands, that's all.

Bayonet training seemed a bit like just another drill. Do you really need training to drive a knife into something? For that matter, would they get that close to the enemy? Many of the claims made about the Lee Enfield with just normal iron sights were, he knew, exaggerated. But even so, it was deadly at vastly greater distances than close quarters. With only a few seconds to take aim, on one knee and an elbow on the other, Guy knew he could reliably hit a man in the body at 100 yards. Prone with both elbows on the ground, 200 yards. With the rifle steadied on a parapet, a good chance at 300 yards. And for quite a distance beyond that he could make people extremely uneasy. Force them to take cover. Moreover, the Germans, who no doubt had rifles just as good, were also well-equipped with machine guns. So how desperate does the army think this will be if it's going to come to hand-to-hand?

Guy discovered later how such theoretical reasoning can reach conclusions at variance with practical experience.

Conditions changed just as the weather started to improve. They were issued with what was recognisably full kit. This included mess and shaving equipment, and lessons on how to use it. New proper uniforms, with webbing and pouches, and each recruit their own rifle. They knew they were going somewhere, and their spirits rose.

Guy reached the vicinity of Ypres in the spring. He didn't know where he was, but he knew he had got there on a crowded slow ship and in some crowded slow trains, plus a lot of marching, much of it at night. Ypres was a sizeable town, filled with a mixture of civilians and troops. He was surprised at how many civilians. You could hear artillery, so they couldn't be all that far from the frontline, yet people were getting on with their lives. Most commercial activity consisted of selling goods and services to the army. Guy discovered that this was 'Wipers', and that the Germans were being held several miles to the north and east after hard fighting in the autumn. There was some shell damage in the town, but at present it was outside the range of German guns. They were billeted around the town in various buildings, including some private arrangements made with civilians, especially by the officers. Guy slept in an empty commercial building, probably an old warehouse, along with the other recruits in his batch.

After being roused in the morning, told to hurry up and shave and have breakfast, they were then told to wait, which they did for several hours, doing nothing. They were eventually mustered for what they were told would be an important speech. A senior officer stood on a wooden crate, praised them for their courage in volunteering, and assured them of the important role they would be playing in the conflict. It was essential for 'Eep' not to fall to the Germans. It was only later their sergeant explained he meant 'Wipers', which was the town where they were. The officer had said it the French way. It struck Guy that the speech told them nothing useful. Bit like school.

Maybe the linguistically accomplished speaker didn't have a chance to get to anything useful, because another officer rushed up and grabbed his attention. The two whispered together on what seemed an urgent basis and then they both hurried away, leaving the crowd of recruits in the hands of a sergeant. The word quickly got around that the Germans had, that morning, released poisonous gas north and east of the town. There were casualties. The Allied line had moved back, the euphemism for 'retreat'. At least this was useful information. Gas? Guy's training had said nothing about gas. He thought wars were fought with guns. In fact, their training caught up with this development with nonchalant promptness. Apparently, you piss on your handkerchief and then breath through it.

Over the next few days Guy and his comrades were told they would be going to different sectors or told nothing at all. They soon became sceptical of anything said to them. But the sound of guns, not far outside the town, and shells now landing in the town, had an eloquence not easily ignored. Despite the damage, the town remained a communications hub. The flow of wounded from the trenches back to the rear gave them all something to consider. The waiting was tedious and made them nervous. At last, they were marched through the town and out east to relieve Canadian troops as what became known as the 2nd battle of Ypres died down. Guy had to get used to hearing shells approaching. He learnt in time to estimate where they were going, just from the sound, and thus choose whether and if necessary where to dive for cover. It wasn't always practicable to take such defensive measures. Your estimate of the shell's destination was fallible. You had to accept there was a large element of luck. Many men became fatalistic, or pretended to be. The concept of whether a shell 'has your number on it' somehow seemed to reassure them, not something Guy could understand.

For the first time, he was launched into the cycle of stealing at night through communication trenches to man a front-line trench for eight days, then four days further back in a support or reserve trench, and then back to the rear for four days of rest. At least, that was the theory. He had his first experience of living, day and night, mostly below ground level, standing-to, peering through an improvised periscope across no-man's land. Sometimes he had to keep watch from what was grandly termed a 'redoubt', or less grandly a 'sap', which was typically a hole in the ground somewhat in front of their wire, to give advance warning of a sneaky attack, and, it was hoped, a location from which to fire at the enemy. Manning one of these holes seemed potentially the most dangerous service he had to perform, at least in the first month or so.

The line to the east of Ypres was now static, and it became Guy's home. In view of his marksman rating, he was offered work as a sniper. This included a few privileges, but the role did not attract him. Typically, it meant choosing an inconspicuous firing position from which a low point in the enemy's parapet could be seen, or some other exposed spot, and lying motionless for hours, possibly all day, hoping to get a glimpse of someone to shoot. Guy quite understood the value of sniping. Both sides practised it to make life less convenient for the other. Guy knew of men who, with a moment's carelessness, had been killed by a shot in the head. But he didn't think he could cope with being a sniper. He had no objection in principle to killing the enemy, just the motionless waiting he would have to endure. It would be too boring.

Raiding was another thing all together. Long night-time duties looking out into dark no-man's land had impressed him with how, much of the time, it could be quiet, with nothing apparently happening. And plenty of shell-holes to hide in. He volunteered for the first raid his company organised. He genuinely volunteered. Raids were not universally popular, and most privates had to be persuaded into the duty. The lieutenant leading the raid had noted that Guy was a steady sensible sort of soldier and was delighted he joined willingly.

For his part, Guy was not at all delighted with the lieutenant's leading of the raid.

To start with, there was almost no preparation. Guy's school gang prepared for a war in the woods by a briefing from Guy so that everyone knew the rules. Then the two sides, each with its appointed leader, went off out of earshot of the other to lay their plans, to which spies from the other side would try to get within earshot. They were then fully prepared to do battle. That was for a serious game in the woods. For something trivial, like a raid on German trenches, the lieutenant gave some sketchy ideas to the NCOs, and off they all went.

To continue with, there was a nearly full moon. 'So we can see what we are doing' said the lieutenant. '*So the Germans can see us,*' thought Guy.

Thirdly, they had the wrong equipment. Rifles weren't easy to carry when crawling through mud, especially if you wanted to keep the action clean.

Fourthly, the party was far too large. It couldn't be controlled, except by shouting orders. Even the lieutenant knew he couldn't do that. As a result, the party acted less co-ordinated than ideal.

And fifthly, they made far too much noise. Their equipment clanked, and with such a crowd there was too much whispered discussion, in fact argument.

It was a fiasco, but they did get up to the German wire. The lieutenant started trying to cut through it, at which point the Germans opened up with rifle fire. The lieutenant had nowhere to hide and was killed almost immediately. The Germans had a pretty good idea where many of the other British troops were and bullets were flying past them, at least, past the lucky ones. Most of the raiding party panicked, running back to their own trenches, in one case shouting the password. Flares went up, and a machine gun joined in.

Guy and two companions, already in a shell-hole slightly back from where the lieutenant's body hung on the wire, froze where they were. Both of the other men obeyed Guy's signals to keep down and still. Guy though it unlikely the Germans would send a party out to find survivors of the raid, but this whole stretch of the line was now thoroughly alerted. The three Britons just waited. And then they waited some more. After something like an hour, with the moon getting low and behind patchy cloud, leaving their rifles where they were, Guy and what was now effectively his section moved very slowly, as quietly as possible, crawling over the lowest mud they could find between shell-holes, back to their lines. There was a hint of dawn in the sky when they quietly introduced themselves and were allowed through the zig-zag passage in their wire and into the blessed safety of their own trench.

The body of one of the fleeing raiders was still hanging on the British wire, where he had been shot just before reaching safety. Guy and the other two had been given up as dead or captured. He was surprised to find that six of those who scampered back under German fire had reached safety, although three were wounded. Of the 20 who had set out, only nine had returned. Moreover, the raid had done nothing useful, unless you accepted the view which could be quietly expressed in the sort of company which would not take exception to some cynicism as to the value of officers, that it did at least get rid of a lieutenant.

Abandoning your rifle was a serious matter, whatever the circumstances. Guy went straight to his company captain. His immediate superior's body was hanging on the German wire, so he thought he was justified in going over his head, so to speak. He gave his frank assessment that the whole technique of the raid had been wrong. There were far too many men to control effectively. We were wrongly dressed and equipped. It is difficult to move furtively with a rifle, and you couldn't keep it clean if you had to crawl. Knives and bombs are what we need. The big thing about a grenade was it didn't go bang where you were, but where you throw it. It doesn't give your position away. The Germans probably had us marked before we were halfway across no-man's land. Trying to cut the German wire was asking to be seen. And heard, too. Wire twangs when it's cut. He particularly stressed that after the shooting started and most of the raiding party had just fled, the last three of them, simply by lying motionless in a shell-hole for over an hour, and then crawling back slowly and quietly, had got back to the British lines without being detected. Oh, and sorry, we had to leave our rifles behind.

Guy was pleased and somewhat surprised that the captain was willing to hear him out, but feeling he might have gone on too long or been over-critical, ended up by asking to lead a raid with many fewer men and with much greater stealth.

Fortunately for Guy, his captain, although an old regular steeped in army tradition, did not have a totally closed mind. The stasis of opposing trenches appalled him, and he would try anything to break it. Well, anything he could get away with and which might just work. He heard Private Beardsley out because he privately had similar opinions on the lieutenant. Beardsley wanted only five other men, so whatever happened it couldn't be any worse than the first raid. This enterprising private wanted to choose them himself, and they must be willing volunteers. Let's give it a go.

Guy also wanted several days behind the lines to get clothing and equipment ready. The captain promoted him to corporal so there would be a chain of command, and effectively gave him a free hand, but ordered him to report every day during his preparations. The captain was relieved that Beardsley didn't ask for revolvers to replace their rifles. It was a silly restriction, but revolvers were supposed to be officers' weapons. Other ranks carried rifles. As it was, Guy didn't want any type of firearm. He wanted his raids to be in the dark when there was little or no moon. It is difficult to line up sights in the dark.

Guy recruited the two who had crawled back from the first raid, and between the three of them they found three more suitable and willing. Over protests from other lieutenants, they all went to the rear, and with the cooperation of the Service Corps, who caught their enthusiasm, kitted themselves out in boiler suits and improvised balaclavas. They modified webbing to make pouches for grenades, and sheaths for knives, making sure nothing could clank or fall out.

Knives were a problem. Bayonets were longer than Guy thought suitable. In the end, they were allowed to take kitchen knives from the catering services, each man selecting his preference. News of their preparations spread around. They were initially affronted by a South African who turned up on the second day to ask them whether they knew how to kill someone with a knife? Particularly if they wished to do it silently? Surely, it's obvious? You stab them. Na, that's no good. Apparently this large slow-speaking man had learnt about such things 'in the bush'. He supplied some gruesome details. Just stabbing a man, even in the chest, may not kill him at all, or it might be a slow process during which he could make a lot of noise. If you want it quick and quiet, cut his throat from behind. He showed them the best way to do it. The demonstrations laid on by this obviously experienced killer created all too clear a picture of what he was talking about. He used the word 'bloody' a lot in his normal speech, but on this topic it wasn't always swearing. Guy found it disturbing, but saw it was excellent preparation. He was also pleased with his team selection. None of them were rattled enough to back out. But Guy totally missed the suppressed eagerness on the faces of two of them, pals from before they joined his special group.

Another problem was blacking their faces. They even used shoe blacking until they discovered burnt cork.

The final effect was that in their loose boiler suits, already khaki and anyway very muddy, if they lay prone and motionless on rough ground in the dark, they just looked like more rough ground. They tested this and found they could be remarkably inconspicuous.

After knives, their other weapon was the bomb, and here was a problem. Guy wanted something that could be armed and thrown silently, which meant the Mills grenade. They were in extremely short supply, and an informal industry had developed behind British lines improvising them from jam tins. These were probably as effective as the Mills, but you had to light a fuse. You could do it with a cigarette, but there was no question of smoking during a slug-like approach to the German line. The remaining alternative was a friction device. Guy was worried that it wasn't silent. The rasping sound could be a warning. Those who weren't slugs had no notion of just how quiet slugs could be. However, it was jam tins or nothing.

This debate led to an important item of identity being established before they first tried out their techniques for real. They were the Slugs. They were inconspicuous. They moved slowly and silently. That was their tactic. It was not a term of abuse. The men liked it because it marked them out as special.

Guy organised the Slugs in three pairs. They had found it best to form pairs when his school gang played hide-and-hunt games. In daylight, it was what you could see that mattered. In the dark, it was what you could hear. The rules were different now, but the principles were the same. They practised crawling silently in the darkest part of the night, testing how close one pair could get to another without being heard. They developed some simple signals between themselves by imitating the scrabbling sounds rats make. They had fun seeing how close they could get at night to any unsuspecting group behind the lines, until they nearly got themselves shot by someone who thought they *were* rats.

Their preparations lasted several hectic days. The army wasn't used to this sort of thing. Guy wanted to get his gang out into no-man's land around the next new moon. He was keenly aware of the danger in not being well enough prepared, but on the other hand he had a feeling their capers behind the lines wouldn't be tolerated indefinitely.

Their first two patrols were pure reconnaissance. They crawled with practiced wriggles to within earshot of a German trench and just listened to the pattern of activity. They then went back home. In both cases, they raised no alarm at all.

The third was intended to be the same. In the event, it could easily have been a disaster. They were lying in familiar holes just outside the German wire, not far from where the lieutenant had been killed, Guy and his partner in the centre, the other two pairs a few holes away left and right. Listening, getting the feel for the enemy's normal movements. In particular, they wanted to know whether there were any special features in front of them. Large dugouts were usually further back, but anything unusual in the front-line could turn into a problem. They were finalising plans for an assault the following night.

Just as Guy was beginning to think they knew enough about this small part of the German line there came unusual sounds. A group of men were moving left to right along the trench directly in front of him. And then clearly audible, and occasionally glimpsed by the light of shelling and the odd flare along the line, a file of men crouched and wriggled through their gap in the wire. The Slugs already knew about this gap. They had intended to use it. Now the enemy was doing so. They came out between Guy and his right wingers and headed out into the churned earth between the lines.

It was encouraging to find their prepared methods now worked. Even while the Germans were passing through their wire Guy signalled to the left pair to come towards him. When he knew they could tell what was happening, he waited for what as far as he could tell was the last man in the enemy file to pass them, and then started to follow them. He was able to detect that the right-hand pair was fully aware. He signalled them to come closer, which in that context meant to follow.

The Germans were doing their best, presumably, but had nothing like the Slugs' expertise. They crouched rather than crawled. They were moving far too fast and making a dangerous amount of noise. With Guy leading, the Slugs had to move faster than their normal pace to keep close to the enemy. In fact, a lot faster. They were still pleasingly quiet. He hoped that any small additional noise wouldn't be noticed by the clumsy oafs in front. With indecent haste, the whole caravan crossed no-man's land, slowed down as it approach the British wire, and then with the odd clink and glint the enemy contingent went to ground. The Slugs had no difficulty in forming a line behind them, where they waited. They knew to let Guy start any action. Guy was by this time worried that the British lookouts hadn't seen or heard any of this, and by what would happen if they did and started firing. They should know that the Slugs were out there somewhere, but nervous men tend to shoot anyway.

When the situation seemed to have settled down, and before the German raid proceeded with whatever they intended to do, Guy decided the chance of nabbing them was too good to pass up. He started moving cautiously towards the German nearest him. He detected that the rest of his men had picked it up and were doing the same.

However, the real action, when it started, was triggered by one of the Germans. He stood up straight, holding a rifle. The nearest Slug could not imagine what the man intended to do, but correctly deducing their concealment was not going to last much longer, leapt into attack.

There were eight Germans and six Slugs, but the Slugs had achieved total surprise. Three of the Germans were knifed. Not perfectly silently as per their tuition, but pretty good for beginners. Guy's German put his hands up with a shaky 'Kamerad', and the other four rapidly followed suit. According to their doctrine, the Slugs forced each captive flat down on the ground with them on top, making it clear, with the point of a knife, that they should keep still and be silent. Guy wondered from which side the firing would come first. But despite the racket, there was none. The lookouts in the nearby British trench *must* have noticed something by now. It occurred to Guy later that both sides in their trenches knew they had a raid out in no-man's land and were showing commendable restraint in not blazing away at the noise.

It was a nervous business, but the Slugs' return with five prisoners was negotiated with the British lookouts. The Germans were pushed towards the passage through the British wire, and they crawled through one by one, with Guy and his men behind them and something of a crowd now in the trench. The Slugs were very slug-like during this process. Their captives didn't maintain quite such a low profile. That suited the Slugs. If bullets came over from the enemy side, there were German buttocks ready to receive them. And in this manner Guy's first active raid came back through the wire last, in their own style, to relative safety and some very impressed colleagues. The prisoners had already been shepherded towards the rear.

Beginners' luck is how Guy characterised it. It was certainly a fluke that the enemy patrol came out just when and where the Slugs were waiting. But everyone who knew about such things recognised the field craft shown by Beardsley's men in tracking them to the British wire, taking over half of them prisoner, and apparently without attracting enemy attention. Or, at least, without the enemy firing at them. Guy couldn't help fantasising, with some personal satisfaction and improbable elaboration, how the enemy would interpret their patrol disappearing without trace.

His captain was greatly relieved. He had been worried that he might attract more censure (there had already been some) for letting Beardsley's ruffians lark around behind their lines. Now it showed they had been doing serious and effective training, and though they might have been lucky, it had achieved results. The interrogation of the prisoners had already produced valuable intelligence.

Guy was promoted to sergeant. He was not exactly given a free hand, but he and his team were taken off regular trench duties, allowed to live in a largely nocturnal routine with a billet in the rear. They worked in step with the waxing and waning of the moon. Around full moon it was largely rest and training, with some welcome daytime living. As the new moon approached, they went raiding.

Both the moon and the weather became important to them. On cloudless nights, they could raid with no moonlight. The stars were enough with fully adjusted eyes. In total overcast, they need quite a lot of moon, since little came through the clouds. The worst conditions were heavy cumuli blowing across an otherwise clear sky. After a few unsettling forays with alternatively too little and too much light, they decided to stay at home during such weather.

The request for proper Mills bombs was repeated, and this time a special supply was laid on.

Their methods remained slug-like. Slow, silent, patient, and well camouflaged. Their services were soon in demand by intelligence officers. They went to a different part of their brigade's line for each dark period. They always dedicated the first few nights to reconnaissance. They only attacked when they were certain they had a suitable spot.

The combination of visiting different parts of the enemy line according to superiors' requirements, and at various times of night accordance to moon and weather, probably helped their raids to be difficult for the enemy to predict. Guy was acutely conscious of how serious it could be if there was a fully alert reception committee waiting for them.

Their attack formation crystallised into three prongs, comprising the three pairs. They chose a trench bay in which they could not detect anything special, particularly any unusual concentration of troops, and which had a passage through the wire. Guy and his mate stationed themselves opposite this passage. The other two pairs put themselves opposite the traverse at each end of the bay.

Guy would, when he thought the time right, start crawling slowly through the wire, using the enemy's own passage. There was a high risk of detection at this point. Guy moved very slowly, flat on the ground, a grenade in hand with the ring pulled, carefully holding the lever. When he thought he could get no further without raising the alarm, or if there was unusual movement in the trench, he initiated proceedings by throwing the grenade into it. His mate would immediately bomb it to the left and right. Guy followed those three grenades into the trench, backed up by his partner. The other two pairs would bomb the adjacent bays and their traverses as heavily as they could.

Early on it surprised Guy how often any German left standing after the grenades was ready to put up his hands and croak 'Kamerad'. Possibly it was understandable. A quiet night on stand-to suddenly erupts with grenades exploding left and right, apparently along the length of the line. Guy also learnt that the hatred each side was encouraged to have for their enemy was not greatly in evidence. He had heard about the Christmas truce. Initially he thought he disapproved. They were there to win a war. But, with closer experience of Germans, he viewed them differently. They were soldiers doing their duty, like Guy. They had no reason to hate each other.

Getting prisoners back was the main problem. The ideal number was one, shepherded, dragged or half-carried by Guy and his mate out of the trench, past the wire by the fastest method, and down into the nearest hole. If possible, no more than 30 seconds in the trench. After going to ground with the prisoner, and fast crouch/crawl using the lowest available route until they were about three holes from the German wire. Then flat on their faces in the lowest part of the hole above any water, on the slope towards the enemy for best cover, silent and motionless, including the prisoner. If he makes a fuss, kill him. *'Sorry mate. Nothing personal.'*

It was at this stage Guy thought it might be useful to have revolvers. If German troops did come after them into no-man's land, the shooting would be at such short range you could aim by the feel of the gun in your hand.

Each wing pair must be at least as fast getting to cover. They will have made more noise and attracted the most attention. On the other hand, they remained outside the wire and weren't hampered by prisoners.

That was about the most they could get in before the line wakes up and shooting starts. Flares go up. Snipers may be taking an interest. It is usually then several hours wait before the line sounds quiet enough for them to start the slow crawl home. Interestingly, they were never challenged by a party coming out into no-man's land after them. It would be difficult to organise such a group at short notice. As a result, Guy never needed a revolver. The response they most feared were trench mortars. These could hit them even in shell-holes as they dropped from their high trajectories. But the three pairs of raiders always spread out on the way back, and there was a lot of no-man's land to cover with these relatively small munitions.

It was made clear to Guy that the main value of his raids was taking prisoners for questioning. The intelligence gained so far had confirmed other information, which indicated that the Germans were improving their trench system behind their lines to make them easier to defend in depth and were moving some of their forces to their Eastern front. They wanted to concentrate on attacking Russia. In the late summer of 1915, this was pure gold to the Allied planners. If Sgt Beardsley can continue to supply prisoners, he can carry on raiding for as long as he wishes.

This was how Guy wanted to continue. Although he had by now unavoidably killed using both grenade and knife, he disliked doing so. It was the politicians who were waging this war, the soldiers were just their proxies. This did not incline Guy to become a 'conchie'. However bad the reasons for the war, or even the lack of reasons for it in the first place, he preferred to be on the winning side. He was working to that end. Killing one German unnecessarily made a negligible contribution, whereas bringing him back for interrogation can make a large one.

This did not suit two of the Slugs at all. The pair who normally formed their left prong had become bloodthirsty. Guy's concept of the wing role was to bomb the adjacent bays to prevent opposition from those directions. The objective was to keep enemy heads down. However, the left-hand pair, noting the stunning effect of grenades thrown accurately from short range, wanted to follow up by getting into the trench to do some short-range killing.

Guy was dead against this. It was unnecessary, and greatly increased the risk of coming under fire before the whole team had melted back into no-man's land. The pair disagreed and refused to accept Guy's approach. Guy was learning that leading was one thing, but keeping operations under control was something else. These two dangerous thugs could spoil things badly. Guy understood the threat they represented to his raids, but he hadn't realised that they were, in fact, jealous of him. Neither of them had so far had chance to knife anyone. Not even in that first mad scramble when they surprised the enemy just in front of the British wire. It was Guy's partner and the other pair who killed the three Germans who resisted. Guy could never have thought that anyone would wish to kill for the sake of it, and, importantly, he had failed to read the growing resentment in his two rebels.

On the topic of raiding, Guy had semi-official leave to bypass his new lieutenant and go straight to his company captain. Despite the volume and value of intelligence obtained from Beardsley's prisoners, there was still widespread reserve about his methods. The term 'private army' came up in discussion around the topic. Regular officers tend to be leery of initiative carried to such a level, and with some justification. Guy's immediate superior, the lieutenant who replaced the first one, wanted nothing to do with him and his brigandry. He was happy to be bypassed. Sgt Beardsley would come unstuck one day. Let the captain remain tangled up with him. The lieutenant wished to keep out of it.

Guy outlined to the captain the problem with the rebel pair, and it was immediately decreed that they must be taken off the raids and returned to normal duties. Much to his subsequent regret, Guy argued that they had completed their current reconnaissance and were ready to make the attack. Could the troublesome pair come on tonight's raid, but then be removed? Alright, but no further extension.

That raid should have gone well. It was turned into a shambles by the pair on the left apparently going berserk. They followed their grenades by storming into the traverse and firing along the adjacent bay. They should not have been able to fire anything. Guy could hear revolvers. A moment later rifles opened up further off to their left, and the revolver shooting stopped. By this time, the other two pairs were haring back into no-man's land, throwing themselves into holes as flares went up and fire started to come in their direction. This was an agreed procedure for the Slugs. If things go wrong, get out as fast as you can. They can't rescue each other in such a situation. All four got back to their lines, but Guy's partner managed it bleeding from a bullet wound in his side.

Guy had lost his grip. He had developed an effective raiding technique, and it had worked well for a while. But he had failed to exercise discipline. Every officer who had deplored his 'private army' considered themselves proved right.

Brigade took a more balanced view. Sgt Beardsley's squad had produced valuable intelligence for negligible losses. They wanted to retain his expertise but needed it under their direct command. He'd been given too much rope. Guy's captain had let it go a bit too far, but wasn't reprimanded, not officially.

Among the senior staff, in fact, it was acknowledged that the sergeant had made an outstanding contribution in pioneering a particular approach to raiding. It wasn't the only method. Others were achieving success with larger parties. But Beardsley had shown how effective pure stealth can be.

Guy was recommended for the DCM and told to go to the rear for some rest. He did so depressed by a sense of failure. He greatly feared that the rest of his gang was going to be taken away from him. Perhaps this is why he was careless. He went for an aimless walk, in daylight, within the range of enemy artillery.

What could be described as arbitrary shelling was practised by each side into the rear area of the other. The volume of such shelling depended mainly on the supply of shells. The guns were sometimes rationed to a mere one or two a day, sometimes many more. Even miles behind your front-line you never knew either when or where a shell might arrive. You could hear them coming but that didn't give you long to take cover. Many just accepted this risk, others were driven to nervous debilitation. Experienced soldiers, those that had survived and adjusted to this hostile world, took precautions when they could.

One of the techniques in this kind of gunnery was to look for places in the enemy's rear where troops or vehicles passed, such as a crossroad. Establish the range by sending over an occasional shell with someone in a forward position to spot where it lands. When you're reliably hitting the chosen point, record the settings. Maybe then set up coordinates for a different busy place on the other side. Then at any time, particularly when it's dark, you can drop a shell behind enemy lines with a better-than-random chance of doing some harm, including a general increase in anxiety.

As a result, there were certain places behind British lines with roughly painted notices such as:

Shell Warning
don't loiter!

No doubt there were similar signs behind the enemy's lines, except written in German.

Guy failed to see, or ignored, one such notice. He was deeply depressed and was hanging aimlessly around at a junction in walkways. There was a yell which got as far as "Look out, you stupid—" when a shell exploded on a pile of masonry which had previously been a house. If a shell lands in mud or soft soil, its effect is limited by being buried before exploding. This shell exploded immediately on hitting a hard surface. A fragment of the casing broke Guy's thigh bone, badly. There was a lot of blood. A smaller fragment gashed his cheek and broke that bone, although without serious damage to the orbit.

He benefitted from not only being in the rear, but close to a dressing station. They brought the bleeding under control, immobilised the leg, wrapped his head up, and a stretcher party took him further from the front to the divisional casualty clearing station, out of the range of shelling. There was no major battle in progress, and he received more attention than might have been the case. This was clearly a 'Blighty one'. The question was whether the leg should be amputated there and then. In his periods of consciousness, Guy pleaded to keep the leg. The doctor noted Guy's robust build and was prepared to give it a go. The wounds were treated with acriflavine, the leg immobilised again, and he was sent back to Base Hospital. Here the doctors agreed that the leg was worth a try. They didn't ask Guy. The wound had been kept open. The pieces of bone were realigned. There was some concern about blood supply to one of the fragments, but they did what they could. Over the next week the wound was allowed to start healing, with frequent observation. There was the expected inflammation, but nothing dangerous. They kept him for another week, and then with the leg in a plaster cast, the cheekbone set and the eye bandaged, he endured the journey back to hospital in England. It wasn't comfortable, but Guy could cope with it.

Even so, it was the worst time of his life. As the pain decreased, a black despair grew in his mind. He was oppressed by his failure. He thought he was trail-blazing a brilliant new development, but he had been blind to the need to maintain discipline, perhaps the most important element of army doctrine drummed into him since he joined up. He had been promoted to corporal, and then to sergeant, precisely for that purpose. But he had ignored his NCO status. His Slugs had been an elite team. They all knew what they were doing. They were the new experts at it. They were a band who stuck together. At no time had Guy spoken to the others, or behaved towards them, other than as a fellow-soldier. As a sergeant he could have called down penalties as soon as that mad pair on his left wing showed signs of insubordination, but he hadn't.

This did not help the healing process. It worried the medical staff. The more perceptive could see Guy's distress. One perceptive nurse made a serious effort to understand it. Guy wanted answers. Would his leg get better enough for him to return to the trenches? Would he be allowed to go raiding again? It wasn't that she misunderstood, she just found it difficult to believe that Sgt Beardsley would want to go back to the trenches. However, she knew an old army veteran who worked as a porter. He would talk sense to Guy.

He did, and it was such a relief to have someone who understood. They had a good old chat, and when the veteran left, he patted Guy on the arm with, "Chin up, lad. I'll see what I can find out." It cheered Guy greatly.

Things started to improve in other ways. After taking the old cast off to check what was going on inside, the leg was given a wash and then a lighter cast, and he was allowed out for Christmas, with two crutches. Whether or not it was anything to do with the veteran, an ambulance was arranged to get him home. The leg felt a lot better but was soon itchy again.

It was good to have somewhat more freedom of choice than being in hospital, but the Christmas leave was difficult for everyone. Deidre and Tom already shared his old small bedroom, so it was crowded at nights. Tom was initially frightened of this strange man he didn't know with a weird leg and screamed if not allowed to sleep in the same bed with his mother. Guy solved that by sleeping on the floor. It was more comfortable than some trenches he'd slept in, even with the cast, although he had started getting used to beds again. The days were awkward until Tom discovered the strange man was fun to play with. Guy then became Tom's best toy.

Deirdre and the senior Beardsleys had been deeply worried when informed of his wound. They had not managed the long journey to the hospital. Now they were delighted to have him at home where they could look after him and he could forget the war for a while. The trouble was, he couldn't. They didn't understand this. They wanted to help but didn't know how. They thought it might do him good to tell them about the misery of trench life, but he didn't want to. He thought he would appreciate quietness, but it disturbed him. He tried to get used to not having to keep his ears open for shells. He was happy enough to hear local news, but it didn't seem important. He did a bit of hobbling around close to home but didn't get as far as WIS. Hobbling was uncomfortable. He had been encouraged to exercise the leg but warned not to over-do it.

He was touched that Mr and Mrs Ingalls, and Lilly from the office, paid him a visit at home. Guy was intrigued and impressed that the firm now had a motor car, with its own driver.

Mrs Ingalls brought a few apples from their orchard, and Mr Ingalls a stoneware jug of cider, also from their orchard, and both much appreciated.

Unexpectedly, however, he found he was disinterested in how WIS was getting on, although he welcomed any news from staff serving in the war. He found it easiest to talk with Lilly. She asked how the medical services had treated him after he was wounded, and whether the hospital in England was doing everything possible. Who had he got to know while in hospital? Did he get to read the papers? Guy found it easier to relate his experience in these areas. But, overall, it was a relief when the time came to be taken back to the hospital for the cast to come off. He didn't get any advance warning. An ambulance just turned up and took him away.

Guy thought about his leave experience. He had already heard of similar cases. The central issue was that he was now a foreigner. He had moved from his old country, the English Midlands in peace-time, to the broken landscape and alien society of Warland. The key point was that he had naturalised. People who had never lived there thought he was the same person as before, and had just been putting up with wet socks, even wet everything, bad food, mud, and, of course, danger. Yes, he had put up with these things because he had no choice. But he had also accepted new social rules. In this strange land, it was now acceptable to kill people. You were, in fact, encouraged to, so long as it was the enemy. And society's attitude to death was different. In England, it was ignored wherever possible, and where it could not be avoided the reality was hidden or disguised. In Warland, you just got used to corpses lying around, because it was not always practicable to clear them away all that quickly. And many of them were in a frightful state. You sometimes tripped over them in the bottom of a trench.

As a side effect, this led to changes in what could be considered ethics. You are issued with shoes on first going to the trenches. They tended to rot quickly. By the time you have settled into trench life and learnt the precautions that must become second nature if you are going to survive, your shoes are falling apart. It is difficult to get new ones. When new recruits arrived to make up for losses, as much as you try to help them, they tend to suffer the most from sniper fire, or not taking cover well enough during shelling. Guy had seen a new lad, despite ample warnings, stick his head above the parapet in curiosity as to what no-man's land looked like. He'd had about two seconds to take it all in. Now, if a new bloke gets killed, with new shoes on his feet, and they are your size, what are you going to do? Is it stealing? I suppose so. But it would be silly not to. You're not much good to the war effort with trench foot.

Even the rules about whether to stay alive are different. If someone does the sensible thing and runs away rather than walk into machine-gun fire, he could be shot for cowardice. Guy accepted this. When a man backs off from a fight, it leaves fewer to face the enemy. One's outlook can change irreversibly in a country run along such lines. On the other hand, Guy did not wholly adjust to the idea of shooting sentries who fall asleep. He had experienced spending half the night repairing a parapet, and then being on watch until dawn. There comes a point in fatigue where it is impossible to stay awake. Fortunately, most junior officers know this as well, and wherever possible they cover up occasional lapses. But, and this was an important but, it is vital to have wide-awake lookouts. The alternative can be surprise visitors in your trench. Guy had been on the other side of that situation. Lookouts should be looking and listening with complete attention. If there is slackness in this area, then maybe shooting a few slackers is the best way to keep sentries on the alert. So Warland society takes a pragmatic approach to the sleeping sentry. It is a matter of judgement, and of fear. Army law can always be invoked. The fear of that happening makes lookouts work hard at staying awake. A once-off lapse can perhaps be overlooked. That's mainly why sergeants and lieutenants do the rounds at night. If it's only known to the two of you, a single offence gives the officer the option of just issuing a severe warning. Repeat offenders shouldn't receive such leniency, because it's a crime against everyone else.

And, of course, some people shoot themselves. When you've heard some poor bod in no-man's land with their intestines lying in the mud beside them screaming in pain, or calling for water, or Mother, all night, perhaps longer, the prospect of a guaranteed quick death can be a tempting alternative. It's a rational choice. Shooting yourself in the head gets it over quickly. It can be interpreted as cowardice, but what the heck if you're dead? Shooting yourself in the foot, on the other hand, shows you are willing to accept severe pain, but firmly intend to get out of this lunacy.

It impressed Guy, on thinking back on his few months in the trenches, and even though there may be logic to support such ways of getting out of the war, how few take them. The vast majority stick with it as long as they can. Guy and his mates lived in Warland. The strongest force keeping them as functional soldiers was loyalty to their own society. Not Britain, but Warland. In other words, not letting your mates down.

But quite apart from the elevation of Death to a living presence, one might say, Warland was a funny country in other ways. One of the weirdest of army regulations was to keep yourself clean-shaven. Great importance was attached to it. It had intrigued Guy. They were filthy, they stank, and they were infested with lice. The sheer physical difficulty and discomfort of shaving, especially ankle-deep in mud in the winter, made it ridiculous. Presumably the brass hats thought it maintained morale. Yet it was a requirement that was generally accepted by the troops. Before long, Guy had found that he regarded it in the same way. It *was* worthwhile. It made you feel better.

He was utterly fascinated that the same regulation required him to grow a neat moustache. But whereas being clean-shaven was enforced, the moustache rule was ignored. Many officers had them, but few privates.

And so, the soldier is now a citizen of this alien country. You no longer feel at home when briefly back in the country from which you emigrated. Guy had heard during his leave of a young wife who was deeply hurt when she found out her man had left their home to return to the trenches two days earlier than necessary to meet some pals in London, by prior arrangement, so they could do a bit of carousing before getting back to their unit. She just couldn't understand it. Guy could.

The hospital kept him under observation for a week, with a nurse helping him to walk again without the cast, with a stick and some discomfort, and he was then pronounced fit for light duties. To his surprise he was given travel papers to a recruits' training camp, where he became an instructor. His marksman rating had been noted, and even with his leg and stick he could help run the shooting range and teach the rifle.

He quickly settled into his new role. He enjoyed it, too. And he was soon shouting at his recruits. He had hated this during his own training, at least to begin with. After that, he got used to it. With the lesson of his raiding activities in mind, he could now see that it worked. It was the army Method for maintaining discipline, and it helped recruits develop the toughness of mind needed when facing an enemy. If you are upset by having insults thrown at you, would you remain functional with someone sincerely trying to kill you?

So, Guy shouted and to some extent insulted. It took a stellar piece of shooting to get anything approaching approval from him. But unlike many of the instructors he did not insult his recruits on a personal level. He kept his diatribes general. There's an important difference between 'You silly little man' and

'What sort of parents could produce you?' and Guy respected it. He got on well with most of the lads, and they learnt how to handle and maintain the Lee Enfield rifle, and how to shoot with it. On the other hand, he came down hard on anyone not taking the training seriously. He was now willing to use army penalties, which could include incarceration for several days on restricted diet. He learnt to be firm and impartial.

In the event, he needed to make little use of punishments. Most of the recruits now were conscripts. Some were older than he was. But, at 20, Guy was a grizzled veteran. A sergeant who, it was known, had killed Germans in hand-to-hand combat, had a badly injured leg still healing, and a spectacular facial scar. Many of his recruits, some of them well-educated professionals, were justifiably afraid of him. They might know much more than he did on all sorts of topics, but Guy had Been There and Done That. He could give them practical and convincingly detailed advice on situations they might never encounter in civilian life but might well meet where they were going.

The rifle training went generally well, but the consistency of shooting seemed to vary with no obvious reason. A man who could put five bullets into a particular circle one day spread them further the next day. Guy did some tests of his own, and wondered whether the ammunition was of variable quality. Was a lower grade supplied to them because they were 'only' training?

He visited the camp's armoury and asked to look at the records. Each ammunition delivery arrived with a manifest produced by the supplier giving details and quantities. He inspected some manifests to see if they showed any indications of quality. They didn't, but to his surprise he saw that some were from his old employer, presumably converted to war work. It seemed strange this hadn't been mentioned when the Ingalls and Lilly visited him when at home with his bad leg, but it was probably just normal to them by that time.

His next leave was during the week before Easter and over the holiday weekend. He made use of this to visit WIS and see whether they made any distinction between ammunition for training as opposed to what they sent to the fighting army.

Lilly was delighted to see him again: "You're walking better now, Guy." Yes, he could run a bit. Only a few steps, but it was progress. In response to his query, she assured him that all their ammunition was made to the same standard. To prove it, she showed him carbon copies of manifests, all of which she had typed. They specified technical details and quantities, but there was never any reference to a distinction such as 'training' or 'war'. She showed him this with the most recent manifest, which covered the last delivery to Guy's training camp. Guy had a good memory, and he was willing to trust it, which might be why it worked well. He had seen the original of this manifest in the camp's armoury, and it had shown 14 boxes. But Lilly's carbon showed 15 boxes. How can a carbon be different from the original? He checked the date again before putting it down.

He had no experience of typing and only a vague idea of what a carbon copy was. "A carbon has to be an exact copy, doesn't it?"

"Yes of course, Dear, except that it is fainter and smudgier." Lilly could see that Guy needed convincing. She showed him how the top sheet was placed onto two pairs of carbon and flimsy sheets. "See? the imprint goes through them all for each keystroke."

Guy was fascinated. "So you can do two copies?"

"Oh, quite a few more, if you hit hard enough and use really thin paper. I normally do two copies. The top sheet goes with the rounds. Mr Ingalls takes the first carbon. I keep the second. It is always sensible to keep copies of your work."

This gave him quite a lot to think about. For one thing, dear old Lilly obviously had been learning about ammunition. She didn't say 'bullets', but 'rounds', which is what the army calls them. Another thing was why did Mr Ingalls need copies of the manifests since he could consult the office whenever he wished? But, right now, he had a further query about ammunition quality.

"At the camp, we get ammunition from different suppliers. When I have rounds issued for training, is there anything on the rounds themselves that would tell me who they come from?"

"My dear boy, yes of course. Just look at the headstamp."

"Err…" This was embarrassing.

"The headstamp. You know, the flat end of the cartridge, where the firing pin hits it. The percussion cap is in the centre. If you twist it so the writing is the right way up, there will be 'WIS' and then the calibre, which is '303' for rifles, curved around above the cap. And below the cap there is the year of manufacture."

"Lilly, that really is helpful. I'm sorry to be so ignorant. I should have taken more interest in it all. The recruits can be a handful and I suppose that's where most of my attention goes."

"I'm delighted to be of use! You're our hero, you know." And she patted his arm in an uncharacteristic manner, for her. Guy was tempted to ask just why Mr Ingalls needed carbon copies of the manifests but decided to sit on that for the time being. He must check whether there really was a difference in the quantities.

Guy first heard news of the Easter Uprising in Ireland on getting back to camp the following Tuesday. There were several Irish volunteers amongst his present batch of trainees. Decent lads in the main, keen, probably brave, but excitable. They were taking different sides in typical style. As far as he knew they didn't come to blows, or even shoot each other, but there were some intemperate remarks.

During this debate, someone dropped a vague hint about the camp doing its bit. The remark was rapidly bitten off. It was the sudden dumbness of these usually loquacious speakers that Guy noticed. It was soon covered by a change of subject matter, and the disputation recommenced. But the thought suddenly came to Guy's mind that the sergeant who ran the armoury, and who kept himself above political wrangling, had an Irish accent.

It did not take much thought to put it all together. Ammunition made by WIS was being smuggled out of the camp and no doubt into Ireland. A box was stolen from the armoury, and the corresponding manifest replaced by a fake showing one fewer boxes, all no doubt facilitated by the armourer. Who is going to remember how many boxes came in with each delivery? The paper records and the stock agree. What more could the army want? How did they produce the false manifest? Carefully typing a new one, matching exactly except for quantity, would take some time. It would require a typewriter. The camp wasn't strong when it came to office facilities or typists, and those they had were not in the armoury. There was a much more likely explanation. Will Ingalls took a carbon copy of each manifold Lilly typed. That was all he would need to type a new original in the privacy of his home and then get it to the smugglers.

Guy tried to reason his way around it. Was there any other explanation? He had checked the discrepancy, and his memory had been correct. The number of boxes had been changed for at least one delivery. Once that was accepted, Will seemed the obvious collaborator. Guy remembered that the Ingalls were said to be from an old Irish family. Was anyone else involved at WIS? The operation didn't seem to need it.

Guy was no moralist. He was indifferent to Irish independence. He'd heard enough from the lads about the wickedness of Britain during the potato famine.

There had been people who couldn't afford to buy what food there was, or to emigrate, and who literally starved to death. And the British government just let it happen. He accepted that the nationalists might have a case. Another aspect of the affair was that he hoped to get his job back after the war. Secret knowledge like this could be useful. Guy had so far mostly enjoyed life, including much of the war and even more his training role. He was obviously a natural leader. If he knew a guilty party at WIS, and the guilt would be dead serious, then he had a strong bargaining position. Guy stored the information away.

The episode had usefully opened his eyes to something else: how to read headstamps. From now on, he made sure to use only WIS ammunition for rifle training. This was partly a sort of loyalty to his old employer. It was also because headstamps from some manufacturers seemed to vary in format and what was included. The WIS ammunition was consistently labelled, so maybe it was made uniformly too. And, if there were queries, he could ask on his next leave.

The WIS rounds did perform well. He thought other manufacturers might be less careful, or possibly there were small differences between the manufacturers. He'd heard snipers discussing such fine points. It was clearly important.

By now, he was in charge of both the rifle range and sniper training. Although he had never worked as a sniper, he could show the best shots among the recruits how to adjust a rifle-mounted telescopic sight. Neither of the two available types were ideal, but either gave you dramatically improved accuracy. He also stressed to his star shooters something he had picked up in the trenches. 'Whatever anyone tells you, don't try to snipe with a bayonet fixed. It increases the spread, and it makes you easier to spot'.

As Christmas 1916 approached, he had a decision to make. Deidre was expecting about the end of January. He could have leave over Christmas, but then not be there for the baby. He chose the baby and arrived the day after delivery. Deidre was pleased with his choice, and happy not to have a husband flapping around at the critical point. She had time to get herself sorted and Julie presentable. They had already agreed via letters that it would be 'John' or 'Julie'. Tom wasn't entirely happy about the new arrival but was adjusting to it by the time Guy had to go back to the camp.

Guy was now sufficiently sophisticated in such matters to associate Julie's arrival with his leave the previous Easter. Of course, he trusted Deidre. But he'd heard so much on the topic of infidelity from other lads that the quick bit of mental arithmetic couldn't be avoided.

There was no hypocrisy in Guy's attitude towards marital faithfulness. He had grown up in a society which expected men and women to play different roles. Only men were sent to the trenches. Women looked after things at home. That was the natural way of things.

When soldiers went to the rear of their lines for a rest, entertainment and sporting events were laid on to help them unwind, but the major issues were the two great itches. Their clothes were boiled, but the relief didn't last long. Either the lice enjoyed the Turkish baths, or their relatives immediately filled the vacant accommodation. As far as the other itch was concerned, the British army sternly forbade their men from visiting brothels and warned that getting venereal disease was a disciplinary matter and could be fatal, it not being clear which was considered the more serious. But what did they expect from fit young men? The French were more pragmatic. Their army regulated the brothels, with separate establishments for officers and men, and their doctors monitored the health of all concerned.

Guy did what he needed. It was part of his old life in Warland. It didn't affect his family.

Another difference which occurred to him is that a woman will normally have no doubt it is her baby, but for the man there is an unavoidable element of trust. Guy checking dates was not just jealousy. It was only natural that he wanted to be sure Tom was his son and Julie his daughter. His knowledge of history didn't cover medieval queens giving birth in the presence of official witness to authenticate an heir, but he would have recognised the principle.

During the journey back to the camp Guy started to wonder whether it was time to be back in the trenches. The leg wasn't entirely pain-free, but there ought to be something he could do. He also wondered whether the army would decide to send him back anyway. He'd been an instructor now for about a year. He enjoyed it, but his sense of duty was starting to fidget. Soon after getting back the colonel wanted to see him, so he assumed it would be about his return to the front.

The colonel was elderly, from Guy's viewpoint, and was in fact a retired colonel. This was typical of commanding officers at training camps. He told Guy to be easy and sit down.

"Good leave? Fine. Have you heard of the Officer Cadet Battalion?"

"No Sir."

"It's a program to train more officers and do it quickly. The brass hats are getting really worried at the lack of progress in winning this war. I want you to go on it."

"I was wondering whether I ought to get back to the trenches, Sir."

"That's out of the question with your leg. You're still using a stick, and you walk a bit lop-sided. Does it still hurt a bit?"

Guy realised that although retaining a walking stick had helped his 'wounded hero' image, it might be delaying complete healing. He decided there and then to go back to unaided walking. Give both legs the same exercise.

"Occasionally, but I can get around."

"Of course, but right now you're not fit for the trenches. Anyway, recruitment and training has got to speed up, and our weapons training is going to expand. I want you to command the whole programme. That's rifle, grenades, machine guns, mortars, and anything else that comes along. We've got more specialist instructors coming to cover all these. This means you need to be a captain. It would be temporary. Only for the duration."

"Isn't that jumping a rank, Sir?"

"Yes, but we're allowed to. You don't quite qualify in other respects, but it can be worked around. For practical purposes, you will command many more men than a captain normally would. Not formally, but effectively. I know you didn't spend long in the Ypres front, but you made an outstanding contribution. I'm told they still quote you on taking prisoners. And I've watched your rifle instruction. You completely understand what's needed, and the men respond splendidly to you. This is why I want you to supervise all the weapons instructors. I'd like to put you straight into the position, but we can't avoid the cadet course. It's only four months. Are you happy with that?"

Guy was unhappy about anything sounding like school, but he had a more serious objection. He hadn't known about the cadet battalion, but there were rumours about commissioning officers from the ranks.

"Well, Sir, officers don't get separation and family allowances, do they? I have a wife and two children. It would be difficult without the money."

That nonplussed the colonel. "Hadn't thought about that. You're probably right. It's this nonsense that officers are meant to be gentlemen, and thus have their own means."

Guy was starting to enjoy this. "But surely you're a gentleman, aren't you Sir?"

Sir half-smiled and paused. Guy had the impression he was revising what to say next. "It really would be difficult, would it?"

"Yes, Sir. I don't know whether I have a choice, but if my family would lose those payments, then I'm not willing."

Sir again paused for thought. He didn't know whether the sergeant had the choice either. "Let me take that away. I'll find out what the situation is and see you again."

Guy went back to training recruits to use the rifle with a sense of anticipation. He liked the idea of being in command of all weapons instruction. He told himself that he must do it using the proper army approach, not to repeat mistakes from his past. He hated the idea of four months in training but guessed it was both inevitable and worth it. In the event, it all happened much faster. About two weeks later he was back with the colonel.

"Things are getting so urgent they've agreed you can skip the cadet training. It's not like you're a captain in the trenches. You know everything needed for this job. I'm going to make it a battlefield promotion. I think I can get away with it. If there is any question of your returning to the trenches, then it's back to sergeant. That's how we're going to do it. We've got to really step up training. Alright with you? I want to get you in position straight away because the extra instructors will be here soon. Better they start with this new arrangement."

"Um. What about the allowances, Sir?"

"Oh yes. I don't have confirmation, but I'm sure they can be continued. Let me know if the payments stop."

It wasn't entirely alright with Guy, but he was starting to think he might be negotiating too hard. And how much longer will the war last if we are making this big drive? He decided it was time to comply. "Yes, Sir. Thank you."

It did, later, strike him as a splendid example of army madness that he could have a battlefield promotion working at a training camp, and which would be taken away if he was sent to a battlefield.

Deidre replied to Guy's letter reporting his promotion with fulsome praise. She was clearly delighted. He had also told her that their allowances should continue. She collected them from the Post Office. Please let me know if they should stop. She was equally emphatic in responding to that.

It took Guy some time to feel comfortable as a commissioned officer, however temporary. There were two problems, both associated with the officers' mess. One was social. Proper officers regarded those promoted from the ranks as 'temporary gentlemen', much their inferiors. The other was financial. He couldn't afford what would normally be expected of an officer.

It was Guy's first direct experience of how deeply the British class system was rooted. Fortunately, he wasn't the only temporary gentleman. There were enough of them to form a sort of junior club within the brotherhood of officers, and they could get away with doing things their way.

In all other respects, his new role pleased him. Overseeing weapons instruction, rather than doing it himself, was a new experience. Having learnt his lesson with the Slugs, he was careful to fulfil his responsibilities as the army would expect. The instructors, sergeants to a man, were all different personalities. Guy just wanted them to teach their weapons correctly, and to transfer an enthusiasm for them to the recruits. Guy watched all the trainers in action and never contradicted them in front of the men. Most of the instructors pleased him. They all did it differently, but Guy was now mature enough not to want them to all do it how he would. All he wanted was results. He made some suggestions privately to some of them and spent time getting to know all of them away from the ranges.

There was one problem case. The mortar sergeant was unsuitable. He expected perfect behaviour from the recruits and had zero flexibility. Guy would offer advice, in small chunks, but although the man listened dutifully, he subsequently continued as before. He just couldn't change. The recruits were laughing at him behind his back, and most seriously of all they were larking about with mortars when they had the chance. Mortars are simple weapons, but they need a careful approach to setting them up, particularly for short ranges. With this instructor, the situation was getting dangerous.

Guy gave Sgt Mortars probably longer than he should have, but then had him replaced. The new man, like him, was recovering from a trench injury, but he had a lot of practical experience with the weapon. He was gruff with everyone, but the recruits learnt quickly under him. In time, they got to like him. It was like having a (fairly) tame bear.

The only other major issue on which Guy had to intervene was range safety. There were regulations, and some of the instructors seemed to view them as inconveniences which just slowed training down. Guy insisted they be followed to the letter. Unannounced inspections and clandestine surveillance were sometimes followed by harsh words or even threats of removal before everyone got the message. Most instructors enjoyed their work and preferred it to the alternative of relegation to the trenches. When they saw that Guy meant it, they fell into line.

Recruitment did increase for the first few months that year, although not as many as the colonel seemed to think and it wasn't maintained throughout the year. With all weapons instruction under him, plus paperwork for which he was glad to have an assistant, Guy was busy. But not so busy that he didn't carefully read the available news from Belgium and France. He was looking for the big push supposed to bring the war to its end. The German withdrawal early in the year was encouraging, but it was known to be a move back to prepared defensive positions, the famous Hindenburg Line. British attacks during April in the northern part of the line had some success. They were intended to support a major French push further south, but this failed with heavy losses and mutiny in their army. Spirits in Britain were not much raised until June with reports of a promising start to the British offensive in Flanders. Advances were indeed made, but the weather deteriorated and by autumn the attacks had ground to a halt in the bloody mud of Passchendaele. The war was not going to end in 1917.

Guy took leave in the following spring, although not over Easter this time. It was depressing. The weather was chilly and wet, a new and major German offensive was pushing Allied forces back, and to cap it all Deidre reported that their family support payments seemed to have stopped. Guy would look into it, but he also had to think about it. He had checked, and it was indeed a fact that officers were not entitled to it. At the turn of the year, the retired colonel who had promoted him had volunteered for active service, even though over the maximum conscription age. With the current emergency status of the Western Front, Guy didn't feel happy about complaining, particularly not being entitled to it. Deidre was sure they would cope somehow, and the war was bound to end this year, wasn't it?

Back at camp Guy made some inquiries about the colonel and discovered he had been killed within a week of reaching his battalion HQ, which was about a month earlier. He had, apparently, visited the front-line to familiarise himself. This tied in with when the support payments stopped. The colonel must have had some way of keeping them going. Could he have been paying them himself, from his own means? Guy was never able to find out, but the possibility made him uncomfortable. Surely an officer shouldn't have to pay personally in such a case. But in a way it made sense. If the colonel thought Guy's training work was worth it, and could afford what it cost, it was a contribution to winning the war. Guy was made to think about his own motivation. He had taken large risks to capture prisoners, but it also enhanced his own prestige. If the colonel had been paying those family allowances, he was doing it secretly. There was a goodness here which Guy couldn't match. Of course, maybe the colonel manipulated the army system while he was alive. Well, however it was, Guy was sincerely grateful for those payments. He concluded that it was not sensible to inquire further. If they came into the open, they might have to be paid back. He'd be in trouble with Deirdre if that happened.

By summer, the German advances were checked. Indeed, it was now clear that the Kaiser's forces were running out of steam. But just as British spirits were rising, there was an explosion at a shell-filling factory in Chilwell. It was under-reported in the press, but sufficient news reached Guy to worry him. Chilwell was adjacent to Beeston. He had known about the factory but didn't know its actual location. He was granted leave, and his journey home crossed Deidre's letter to him. They both appreciated the prompt reaction of the other. The factory was at the far end of Chilwell from Beeston, and although everyone in Beeston heard the explosion, which was during the evening, the Beardsleys and Deirde's family were all safe. It was impressive to learn that the factory resumed production the following day despite well over 100 deaths among the workers. And most of those were 'canary girls' who already suffered from the effect of handling TNT.

The war had reached closer to home. The German air raids, both with Zeppelins at night and the Gotha bombers by day, had mainly been in the East and South-East, particularly London. Guy had been glad that the Midlands weren't normally visited, although at least one airship had apparently reached Liverpool. If the Germans knew shells were being filled in Chilwell, they might make it a target, which would mean bombs scattered around the district.

The best way out was to end the war as soon as possible, and Guy's role was to carry on making sure recruits knew how to use their weapons. He continued to work hard with the instructors. By now, he fully understood that issuing orders was one thing, making sure they were carried out was another.

And the war did end that year. By late summer, it was clear that not only had the German offensive lost momentum, but its army was collapsing. There was still hard fighting, but the Allies advanced. It was galling to many in the British army that American troops joined the war just as the enemy was caving in. Obviously, at least to the Yanks, they had arrived and showed us how to win it.

Guy was demobbed unusually quickly. His training programme was closed in November, and by waiving his right to a demob suit he was home in time for Christmas.

Deidre had been working her magic again. There had been many comings and goings around Beeston during the war, and with some help from Mr Beardsley Senior she had secured a rented terraced house in the village. It was small, but it would be all theirs. Christmas had worked out well enough over the butcher's shop, but it had been a crush.

Although it was a major change after the camp, Guy was pleased to realise that he no longer had the same sense of alienation when he was in the trenches. Two years at the training camp had been a useful intermediate stage in re-naturalising to a land at peace.

He went back to WIS, and yes, it was welcome back, we're glad to see you in one piece. You're walking OK now, it seems? Yes, thank you, he was completely back to normal. Not quite true, but close enough. The ammunition manufacturing had come to an end, and they were back to their proper function of steel fabrication and construction, although business was still slow. Guy also went back to it. It had never completely stopped during the war, and it now gradually started to expand again. By Easter 2019, several other ex-WIS men had been demobbed and were back with the company, and on the Monday holiday Will held a staff garden party at his home. Will loved his staff, but he wasn't going to give them a workday off for a party.

Guy had been part of a construction crew for a few months by that time. He knew he was good at putting up steelwork, and he enjoyed it. Will's foresight in offering their services to Marconis before the war was paying off. Designing and supplying masts for wireless installations promised to become an important part of their business. These often tall but thin structures were technically the most advanced things they made.

Guy wanted to lead a gang, in fact the best gang in the company. He had quite a lot of experience with different types of gang by now, and he reckoned he could make an outstanding go at it. And it seemed likely he could twist an arm.

He knew it would be taking a risk. Will might strenuously deny any suggestion he was involved in smuggling, and demand Guy proves it or else it's the sack. Might Will take carbons of his falsified manifests and swap them into Lilly's filing? Would that be practicable? It would be if Lilly herself had been in the racket as well. Guy found that impossible to believe. He decided to go ahead but say the least possible.

Towards the end of the Easter party, an opportunity presented itself to have a quiet word with Chairman Will. "You know we used Wiz ammunition in the training camp? I learnt the importance of consistent ammunition. The Wiz rounds were as good as anything we had. It made me proud of my old company. I took a lot of interest in Wiz deliveries. The manifests were interesting." Will's expression changed just enough to convince Guy. He had lowered his head a little and was regarding Guy slightly sideways. "Look, Sir, I'm not greedy. I would just like to be the foreman of our best construction crew, particularly on the large wireless projects. If I can select my own men, I'll make you proud of us. That's all."

Will thought long enough, looking down at the ground, to make Guy certain that the WIS Chairman was guilty, and understood that Guy knew and was offering a deal. Will was wondering whether Guy would stick to his side. This was blackmail, although a mild form at this stage. Would Guy later ramp up his demands? A characteristic of Guy was that he had an open-looking honest sort of face, and he matched it with a frank nature. It had stood him in good stead in the past, and it did now. A characteristic of Will was that he had a high opinion of his ability to judge men. He decided it would be safer to go along with Guy than to refuse. "Hmm. I'll think about it."

In fact, it worked well. Guy was given his head in selecting the best men for an elite crew. He bossed them around and was rude to them, but they got the most advanced jobs, and the best money, and they were, if privately, proud to be in his gang. They consistently completed work on time and without incident. Guy really did seem happy. As far as anyone could tell his leg was now completely better. It seemed to give him no trouble, even when clambering around high above the ground. Will arranged for his pay to go up a little. Guy made sure the rest of the crew got similar rises. Not everyone in the company was happy about it, particularly those on the less-specialised construction crews. There was even open discussion, in quiet corners, as to what on Earth was this handle Guy had on the boss? But WIS was doing unusually well, for a small company in the difficult post-war period, and its people were glad to be part of it.

What Had Been Happening: Sid

'Sailor Sid' they called him. He grew up in the Borders fishing port of Eyemouth, from where his father fished the North Sea for haddock and herring. When old enough, he helped crew his father's smack when there wasn't school. Sometimes when there was school. Like his dad, he was small and wiry, handy around deck, and good at climbing up the rigging for a more distant view. The scope for getting up the rigging in Pa's small boat was limited, but Sid could make better use of it than anyone else. This included Pa, who was getting old, and pleased for Sid to be a lookout when needed.

Sid was told how the town had once prospered, with a large fishing fleet and good takes. But this prosperity had to be fought for, and it didn't last. They were the last Scottish fishing port to throw off the Church's hated fish tax. This had been a tremendous struggle, led by the village hero, William Spears. Pa came from the same family and remembered William well. Although he could not claim descent from William, just bearing the same surname counted for something in Eyemouth. Sid was born too late to have known the great man, but he grew up hearing a great deal on the subject. Pa also said they were the last port along the coast to get government funding allocated to improve their harbour.

The final blow was a real disaster. Before the promised development took place, the storm of 1881 hit the coast. It was said that the fishermen of Eyemouth were more desperate financially than at other ports, and many sailed out into what was only a lull in a major storm. Over 100 men lost their lives from a total population of about 3,000. A few reached shelter in other ports. Over half the fishing boats based at the village were lost.

At the time of the storm, Sid's father had been a deck hand on Grandfather's boat. The old man desperately wanted to sail, but he looked at the sudden lull in the storm with experienced eyes and decided not to. Even when quite young, Sid had worked out that he owed his existence to his grandfather's wisdom. Not only wisdom, but patience. And as Pa pointed out, willingness to be looked down on as not bold enough for a true Scottish fisherman.

Pa didn't explain to his children a further disaster connected to the church tax and the Great Storm. They found out for themselves anyway. The planned harbour improvements were mainly to make it easier and safer for boats to get out of it, and more importantly, to get back into it. Stopping the fish tax was finally agreed years before the storm, but the church strung out the negotiations by demanding a one-off payment in compensation for losing the tax. The government didn't want to get on the wrong side of the church by providing financial assistance to the town before this was settled. As a result, the proposed work was agreed only a month or so before the storm. During the disaster some of the boats foundered just outside the still-unimproved harbour entrance, in full view of townsfolk on the sea wall.

Eyemouth was still stunned by these events when the government decided their harbour was no longer worth developing, and the money was spent elsewhere. This callousness, coming on top of the reason for the delay and then the storm itself, left a deep reservoir of bitterness.

The survivors of the storm, those that made it back to port, and those who never left it, carried on fishing. It was all they knew. They clung to it resentfully, not inclined in the slightest to be charitable towards any form of authority. Nor, for that matter, conspicuously religious. Sid drank all this in with his mother's milk, so to speak. It seemed grossly unfair. "Pa, why didn't guv'nt take our money away? They should've 'elp'd us."

It was difficult to explain to a young child. "Aye, lad, it's 'ard. They didn'a reckon we were worth 'elping after the storm. Sorry, lad, that's 'ow things happen, oft as not."

Pa Spears reflected on this reply over the next few days. His young son hadn't seemed convinced. He tried again. "Y'ken, lad, gov'ments 'ave t' please as many people as they can. Suppose they gave us t'money and we get a better port? Along the coast, say down at Berwick, they'd say it were wasted on us. We didn'a 'ave the boats to use it. Gov'ments 'ave to put money where it does most good. We just weren't worth it."

"But Berwick's England, in'it?"

"Same gov'ment, lad."

"… Oh."

Pa could see further explanation might help his young son but put it off to another day. Neither geography nor politics was his strong subject.

The Spears were a large family. Sid was the youngest. Not all the children had survived childhood. Several brothers worked in fishing from various ports along the coast. The Eyemouth fleet, although it had grown again since the Great Storm, offered too few opportunities. The boys did not own boats, just got work on them where they could. The oldest boy had gone a few miles inland and had a steady job on a farm near Ayton. The scholar of the family was studying engineering in Glasgow. Whether this needed to be paid for did not cross Sid's mind. He was well into his teens before he even handled cash. There wasn't much of it floating around in Eyemouth. His academic brother benefitted from philanthropy. He was one of the earliest from a poor background in Scotland to attend university.

Most of Sid's sisters were, or had been, 'fisher girls'. These followed the herring fleets along the coast in teams of three, gutting and salting the catches. It was tough work in all weathers, but you could earn money. It was also an efficient and discriminate way to find a husband.

Ma was worn out. She was glad her offspring were getting work, even though it meant leaving home. On balance, it was better for them to get away. There was an air of depression in Eyemouth, and far too much drunkenness. She was greatly consoled by Pa not being like that. He was sad and getting old now, but he was sober and thoughtful. Ma had long since given up the dream of being the matriarch of an extended family, perhaps running their own fishing fleet, or, even better, an inland farm. She didn't spend much time wondering what Sid would do. He was a bright lad. He'd find something.

Sid did find something. He joined the Royal Navy. His greatest delight was to sail offshore, even if the fishing wasn't as profitable as they would like. The movement of the boat with the waves and wind, keeping the sails filled, going neatly about when needed, the vast sky, the distant sight of the shore. These were the things which gave him the most pleasure. But he could see there was not going to be much of a future in this kind of fishing. On leaving school, he had the choice of looking to join a boat in one of the larger ports, like some of his brothers, or going into the navy. He was already captivated by stories of Nelson and Trafalgar. He'd read enough about his hero to know about Santa Cruz, Nile and Copenhagen as well.

Moreover, Sid knew that Britain had the most powerful navy in the world. It would never be defeated, and just to make sure it was building even larger battleships, the most powerful in the world. Choosing the navy was an easy step for Sid. Pa did not argue, he was proud of his son. Another Nelson perhaps. Ma thought it wasn't too bad either. One boy at university, another in the navy. That's good going.

The recruiting officers at Rosyth, by contrast, thought Sid a bit on the small side. Strictly he didn't quite meet the physical requirements. But they liked him being a sea fisherman's son, with experience of sailing and Nelson his hero. At 16, he could become a boy recruit, and maybe he would grow a bit more anyway. With the rate at which dreadnoughts were being built, they needed more men. What's more, Sid was clearly a bright lad. He had a dour look about him when relaxed, but brightened up when talking about something which interested him, which was anything to do with the sea and ships.

Before joining the navy, Sid had never been further from his home than Glasgow. Within a few days, he was travelling to a place called Devonport, which he had never heard of, by train, with a group of other recruits and a petty officer. He had very little idea of the layout of Britain south of about Hull, but he proudly gathered that he was going to join HMS *Impregnable*. It took two days to get there, with a night at barracks in London. *Impregnable* was at least two ships, one with *'II'* added to the name. Later he found there was even a third. But the essential point, which thrilled him, was that they were all genuine old wooden three-mast warships. They were basically stationary hulks, but the masts, yards and rigging were all there. He would be living on one of the *Impregnable* training ships.

Sid quite understood that modern warships were made of steel and driven by steam and propellers. But these training ships were like those his hero had lived and died on. He revelled in it. On deck, he was always aware of the towering masts and yards above him. In time, the boys gave demonstrations of manning the yards, proudly standing on them rather than lying over as when handling sail. Sid found this much more demanding than shinning up the mast of Pa's boat off Eyemouth. Being small he was sent to the highest yard. It was a great deal higher than Pa's gaffs. And the wide and essentially stationary deck below had a very solid look about it. He had to concentrate on his immediate surroundings during the first few climbs. Foot here, hold on to this. Next hand goes here. But in time the exhilaration of being up there took over. They would put on displays for visitors to the ship, the yards covered in boys, standing upright, their legs apart and arms spread to hold onto ropes rigged for the purpose. They all felt the thrill of being where very few of the visitors would dare to go. And the view over the harbour gave them a quite inappropriate sense of superiority.

He did not revel in all the training. The discipline was strict, and the available punishments bordered on the savage, although Sid was sensible enough to keep out of serious trouble. The food, clothing and general conditions were an improvement over his childhood, but he was worked a great deal harder. Although he had been an active lad growing up, and working on Pa's boat was strenuous, he had never been forced into such a level of exertion. The navy seemed to control his every moment. He never had to decide what to do, it was decided for him. All he had to do was jump to it.

A lot of what he had to jump to was extremely physical. Sid was surprised by the emphasis placed on moving heavy objects around. Previously he would have thought that shipboard equipment would be fitted by the dockyard and that would be that. But the boys had to, for instance, practise taking old naval field guns apart, carry the pieces over some artificial barrier, perhaps representing a river, and then assemble them again. They had teams racing each other doing this. Part of the skill was in improvising cranes and slings to get the guns over the obstacles. There were well established and ingenious ways to do this. To start with it was just yet another laborious bit of training. Then it became an enjoyable competitive sport, of which the pinnacle was a recently introduced event at the Royal Tournament in London. That pinnacle was as unreachable as Everest to the boys. The teams who competed in it included the strongest and toughest men in the navy. But the boys on HMS *Impregnable* pursued their humbler version of it with similar enthusiasm.

With the food and exercise, Sid did in fact grow a bit taller and put on more muscle. He generally went to sleep exhausted, and they weren't given much time to sleep. He had wondered before joining the navy whether hammocks were comfortable. With his agility, he was one of the first to master the knack of getting in and out of them. But were they comfortable? He normally fell asleep so fast he couldn't tell.

Some of the classroom material was boring, but much of it was a revelation. He had not realised how complicated modern warships were. He also discovered that despite his offshore fishing with Pa, he didn't know much about real seamanship.

Nor did he even know much naval language, beyond 'port' and 'starboard' and the points of the compass. Compared to Pa's boat their three-master was a different world. Your food came from the galley, and for the other end of the digestive process you went to the heads. Stairs became companionways. The floor was now a deck, a ceiling the deck-head. And so on, with many others, both nouns and verbs, and a great deal of slang. Sid now belonged to a different tribe, with its own language.

They also studied gunnery, and in the process a particular question of terminology was clarified. He joined the navy thinking, like most people, that a 'dreadnought' was simply a much larger and more powerful battleship which made all the others obsolete. It was a common misconception, although up to a point it was true. There was indeed a battleship named *Dreadnought*, although she was now outdated.

More importantly, 'dreadnought' was a response to the increasing range of naval guns. They could now fire shells well over 10 miles. If your target is that far away, it is difficult to know the exact distance, and thus the angle to which you should elevate your guns for the right range. Optical rangefinders were a useful starting point, but the most reliable way to adjust your range is to watch through binoculars to see how many of your shells fall short into the sea, by counting the splashes. If you know how many shells were fired in one volley, either a salvo or a broadside, then you want to see half that number of splashes in front of the enemy ship, where they are easier to see. You then assume the other half, which are more difficult to spot, fell beyond the target. This means your shots are straddling the enemy ship, and one should occasionally hit it. Sid had to face the harsh fact that in a future battleship engagement no one expected more than a small fraction of your shells to hit the enemy ship. It was a revolution in thinking for a lad who in his youthful dreams imagined himself on a Nelsonian gun deck blazing away point-blank at the enemy. Then, you could hardly miss.

The 'dreadnought principle', as it was known, was to have only one size of long-range gun. Up to HMS *Dreadnought*, battleships generally had guns of different calibres, requiring different elevation angles for the same range. If they all fire at the same target, you can't tell which splashes come from which guns. This problem had been noted in various countries, but Britain was the first to do something about it. Dreadnoughts had perhaps fewer big guns, but they were very big, and they were all the same. There was only one set of splashes to worry about during a long-range duel. Sid found the whole topic fascinating. He could understand it readily, as well as associated equipment like the range clock and the Dreyer fire-control table. What they do, if not how they do it.

Sid's classroom reports reflected his tendency to ignore subjects he found boring. They only tried to teach the elementary principles of navigation to the boys. It wasn't even worth starting with Sid. But he threw himself into the topics he thought would be useful, or at least those he enjoyed. Along with a tendency to ask the wrong kind of question, and his glum facial expression when not animated, it resulted in one lecturer commenting in his report, while recognising Boy Spears' strong points, that it would be better if he allowed the Admiralty to run the navy.

The best part of it all was sail training. The actual school ships were permanently moored, but the boys spent time crewing smaller vessels. They started with rowing boats, which tended to be called barges, then small sailing boats such as the simple sloop, working up to sea-going ships. Sid was a natural. He finished his sail training in a brig, square-rigged sails on both masts, plus a large spanker.

It was hard work. They had to learn the proper terms for every single item of fixed and running rigging. On the brig, there were hundreds. And then there were the many commands from deck to be learnt, and how to wear ship or, trickier, go about.

Amidst all this, for the first time, Sid was out on a yard, letting fly or reefing sail, with the ship riding the waves and heeling with the wind, the sea and the sky forming a vast and ever-moving backdrop, and what now looked a rather small area of deck below him, very mobile, to which he must keep his ears tuned for orders. Sid thought it was heaven, but on reflection wondered whether Heaven would include anything so good. Later on, working aloft in cold rain moderated this immediate enthusiasm, and of course he remembered that he didn't believe in Heaven or Hell, but he still thought this was the work he would most like to do. Of course, he wouldn't be handling sails, not on a dreadnought.

Experience at sea expanded his perception of masts and sails. Pa's smack was ketch-rigged. It had a main mast which was one piece of wood, with a gaff and a boom, each single bits of wood. Aft, there was the smaller mizzen mast, again just one piece of wood.

On the brig, things were different. The two masts were each assembled from three separate sections, lower, topmast and topgallant. Each of the top two sections sat in an iron socket on the one below. Each section was held in place by its own shrouds and stays.

That was the arrangement, along with the corresponding spars forming the yards, for up to moderately stiff winds. If a storm was brewing, typically the topgallant spars, and if considered prudent the topgallant masts, would be lowered to the deck, 'struck down' for dirty weather. When winds abated, they would be 'swayed up' again. This was all done with improvised derricks, from a pitching and rolling deck. For a violent storm, even the topmasts might be struck. The earlier practice the boys were given in moving heavy and awkward items around now made a lot of sense. Give sailors some lengths of wood, rope, and some pulleys, known as 'blocks', and they'll move anything. For that matter, they'll rig almost anything. Sid did wonder where such skill would be needed on a modern warship, but he was beginning to accept that maybe the navy did know best. After all, it was the best in the world.

After slightly less than a year of such training, Sid was rated up to Boy 1st Class, and assigned to the crew of the brand-new first-of-class battlecruiser HMS *Queen Mary*. He had already given some thought as to where he would prefer his battle station to be. Many people thought there would be a war. The more bellicose were eagerly anticipating one. It still seemed unlikely to Sid. Britain had maintained her navy at the strength of the next two strongest navies combined. At the rate Germany was building dreadnoughts, this had cost Britain a great deal of money, but she had nevertheless kept well ahead. It showed how important it was to control the seas, particularly with the Empire in mind. Who would challenge us?

However, it is sensible to prepare, if you can. Where would he prefer to be when the big guns were firing at each other? Their shells could weigh something like a ton, more for the largest calibres. They were designed to penetrate armour, and they exploded.

Sid's naval education had stressed that warship design is always a compromise between armament, armour, and speed. The Royal Navy favoured attack, and thus tended to specify larger guns and thinner armour. It was understood that the German navy had heavier armour. Their guns were not so large, but they had a good reputation for accuracy with them. This gave Sid and his mates something to think about.

The instructors had also made sure the boys understood another important naval principle. The days of point-blank gunnery were gone. Future naval engagements were expected to be fought at ranges which made an enemy ship difficult to see in any detail. (The boys had to get used to distances they would think of in miles being expressed in yards). The first thing they took from this was how difficult it made the gunnery. But there is another implication which was not so obvious, so it was spelled out. The damage the enemy is doing to your ship is all around you. The damage you are doing to the enemy ship may be impossible to see, unless she blows up or has a major fire. Don't assume you're losing just because your ship is taking hits. If your guns can still be fired, the fight continues. They were taught the importance of reporting damage, and of damage-control parties.

"Oh, another thing. Don't get carried away by the old idea of your gallant captain, when things get too hot, striking his colours and nobly surrendering. That isn't going to happen. Your captain, or his admiral, may decide to run from an engagement, but that decision will be made for you. Well, until you *are* the captain, of course. In the meanwhile, your ship keeps on fighting. Get it?"

Sid was no coward, and he was attracted to the idea of being a naval hero. But he was also prudent, and decided that, taking everything into consideration, below decks was preferable. This wasn't shameful, most of the crew, even at action stations, were below decks, running the large and complicated machine that makes up a modern battleship. The ship wasn't going to sink, but it might receive damage. The stations deepest in the ship were the engine rooms and magazines. But although Sid had distinctly filled out during his training, he did not have the ideal physique for a stoker, and working in coal dust did not attract him. The lessons on damage control, however, gave him the idea of working in the sick bay. All large warships have the equivalent of a small hospital. They are not so deep below decks, but he thought they must have at least a useful degree of protection. The equivalent of nurses are the sick-berth attendants. He could be one of those. He mentioned this interest towards the end of his training, to the surprise of the officer concerned, and to his own surprise was sent on a short first-aid course. This turned out to be his only formal medical training.

He was pleased, on joining *Queen Mary*, to find his preference had been noted. He was appointed to the sick bay. He was less pleased to discover his uniform would then be that of a steward. This did not suit him at all. He fancied himself in the sailor's square rig, with the bell-bottomed trousers. However, he had learnt to mentally shrug. That's how it's going to be. The navy was getting through to young Sid.

His ship was assigned to the 1st Battlecruiser Squadron. During the first six months of 1914 they showed the flag in some European ports and conducted various exercises in the North Sea.

To his surprise, and along with most of the boys, he was seasick. This seemed grossly unjust after being in and out of boats since he was a child. The motion of the large steam-powered cruiser felt entirely different from any sailing ship he had been on. Most of the time he was below decks and couldn't see the horizon. And the smell of fuel oil, which was sprayed onto the coal before it went into the boilers, permeated everywhere.

The officer in charge of the sick bay did not want sea-sickness cases. Just do it over the side or in the heads, please. Moreover, from Sid's point of view, it seemed unprofessional to be ill. He was supposed to look after any real casualties. It took a few miserable days before he was properly well again, but then he had his sea legs. In his opinion, it was a matter of getting his sea stomach.

The training exercises included real gunnery with floating targets. Sid could never adequately convey, in later life, the sensation of being below decks when a full broadside was fired. You should imagine a large giant hitting the ship with an enormous hammer. He could, accurately, report that damage was sometimes caused to items not properly secured. But like all impressive sensations, it was not the same put into words. This did not stop Sid being pedantic, in later life, on the difference between a salvo and a broadside.

Shipboard discussions ensued as to whether a broadside moved the ship sideways. It felt as though it did. Some pooh-poohed the idea, pointing out that the length of the ship's hull presented too much resistance in the water. The deep thinkers said, '*Yes, but the resistance can't be total. Mooring lines can pull the hull sideways. So can the wind. Slowly, of course, but it moves.*' Sid thought, '*Yes, but would it be enough for us to feel?*' Perhaps the recoil temporarily distorted the ship's shape? You certainly felt something.

Queen Mary and her crew were worked up into an efficient unit. Some wrinkles in both crewing and machinery were ironed out. Sid turned 18. In recognition of his new maturity and after some delay, he was officially no longer a Boy but an Ordinary Seaman. It didn't get him back into the square-rig uniform he preferred, but it was progress of a sort. The ship was starting to feel like home.

And then, within a few weeks, the political situation went rapidly downhill, and Britain, along with OS Spears, was at war. Every sailor hoped for an immediate engagement between the British and German fleets. The enthusiasts lusted for one. *'Germany has been spending all this money trying to catch us up, let them prove what they can do.'* This sentiment was largely shared by the population. What was really wanted, of course, was another Trafalgar. Would destroying the German High Seas Fleet win the war? Possibly not. At least, not all in one go. But it would put the enemy where he belonged. Sid was thrilled, not so much at the prospect of war as such, but that he was part of a large body of men who were, like he was, inspired by the Nelson spirit.

However, as war news started to get through to the sailors, the real danger seemed to come from subversive weapons, mines and submarines. British naval ships, sometimes substantial ones, were getting sunk by these unseen hazards, things which until then Sid had hardly thought about. For the first few weeks of the war, the cowardly techniques of the enemy formed the main topic of conversation. The desire for a straightforward shooting-match changed to resentment of a dastardly foe. Perhaps even a cowardly foe.

Then came the action off Heligoland. German light cruisers on a routine patrol were ambushed by a much stronger British force. The *Queen Mary* was part of the battlecruiser squadron. She fired her great guns in anger for the first time and suffered no casualties. The Germans lost three light cruisers and a destroyer, with substantial loss of life and damage to other ships. Britain lost no ships, and only 35 of her sailors were killed. Sid felt proud. He had been below decks the whole time, but that was his role.

It was much less than an engagement between the two main fleets, but it was an encouraging start. It was hailed as a victory. Royal Navy spirits rose. It was a proper engagement and they had won. Less attention was given to how uneven a match it had been.

Spirits spiralled downwards again for the next few months, as activity in the North Sea and English Channel had to focus again on protection against underwater threats. British losses mounted from these weapons. They seemed to give the advantage to their enemy.

Things appeared to deteriorate further when the entire British fleet based in Scapa Flow unexpectedly sailed out to the west of Scotland. This upset Sid and his fellow-matelots because it took them by surprise. They liked to think their rumour-mill was infallible. Various explanations circulated, not all of them authorised, but they learnt after sailing back a few weeks later that submarine defences had been added to the entrances to Scapa Flow. It was strongly believed that there had previously been none, and that a German submarine had attempted to enter the fleet's anchorage. Or possibly even succeeded. Sid, along with many of his naval colleagues, began to wonder if the navy had seriously lost its edge.

In addition to further losses caused by such underhand methods, including a minesweeper sunk within sight of Deal pier, a further outrage was the shelling by German cruisers of several east coast towns. The *Queen Mary* was part of the force sent to trap them on their way back to port, but poor visibility and confused signalling allowed the enemy ships to slip past them and get home, almost unmolested. There was outspoken public dissatisfaction with the navy over this. It had neither prevented the raid, nor punished the raiders, despite advance warning from intercepted German wireless signals. The battlecruiser squadron was moved to Rosyth to be closer to the threatened towns in future.

Just after Christmas HMS *Queen Mary* was docked for a refit. A week later OS Spears was granted two weeks leave. He had lost confidence in the navy. Maybe some recuperation would help him feel better. He was an old hand at rail travel by now. During journeys to or from Devonport while training he had even become familiar with parts of London. For this leave, he was allowed to go in square-rig uniform, which made him look much more like a sailor. He never found out whether it was a concession, or the normal regulations. There were quite a few things like that in naval life. They had stopped bothering him. Go with flow.

Neither his family nor the village had any advance notice of his arrival, this genuine son-of-the-town sailor man with a slightly rolling gait walking from their branch-line railway station to his home, unnecessarily via Harbour Road. It was a minor sensation. He was warmly welcomed.

At home, Ma's sister Aunt Mabel had come to live with them. Pa was getting old. He had stopped fishing, and he seemed smaller than Sid remembered. Steam was replacing sail for offshore fishing along the coast, and Pa's old boat could not compete. He had sold it but didn't get much for it. There had at last been some harbour improvements. But food prices were going up. Those who could get out fishing made it pay. You could also make a living chartering your boat for minesweeping. Some fishing boats caught mines without meaning to. The war reached into even this remote stretch of British shoreline, and it could be dangerous.

Sid did indeed feel better on getting back to his ship. A few days later, however, the ship's company was disappointed to find they had missed the Battle of Dogger Bank. It was another intelligence-based ambush of a raid to shell the

East Anglia coast, and this time the British response worked better. The German cruiser *Blücher* was sunk, and other enemy ships were damaged. The victory should have been more decisive, considering the size of the Royal Navy force, but it was still a victory, and was hailed as such. The rest of their cruiser squadron took part in this glorious success, but the *Queen Mary* was still in dockyard hands and had missed it. Sid reflected that it was at least comforting to know the navy had got something right.

An important result of the Dogger Bank action was that it discouraged the German fleet from entering the North Sea in any strength for more than a year. Instead, the naval war went back to the attrition of mine strikes and submarine attacks. The U-boats were getting more numerous and their captains more skilful. The navy continued to lose ships to torpedoes, and such attacks were extended to merchant shipping.

Sid, ahead of most of his shipmates, started to think in a more balanced manner about submarines. From time to time, there would be rejoicing that a British submarine had sunk a German ship. Sid hadn't thought about it much before then, but of course the Royal Navy had submarines. Are they really a coward's weapon? It isn't a coward's job to crew them. And they're far more effective than their size might suggest. A tiny boat with a ridiculously small crew, 30 or less, could sink a massive warship with a crew of over 1,000. And get away with it. For someone on the massive warship, it was worrying.

Part of the controversy centred around the use of submarines against commerce shipping. The Germans became increasing aggressive, epitomised by their sinking of the Lusitania. As far as Sid knew, the Royal Navy used its submarines only against enemy warships. But that was only as far as he knew. He was quite aware by now that the government could be selective as to what got into the news.

A depressing item of gossip of a different sort was HMS *Bulwark* blowing up in Sheerness harbour, with heavy loss of life. Sabotage was ruled out. It was thought to be an accident. Obviously, war is dangerous, and warships carry large amounts of explosives. But a disaster like this must mean something is wrong. There were dark mutterings that apparently a *Bulwark* magazine was adjacent to a boiler room, and cordite was stored too close to the warm bulkhead.

Later in 1915 Sid was distracted from such thoughts by being transferred, with little notice, to another brand-new ship, the Queen Elizabeth Class HMS *Barham*. This was the latest and most advanced class, described as a super-dreadnought. Her guns were as large as any in the battle fleet, but she was faster, almost as fast as the cruiser squadrons. Sid didn't know what to think about the move. He had grown to like life on the *Queen Mary*.

There was time for only a few quick goodbyes. The navy needed over a thousand men for the crew, and although many would have to be newly trained recruits, some more experienced sailors were needed. Sid was now in that category.

He was issued with the normal rating's square-rig uniform. No one told him whether he would be a sick-berth attendant in his new ship. He wasn't. The gunnery officer knew that youngsters tend to have the best eyesight. The fire-control system might have advanced rangefinders and ingenious calculating machines, but its most important element, in his opinion, was fall-of-shot spotting by keen-eyed observers. 'Guns' had taken the trouble to look through the training reports of the younger new crew, and a sentence in Sid's caught his eye: *He is particularly good at distinguishing whether a smudge on the horizon is coast, cloud, or a ship.*

The first Sid knew about it was while he and some of his old shipmates were admiring their new accommodation. It was slightly roomier than what they had shared in the *Queen Mary*. This was because *Barham*, along with the other ships of her class, burned just oil. This allowed the boilers to be smaller, and the crew accommodation larger. Their living arrangements were not what many people would call spacious, but compared to their previous berths it was a distinct step towards luxury.

Sid's appreciation of this benefit was interrupted by a message: 'OS Spears report to main deck.' Whereabouts on the main deck? And what had he done wrong? Sid couldn't think of anything serious, so he was just intrigued as to what this could be about. On deck, an officer checked who he was, said he was the gunnery officer, and that he wanted to try him out for spotting fall-of-shot. Guns was none too impressed with Sid's normal dour face but took him up to the foretop to find out what he could see. They climbed to the cabins and platforms high on the tripod mast abaft and above the bridge superstructure. From this vantage point, directors and range finders were used during gunnery. It was here that shot spotters operated.

Sid's expression changed markedly as he looked round at the view, mainly naval ships and dockyards, but still an impressive sight.

"Can you find *Warspite*?" Guns could see the name but could identify it only because he knew what it was. There were several ships around them. Sid looked from one to another. It took a while since the required vessel was one of the more distant. Finally, he pointed to the right one. "You can read her name?"

"Only just, Sir. I'm going by the shape rather than each letter."

"Fair enough. Now let's look at some detail. See the companionway just abaft the bridge?"

"Yes, Sir."

"Just aft of that there's a fitting on the side of the compartment. Can you make out what it is?" The officer had binoculars. Sid didn't.

"There's something there, but I can't identify it. I think it's too small to be a storage cabinet. It seems about the right size for mounting a life-raft, but with the raft missing. That's just a guess, Sir."

His questioner took the glasses down and looked directly. He could only just see that something was there. Spears could see alright. But what about the horizon? That can be deceptive. There wasn't much sea horizon visible from where they were, but the glasses showed him something.

Sid spent a while tracking his eyes along the line between sea and sky. Often a hazy transition, it was reasonably distinct that day. He covered the whole segment of horizon, and then came back to the speck he had spotted. "A bit left of centre. I think there's the tops of a hull-down ship."

"Merchant or navy?"

Sid looked some more. He flicked his eyes away and brought them back. No, nothing was going to make it clearer. "Can't really tell, Sir, but it seems more of a top than you would expect for a merchantman. I guess a warship. But I can't definitely identify fighting tops."

Nor could Guns, not even with his binoculars. He passed them to Sid. "See what you can make out with these."

Spears checked the focussing for both his eyes, using the approved sequence, and then showed he knew how to hold binoculars. There was no vibration from the moored ship to suppress, but he supported them between fingertips with his thumbs braced against his cheek bones. "Still difficult to make out details, but it strengthens the case for a warship."

"Your dad a lawyer, Spears?"

"No Sir. Fisherman."

"Oh yes." That had been in the report.

Guns was pleased. OS Spears had understood what he was doing and had co-operated sensibly. He hadn't pretended to see more than he could. He also discussed an uncertain identification intelligently. And he obviously liked being aloft. Another plus was that he didn't exaggerate his accent. His vowels were softly Scottish, but he spoke clearly, important when using a voice-pipe. Some Scottish ratings could be incomprehensible, either as an aggressive assertion of identity, or simply to make it difficult for an officer to understand. Or even in pursuit of both objectives. Guns guessed that this one spoke to him just like he would at home. That would be true now, but not while Sid was growing up. He had felt a strong affinity with the other boys with whom he trained and had subconsciously blended his accent with those of the others.

"OK, young Spears, I want you in my Gunnery Branch for shot-spotting. Any questions?"

Sid interpreted this as not whether he wanted to be a shot-spotter, or even whether he knew what a shot-spotter was, but whether he had any other type of question. "No, Sir."

So, he was going to be a shot-spotter in the gunnery department. It wasn't a question of whether he would like to be. His immediate reaction was to feel somewhat flattered, although not totally sure whether he was pleased or not. Guns also said he would launch the process of up-rating Ordinary Seaman Spears to Able-bodied Seaman Spears. Well, OK, he could handle that alright. 'AB Spears' sounds good.

On getting down to the main deck, Sid looked back up the tripod mast supporting the fighting tops and paused with a hand to his chin.

"Something on your mind, Spears?"

"Yes, Sir. I think I do have a question. It is only about a general principle. Why isn't the foretop built up from the top of the bridges? We have all the steel in this tripod from the main deck up to some quite small cabins. They could be supported by a much shorter mast extended from the bridge superstructure. Wouldn't the tops be just as effective directly above the bridges? It would place them further forrard from the smokestack, which could be useful. And it would save weight."

The gunnery officer had not been asked this before, had never met a rating who asked such a question, to which he didn't know the answer. Was young Spears a lower-deck intellectual? Even worse, was he a left-wing agitator intent on starting a revolution? Like many officers, he was not too keen on the former, and along with the Royal Navy in general, verged on the pathological regarding the latter. Ah well, it looked as though he will do the spotting job well enough. Let's see how things go. On the other hand, it was a good point. Why not just build up from the bridge castle? Maybe our Spears just has a working brain. Shouldn't penalise him for that. I'll put him with PO Murphy. They'll get on famously.

Sid didn't quite know what to think, either. Before his first shipboard appointment, to the *Queen Mary*, he had carefully and analytically considered where he would like to be during an engagement. He thought he'd reached a sensible conclusion. There's bound to be some risk in the navy, but there's no point in overdoing it. A useful job a few decks down seemed a good choice. A sick-berth attendant is a worthy and necessary role. It had been a good idea. You might have to go out with stretcher parties to bring in the injured, which would certainly be risky during gunnery, but it wouldn't happen all the time. The arrangement had about enough of a heroic feel about it to satisfy his ambitions in that area. Perhaps even a bit more than strictly necessary, but that was alright.

Moreover, having reached that conclusion, he had, to his surprise, achieved the role of a sick-berth attendant in *Queen Mary*. Now, transferred to *Barham*, and by a process entirely outside his control, his position would be about as far above decks as he could get. Should he have fluffed the tests of how well he could see? He didn't think he could have. And it was truly exhilarating to have such a commanding position above the ship. Shot-spotting was something he could do, do well, and it was a vital job. He mentally shrugged. He didn't want to become fatalistic, but there are times when you wonder whether it is worth bothering. Perhaps just let life take you along? And it was as close as he would ever get to his boyhood dreams of being one of Nelson's gunners.

His action station was now a small cabin at the top of a tripod mast just behind and well above the captain's and admiral's bridges. The view was spectacular, and it wasn't spoiled by looking through glass. The windows were openings in the metal walls. Sid was elated at sort of being up in the rigging again. He was much more part of what was going on during their working-up exercises than he had ever been in the *Queen Mary* sick berth. During live-firing practice he saw the big naval guns firing for the first time. And these were indeed big, 15 inches. He was told to protect his eardrums by keeping his mouth open. The vast belches of flame and the amount of smoke took him by surprise. Having had them pointed out, he could also spot the shock waves which radiated from the muzzle of each gun at the speed of sound. And he could certainly feel something move when they all fired. He suspected it was the tripod mast flexing.

At his spotting station, Sid got to know the petty officer manning the large range-finder mounted in their eyrie. A large solidly built man, older than Sid, with a mild Irish accent, close-cropped gingery hair, and an easy-going attitude.

Towards the end of 1915, during manoeuvres complicated by occasional fog banks, they had an interesting discussion. Sid had raised the question of relative risk in different parts of the ship during an engagement. This experienced sailor cheerily gave Sid the benefit of his expert opinion. "My view is that this is the safest place in the ship. Down in the magazines or machinery spaces you are less likely to be hit directly, but the ship could sink quicker than you can get out, and of course you stand no chance if it blows up."

Sid knew by now that Royal Navy ships can blow up even without the enemy's help.

"If you are on one of the higher decks, or in the superstructure, a shell landing 30 feet away is a serious matter. Splinters and fragments fly outwards when it explodes, and of course there is a sheet of flame. Now, up here, a shell passing 30 feet away could miss us completely. It would just fly by. In other words, our cabin is a small target. After the distance, it has travelled the chances of a shell actually hitting it must be very small."

He appeared thoughtful for a while, perhaps wondering whether the following comment was a good idea. But... what the hell.

"And it could be to our advantage that we are not behind thick armour. I think a big shell would go straight through us without exploding, or possibly explode after it has got some way further. That's not so bad."

These observations seemed logical to Sid, apart from how you interpret 'us' in that last comment. "It must be a question of *what* the shell hits, surely, on its way through?"

"Ah, yes. Well, that's a point, but individually we really are small targets. Especially you."

That wasn't tactful, but it was accurate. The petty officer wasn't what you could call petite. He made up about twice Sid's cross-sectional area. It could be viewed as comforting. It made it about twice as likely that something passing through the fighting top would hit the PO rather than Sid.

These thoughtful reflections were interrupted when something caught the eye of the senior man. He transferred his attention outside. "Look you now! That's wrong."

It was indeed. Their sister *Warspite*, also Queen Elizabeth-class, was sailing out of a patch of fog straight towards them. There wasn't room for her to turn, and as pointed out later, ships don't have brakes. The PO offered helpful advice: "Hang on."

They did hang on. Compared to a broadside, the ship's reaction was slower but more damaging. The closing speed between the two hulls had not been all that great, but each weighed well over 30,000 tons, and a lot of steel became bent, torn and tangled. *Warspite* had a spectacularly shorter and blunter bow when the damage had all been done. Neither ship sank, or was even in danger of sinking, but both needed to return to base, and then into dock for repairs.

"Er…Sir…I know we mustn't criticise the navy…" A sardonic grin. "But shouldn't captains know how to steer their ships?"

"No, not at all, that's the helmsman's job."

"But surely it's the captain's job to avoid collisions?"

"Well, there have been a remarkably large number of collisions, so we must draw our own conclusions. But this is a mild case. You're too young to remember, but there really was a collision in the Mediterranean last century. The *Victoria* was rammed by *Camperdown* and capsized within quarter of an hour. I think about half the crew were drowned. It was during fleet manoeuvres. The commanding officer was a well-known old admiral with a good record but who didn't expect his orders to be questioned. And I don't think anyone is completely sure what went wrong, except it had to be something to do with his orders or how they were understood. Some think the admiral might just have confused the diameter of a turning circle with its radius. Or even got port and starboard mixed up. Anyway, he had the decency to go down with his ship.

"Oh, and another thing. Our admiral of the Grand Fleet, John Jellicoe no less, was one of the survivors of the *Victoria*. He has a reputation for being cautious. Maybe that's where it started."

The events of that day gave Sid things to ponder. Quite apart from the collision and its implications, he reflected that this PO must be relying on him not to quote him around the lower decks. Sid wouldn't anyway, but he took the implied intimacy of their banter as a distinct compliment. They spent enough time together in the foretop to get to know each other quite well, taking the difference in rank into account. Sid could not remember anyone else with such genial approach to life. The PO wasn't slack when it came to their duties, or anyone else's duties for that matter, but nothing seemed to disturb him, even when he had occasion to point out something he didn't think was quite as it should be. Outright bloomers and disasters like *Warspite* ramming them caused him apparently to reflect on what it all meant, stroking his chin with raised eyebrows. Quite often with a witty remark as well. But even if it was something about which everyone had good reason to be worried, he gave the impression of just viewing life's vicissitudes with bemused wonder. Probably thinking up another joke.

The deprecation wreaked by *Warspite* resulted in *Barham* going into a floating dry dock at Cromarty Firth, and Sid for the second year went on leave in December. This time it included Christmas Day. Ma and Aunt Mabel seem well settled and cheerful, delighted to have him home for Christmas. Pa did not look well. Not being able to fish and therefore not bringing in much money, he didn't have a purpose in life. He helped with a bit of net mending and other minor repairs, and these brought in a little cash, but he had started to drink some of it. Ma, and especially A. Mabel, were not happy about this. Nor was Sid, but he couldn't tell his Pa what he should or shouldn't do.

Back onboard *Barham*, Sid was further depressed to learn that another cruiser had blown up, this time in Cromarty Firth. An investigation could find no evidence of enemy action, so again it had to be some form of accident. The ship was entertaining guests at the time, including officers' families and some local nurses.

The weather frustrated some naval activities in the early months of 1916. Gales in the North Sea caused several operations to be curtailed, mainly because the sea state was too much for the supporting destroyers. These much smaller ships were considered essential escorts to the capital ships for protection against U-boat attacks. It was becoming clear that submarines, perhaps the most seaworthy of all naval vessels, can operate in weather which keeps destroyers in harbour. And dreadnoughts *do* dread something, the threat of submarines without the protection of destroyers. Some of the more active and logical brains in the navy, and there were some, found themselves wondering whether the dreadnought-building race had been an expensive mistake. It was time these pinnacles of naval engineering did their job and had a good slugging-match with the Germans.

Another aspect of weather showed its hand during some routine firing exercises. They were steaming downwind, and the tail wind was strong enough to carry the smoke forward from the funnels and thus around the fighting top. "What," Sid asked his petty officer friend, "do we do if this happens in action?"

"Look you now, this is nothing." PO paused, for effect. Should he be frank here? *This youngster hasn't seen much of naval life yet. We mustn't frighten him.* But perhaps he ought to know. "I started my gunnery career spotting in *Orion*. In your youthful innocence, young Spears, you wouldn't expect anything as silly as the arrangement we had there. But please be assured that I am not playing games or trying to deceive you. And I am not exaggerating. This is true. On *Orion*, as with several of the early dreadnoughts, the foretop was *abaft* the first smokestack. We could hardly see anything, but that didn't matter since we could barely breathe either. Nothing could be done about it. Gunnery exercises were just short of fatal, as far as we were concerned. It was just as well we never went into action."

Sid did indeed find it difficult to believe. He frowned. "But how could anything so stupid ever be constructed? It would take a lunatic."

The PO brightened up. He raised a finger in emphasis. It is so encouraging to have a bright pupil. "You've put your finger on it exactly. That's just what did happen." He looked round, somewhat theatrically, but not overdoing it. "I'll let you into a secret about battleship design. What I am about to divulge is not widely known. And those dimwits at the Treasury can't know about it. All the detailed design inside a battleship is done by specialists who know what is needed and how to make it all work. Well, most of it, anyway. But every so often our Sea Lords want a dramatic advance in design, something to strike fear into the King's enemies, or the Germans at least. They want a bold new concept of a warship. So, what do they do?"

He leant forward and spoke a little quieter.

"At that point, they turn to a genius they have at the Admiralty. They keep him locked in a special room, and only let him out occasionally. You see, they want his ideas to be original. If he spoke to us sailors, we would muddy his thinking. We might have different opinions on all sorts of things. That could confuse him. Quite a sensitive soul, the Admiralty's genius. Our Lords want the pure spark of his thinking to come straight out and into the new ship. So, what happens? They give him the broad requirements, how much bigger than last time, how many guns, and so on. And then tiptoe out and lock the door. And what does he do? A new page in his sketch book, and he starts on an outline drawing to lay out the overall scheme. He knows the front is sharp so it can cut through the water, and the other end is blunt because that's where the propellers are, or whatever it is pushing it through the water. And then the guns. He says to himself, 'They like to have some pointing forward for when they are going towards the enemy, and some at the back for when they are running away, and then they need room for them all to point sideways, which is funny since they never travel sideways. At least, I don't think so. Never mind. Now, what do they want between the front and back guns? It's written down somewhere. Oh yes, here it is: three chimneys and two masts. They do like masts. I suppose it reminds them of the old sailing ships. I don't think they have sails any more, do they? Anyway, if we want a nice balanced layout with two masts and three chimneys, it's obvious: chimney; mast; chimney; mast; chimney.' He sketches them in. 'Yes, that looks nice. Hold on, that's not right. Here's the note they gave me. Two of each. Oh well, rub out the middle chimney. Let's leave the gap, they sometimes want space to fit other things in. The dockyard people can do the details. Right, I like that: chimney; mast; gap; mast; chimney. Like two pairs of marching soldiers. Hold on, I'm not certain it looks right now being symmetrical around that gap. Let's swap the last two: chimney; mast; gap; chimney; mast. Yes! Looks good. Quite easy. I sometimes wonder why they pay me. Well, do they pay me? I can't remember. Now, will they let me out for lunch?' So, see how it works, young Spears? That's the Admiralty's secret weapon. That's how a battleship turns out to be a machine for producing smoked sailors. I may be wrong, but I don't think Nelson had that sort of problem."

Smiling and laughing weren't Sid's strong points, but he couldn't help grinning. "Couldn't you be sent to the Tower for telling secrets like that? Suppose the Kaiser heard!" He had come to like this large, genial, and calm man. Sid had never seen him get flustered when things went wrong. He could demonstrate a caustic sense of humour but didn't get into serious arguments. It was difficult to imagine him getting much upset over anything.

The war went on, and with it the routine of shipboard life. Much of it cleaning. Being on an all-oil-fired ship provided a merciful relief from the scrubbing needed after coaling the old *Queen Mary*. They went out on exercises and patrols in the North Sea. At least, when the weather allowed their destroyers to come along too.

A major disruption to such routine occurred when the Queen Elizabeth cruisers were moved from Scapa Flow, where they had been part of the Grand Fleet, to Rosyth, where they were placed on attachment as the 5th squadron of Admiral Beatty's battlecruiser fleet. It made a change, and the view wasn't quite as bleak or the wind so biting as at Scapa.

Then came the day late in May when major preparations for sailing became evident, and during the night Beatty's entire fleet sailed. Dawn found them steaming across the North Sea, and after the morning stand-to the squadrons manoeuvred into line-ahead, with the 5th squadron last, despite having the biggest guns in Beatty's force. The trouble was that they were also the slowest of all the cruisers. Not by much, but enough to make a difference. In the absence of *Queen Elizabeth*, in dock for maintenance after service in the Mediterranean, *Barham* led the squadron as its flagship, followed by *Valiant*, their old friend *Warspite*, now with a new bow, and *Malaya*.

It was a grey day, with broken cloud and patches of mist, and a moderate sea state. The squadron of four large and near-identical warships looked majestic to Sid, but they seemed a long way behind the tail-end of Beatty's regular squadrons.

The routine watches continued. Sid came off duty at midday. He was having a nap when the ship went to battle stations. When he reached the foretop, the main part of Beatty's fleet was nearly out of sight. They had increased speed earlier, changed course several times, and were now steaming approximately south. Sid found it unsettling how little they knew about what was happening, and how far they had been left behind. Surely Beatty hadn't forgotten them? There was a delay before the 5th squadron changed course to follow the other British cruisers. They weren't quite as fast but could cut off a corner to help catch up.

There was a smell of fumes in the top. "We've got a bit of a tailwind, haven't we?" holding his nose. The smoke from the stack just aft of them was hanging around, not streaming straight towards the stern, as they would prefer.

Petty Officer thought it wouldn't be a problem. "I think our speed will always beat the wind, today. It's about north-west, so it's chasing us on this course. Might make us a bit faster."

He reflected a while, then decided to come clean with young Spears.

"You know, the other day, about having smokestacks forrard of our tops. I might have been just a little unfair to our Lords at the Admiralty. It's not entirely down to that genius they have locked up. And it's not restricted just to the Orion Class, either. The original *Dreadnought* was the same. There's a certain logic to it. You see, putting the foremast abaft the forrard stack means that it can be used as the boats' derrick. It's a convenient place to keep the boats. Now what's more important, hoisting boats in and out, or gunnery? Well, consider what occurs most. How often are boats used? In port, several times a day. Our captain needs his barge for all sorts of important engagements. Like dinner ashore. Even more so if we have an admiral on board. And, moreover, how much of our time do we spend in port? Most of it. On the other hand, how much time do we spend shooting at Germans? Or shooting at anything, for that matter. A great deal less, you must agree. So, it's obvious. Hoisting the boats around is much more important. It's logical, when you think about it."

Sid decided it was time he contributed to this repartee. He put on his thoughtful expression. "Are you sure that's right? If something's logical, surely it must be logical whether I think about it or not."

"Er, well, yes, I suppose so."

Refreshed with such scintillating discourse, the crew of the range-finder platform passed the time as their squadron chased after Sir Beatty. They were largely in the dark as to what was going on, but a substantial buzz had gone round the ship that the German High Seas Fleet was at last coming out. Beatty's cruisers were sailing for a rendezvous with the main British fleet somewhere off Denmark. This could be the decisive battle they had all longed for.

Sid's confidence in the Royal Navy had taken damage below the waterline, but it was still afloat. He was eager, if apprehensive, to prove that Britannia continued to rule the waves. As far as the PO was concerned it had been all hands to the pumps pretty much since he joined up, but he had decided to make the navy his career, and that was that.

As the *Barham* closed on the squadron in front, more of the British ships became visible. Patches of mist made it difficult to keep track of them. You would see a new ship, then it faded out of view. About an hour after going to battle stations there was a dramatic change. A ripple of flashes stabbed out of the grey mist to port of the cruisers ahead. It was Sid's first sight of gunfire pointing generally towards him. There was a worrying delay, several minutes, before Beatty's ships started firing back. Sid studied what he could see of the shell splashes around the rear-most British cruisers. German gunners seemed to find the range in disturbingly few salvos.

Only a few minutes into this action no one in the *Barham* tops could ignore a set of large explosions. They occurred a long way ahead amongst the British ships. There were several flashes of flame, but the lasting memory was of a tall column of smoke rising far above the patches of mist over the sea. They already knew their ships could explode by accident. This one must have been by enemy action.

As they continued to close on the cruisers, the German ships started coming into view. At last, they were given a target. Sid trained his glasses in that direction and there was his first reasonably clear sight of the enemy. It was closer than he had expected, approximately on the same course as *Barham*, somewhat ahead and to port. There was no spotting to do until the first ranging salvo was fired, but Sid kept his gaze on their target while waiting. Target angles can change, and more than one German cruiser was now visible. His spotting wouldn't do any good if he was looking at the wrong ship.

The gunnery department in *Barham* took great satisfaction, later, in how quickly they got their first target's range and secured hits on her. At the time their attention was wholly occupied with the battle, which progressively increased in tempo. German shells splashed into the sea to port, screamed overhead to splash to starboard, and before long they received hits. The first one seemed like a hammer blow through the hull, up to the foretop. It seemed to hit Sid through his feet. The second hit was on the superstructure aft, with a burst of flame and debris flying past his spotting position.

Before long, there was another appalling multiple explosion amongst the British cruisers ahead of them. Another huge column of smoke.

Sid was quietly terrified. He combated it by concentrating obsessively on his spotting. He counted off his own unofficial fall-of-shot-time estimate to make sure he was on peak attention just before their shells were due to drop around the distant target. Reporting how many of their splashes were short the moment he was certain. Always stating when he couldn't get a clear sight. None of his reports were made up to impress anyone. Then looking quickly around without the glasses, waiting for the next broadside, just in case something significant changed around them. At their next broadside, starting his mental fall-of-shot clock, adjusted by the previous real one, then eyes back to the glasses. None of their exercises had included the complication of enemy funnel and gun smoke, nor the distracting scream of his shells falling around you. Nor, of course, those that hit you. These, and the poor North Sea visibility, turned gunnery from an almost analytic exercise into a desperate struggle.

Just when Sid was starting to feel that both sides had done enough damage to each other and should start to break away, he saw new gun flashes further to the south, ahead of them rather than to port. It suggested that there were further enemy ships coming from the south. He was sufficiently well informed to guess the British cruiser squadrons, on a roughly southerly course, were sailing head-on towards the approaching main German battle fleet. If so, the British ships would soon be outgunned and outnumbered. From what he had learnt about naval tactics, Beatty and his cruisers, including the Queen Elizabeth ships, should now be racing to the north from where it was now thought Jellicoe and his main battle fleet must be approaching. He expected, and earnestly hoped, that all the British cruisers would immediately be signalled to turn individually away and flee north. But there was no sign of it. They continued to steam towards the enemy battleships, while still engaged to port with the enemy cruisers. Beatty's squadrons were heading straight for a cauldron of incoming fire.

The first sign Sid observed of a tactical withdrawal was the sight of Beatty's flagship leading his 1st squadron past them back northwards. Using his glasses briefly while waiting for *Barham* to fire her next broadside, Sid could see that *Lion* was damaged. In particular, Q turret seemed to have lost its roof.

This was Sid's first real naval battle. He was in no way a naval tactician, but he thought initially Beatty had made a bad decision. He was turning his ships away from the new threat *in succession*. Each ship would change course away from the danger in roughly the same area of sea, with the enemy getting progressively closer. The new threat had to be the main German fleet, composed of battleships, slower than the Elizabeth-class ships, but more heavily armed than the cruisers they had been engaging. And the 5th squadron was going to be the last of Beatty's fleet to go through the concentration of German fire.

Even while concentrating on his job, a part of Sid's brain was turning the situation over. Was it in fact a good decision? The Queen Elizabeths were Beatty's largest guns. He was putting them closest to the large enemy fleet as the rest of his cruisers withdrew. Had he kept the Queen Elizabeths to the rear so they would be less damaged at the start of any withdrawal? It was a logical decision. Just a bit rough on the Elizabeths.

As they continued south into the turning point, known subsequently as 'windy corner', Sid's concentration on shot-spotting was interrupted by various changes to their targeting. The intensity of incoming fire produced something like battle-frenzy. He was snarling, at least in his mind, "Take that, you bastard! What do you think of that, then? See, we can hand it out too." He hoped, later, that it had indeed been only in his mind. Even if he had used his voice, it might not have mattered much in windy corner. It was an extremely noisy corner. Shells arrived from different directions. They took more hits. But their ship was still working. It was under power. In the foretop, they continued to receive orders and could still report back. After all, it only required the voice-pipe to be in one piece, and, of course, someone alive at the other end.

Barham sailed northwards from windy corner as *Valiant* followed her into it, and then *Warspite* and *Malaya*. They all came through, with damage, but all functional. With their superior speed, they pulled away from the enemy battleships. As the afternoon wore on, they followed Beatty's remaining cruisers north, duelling with enemy cruisers, running north again on a roughly parallel course. They settled down to the simple process of engaging just one enemy ship at a time. Sid and his colleagues in the fighting tops were now battle-hardened. A two-ship duel was just their normal function.

Sid had no knowledge of the overall battle plan, if there was one. At this point, he only hoped they were leading the enemy towards the main British battle fleet. Or were they simply running away from the High Seas Fleet? No problem if they were, they had the speed. At least, the Queen Elizabeths and the other cruisers did. But a master plan should have them leading the enemy battleships into a trap. It was thus a thrilling sight when the northern horizon became dotted with ships. It could only be Jellicoe with the Grand Fleet. As they brought up the rear of Beatty's cruisers and closed with the main fleet, the battleships were deploying from columns into a battle line to port, initially eastwards, and then turning more to the south. It was the classic 'crossing the T' trap for an advancing enemy.

While this was taking place, the 5th Battlecruiser Squadron conducted their own special type of manoeuvres. *Warspite* left their line, performed two complete circles, stopped, and then made some irregular and slow course changes. She attracted a lot of fire. Amongst Sid's colleagues there were unkind comments about *Warspite*'s handling. They weren't being callous, and they recognised that it was a dangerous place to have trouble with your steering, but they considered themselves fortunate not to be rammed by her again. They were not privy to whatever signals went to *Warspite*, but at last she managed to get herself pointing west and sailed slowly off in that direction, and out of the battle. Sid's PO commented that *Warspite* still seemed to have a difficult relationship with her helm. They heard later she had received damage which locked the rudder position.

A major engagement developed between the two fleets. With the sun in the west, the British, now further to the east than their enemy, had the better light. Their ships were spread out in an arc, and they outnumbered their opponents, who were more bunched. The Grand Fleet could deliver heavier fire than could be returned. Even so, it was a ding-dong affair. Throughout the long early-summer evening the German admiral, Scheer, manoeuvred his fleet skilfully, with several turn-away moves. With the light fading, *Barham* engaged in several episodes of sporadic firing, but without observing hits. The action continued into a moon-less night, in the confusion of which Scheer's ships slipped past the British with only a few exchanges of fire and headed back to their ports.

When they were stood down, which for the men in the foretop really did mean coming down, Sid caught up with some of the details. The first ship he had seen explode during the cruiser action when sailing south had been *Indefatigable*. The second was his old berth *Queen Mary*. Both were horrible to consider, but the *Queen Mary* was a particularly nasty shock. He had old pals on her. For that matter, he could easily have been with them.

They also learnt that two other British ships had been lost by magazine explosions, *Invincible* and *Defence*. Beatty's famous observation to the effect that there must be something wrong with our bloody ships today was not yet in circulation, but similar thoughts must have been occurring to many of the tired crews.

But Sid's worst shock was to learn that a shell early in the cruiser action had penetrated the *Barham* sickbay, killing everyone there. And by a horrible stroke of bad luck, eight of those were boys who were only there because they had been taken poorly by inoculations.

That was his old job, a sick-berth attendant on the *Queen Mary*. It was difficult to settle down to the regular watches as they sailed back to port. The battle damage was under control, but his thinking had taken some harm. If he had not been selected to transfer to *Barham*, he would have been on the *Queen Elizabeth* when she was destroyed, and he would be dead. If he had kept his sick-berth role in his new ship, as he initially would have preferred, he would also be dead. He had the *Barham*'s gunnery officer to thank for his life.

According to the subsequent official analysis of the battle, *Barham*, along with their Queen Elizabeth Sister *Valiant,* scored highly with accredited hits. That pleased the gunnery department no end.

Overall, however, the action had been a disappointment. Britain lost more ships than Germany. Many of the German ships, even though heavily damaged, had been able to get back to their home ports. Far too many of the British ships had blown up or sunk. The navy at large did not understand how this could happen, although the rumour-mill had it covered. It was suggested that in Beatty's cruiser squadrons they were encouraged to ignore safety procedures by leaving flash doors open. This allowed faster delivery of ammunition to the turrets but made the ship vulnerable to a shell explosion sending flame down to the magazines. It wasn't something wrong with the ships, but the procedures used on them. It was thought that German ships had interlocked flash doors on each ammunition hoist to make it impossible for them to be open at the same time.

The most galling element, at least to Sid, was the public's anger. He had not witnessed it personally, but apparently some ships were booed upon docking. The news had got there that fast. How could the heirs to Nelson have failed to destroy the upstart German fleet? In Royal Navy circles it was accepted that German designers concentrated more on armour than firepower. But at Jutland we outnumbered them, had larger guns, and by luck or judgement had deployed into a highly favourable position. We should have pulverised them.

Sid took a keen interest in all the news he could gather. A widespread view was that Beatty had shown the Nelson spirit in throwing his ships against the enemy, whereas Jellicoe was too cautious and should have pursued their beaten foe more vigorously. The better-informed naval view leant more towards Beatty being to blame for prosecuting a private war with the enemy fleet, at great cost, and failing in his main role of scouting and reporting its position. In chasing north with the High Seas Fleet coming up behind, he had in fact led the enemy into a trap, but he had failed to give Jellicoe advance information on how events were unfolding. Jellicoe, with the weight on his mind of Churchill's tactless comment that he was the only man on either side who could lose the war in an afternoon, had to bring his battle fleet to action without knowing where the enemy ships were until he could see them. His deployment of the battle fleet to cross the German's T was a major achievement, expertly conducted under difficult circumstances. And after the main engagement he was probably right not to chase the retiring German fleet aggressively, due to the threat of underwater weapons. The enemy had demonstrated disturbing competence with them.

On reflection, Sid came to see it was the strategic implications which were the most important. If the Germans could win control of the North Sea, they could shell London and largely shut down Britain's merchant shipping. That could starve us out of the war. Although the Germans acquitted themselves well at Jutland, it was they who withdrew from the battle. They escaped from the trap and ran for home. And, as events turned out, stayed there. Britain may have lost more ships and more sailors, but she still had much the larger fleet. An American journalist commented that Germany had assaulted her jailor but was still in jail.

The *Barham* and her crew saw no further action. In the November following Jutland, there was a major sailing on reports of the German fleet coming out again. Apparently, they were using Zeppelins to scout for them, though experts later doubted whether they achieved much. Both sides operated with submarines, and these seemed to have been the only vessels to inflict damage on the other side.

The rest of the war was something of a drag. Routine patrols, relatively minor operations, elaborate precautions against torpedo boats and U-boats. The news was mildly enlivened, although you could not call them jokes, by reports of two more collisions by *Warspite,* both with ships she would be expected to consider friendly. PO Murphy again had occasion to comment that she still didn't seem to have a sensible working relationship with her helm. Perhaps it was her name. If she couldn't have a bash at the enemy, any nearby ship would do.

Sid's native cynicism was not abated when the supremely professional Jellicoe lost his position as the head of the Grand Fleet, for it to go to the gung-ho and perhaps careless Beatty. He was reminded of Nelson's dictum. In effect: '*Just throw yourself at the enemy. We won't criticise.*'

The only other naval event in Sid's war was the internment of the German fleet following the armistice when it meekly followed HMS *Cardiff* into the Firth of Forth between two lines of Royal Navy warships. *Barham* was in the northern line, and at full readiness. There were some thoughts that the German ships might open fire in a final blaze of defiance. Some British sailors thought the whole business shameful and would have at least understood had they done so. One aspect of that day was beyond dispute. No one had ever seen such an assembly of naval ships before, and probably never would again. Sid thought it a sad ending.

He had much else to think about. He was proud of the role he had played at Jutland. He wasn't boastful by nature, but he held the sentiment to which the veteran is entitled: 'I was at the battle. I did my job'. But now he wanted to leave the navy. He was disillusioned about how it was run. He had signed up for 12 years, but no longer wanted it to be his life's career. There were possibilities for leaving early and going onto the Reserve. He started those wheels turning and voiced his wish for an early release. In due course, he was able to sign a form to that end. He hoped the wheels really were now turning. There was no other indication that they were.

Peace-time naval life returned, but in a much-changed country. The nervous but militaristic pre-war years seemed in retrospect to have been a phase of national madness. The benefits of peace were now in demand but slow in arriving. The navy was no longer the national hero, and it urgently needed to reduce costs. The priority was to decommission the older ships and demobilise their crews. *Barham* was one of the most up to date, so she was expected to remain in commission for years yet.

Sid settled down to serving his time. He was, in fact, comfortable in *Barham*. He had grown fond of the ship, and many of its company. Like the poor old *Mary*, it was now where he lived. If he had been asked to say where his home was, his ship would now win over Ma and Pa's modest place in Eyemouth. He was genuinely fond of his parents. He regretted the way his father's life had contracted so much, no longer able to earn a living from the sea. But although he had fond recollections of his childhood there, Sid did not see himself having a career in Eyemouth. He reflected that his attempts to steer his naval life had been overridden by a sequence of events over which he'd exercised precious little influence. Maybe the one sensible decision Sid could make now was to stop trying to plan his future.

But to look at it another way, you can't go through life without making any decisions at all. For one thing, if he leaves the navy, he will need a job. '*No one is likely to offer me employment unasked.*' Therefore, he would have to apply for work. Maybe the secret is to make decisions for the near-term, but don't try to plan your life far into the future. It's a waste of effort. That would be his strategy.

Having thus finalised a philosophy for the rest of his life, Sid decided he might as well learn about things which could be useful. In any case, he was fascinated by machines and engines, and what electricity and wireless could do. Aboard ship, a pointer set by hand at one station could make a pointer elsewhere in the ship move to the corresponding position, by electricity. It wasn't like using a mechanical link. It didn't matter how far apart they were. They only needed to be connected by wires. This type of system was used to control a variety of functions. In his department, gunnery, it was used to train and elevate all the big guns to the same target. Even more fascinating, as well as mysterious, was the growing science of wireless telegraphy. Sid had learnt how flags were used to signal between ships. They still were. In theory, he knew how to do it. He had also learnt that they didn't work over the distances and through the mist and smoke they'd had at Jutland. But wireless did. A major problem, apparently, was that their commanders didn't trust it. Maybe the equipment wasn't installed or adjusted right. More likely, many thought, it was not used because it was not yet part of naval tradition.

As it was, the Battle of Jutland had been along the lines of a heavyweight title fight with a vast sum at stake but with blindfolded boxers. Jellicoe not only spent much of the time not knowing where the enemy ships were, but not even knowing where his own cruiser fleet was. Wireless telegraphy could have given Jellicoe a crucial advantage in the initial engagement of the main fleets and would have transformed the night action. In the event, wireless was almost ignored, and the German ships had escaped.

Sid greatly appreciated the Royal Navy's attachment to tradition. Nelson was still a real presence. But Sid was clear minded enough to see that failure to use wireless signalling as soon as it became available had turned what could have been a decisive and convincing victory into an unsatisfactory muddle. Fortunately, he was not the only person in the navy to appreciate this. But as far as Jutland was concerned a great opportunity had been allowed to slip by.

Sid made use of what formal training in these modern methods the navy made available, but he mainly learnt by making friends with the engineering and signalling people who used them. Wireless depended on electricity, and electricity came from dynamos, and dynamos had to be driven by engines. Batteries might be used, but they had to be charged from dynamos. This was the modern world, and the more he found out about it the less Sid worried about getting his demob. This was better than college, at least for him.

During the winter after the armistice came the event which launched his release. Sid learnt about it in a telegram from home. Someone must have helped

Ma send it. Maybe Aunt Mabel knew enough. Pa was dead. The funeral date was given. He could get to it if he took a train the next day. He applied for leave.

The officer who looked after such matters had already seen the telegram and was ready for him. "This is for two week's leave, Spears. Sorry to hear about your father. Your mother is going to find it difficult; I expect."

"Yes Sir."

"She would probably prefer to have you at home, wouldn't she?"

At that point, Sid spotted what the officer was working towards. He had enjoyed informally improving his education and had lost sight of getting an early release. But he might be near the end of what could usefully be gained as an AB. Yes, he still wanted to get out. Ma prefer me at home? Not certain. She and Mabel were well settled. Dad had been their main concern. Sid didn't like lying. It tended to complicate things. He framed a factually correct reply.

"I could be a help, Sir."

Sir interpreted that as a modest 'Yes'. "Right, you've already applied for release. This gives us grounds to increase your priority. Don't be late back. Your demob won't happen immediately, but it shouldn't be too much longer. Best wishes to your mum."

That last comment was sincere. It nearly brought tears to Sid's eyes. There were plenty of disadvantages being in the navy, but Sid had experienced much kindness as well. Sailors could be a rough lot, but they mostly looked out for each other. And most officers showed a genuine concern for their men. In the meanwhile, he had a train to catch.

A substantial fraction of Eyemouth was at the funeral. Many of them remembered Pa when he had been a hard-working and respected sea-going fisherman. They had witnessed his decline sadly, but with the tolerance of familiarity. Pa wasn't the first retired skipper reluctant to end his days mending nets for others to fish with, even if they did pay him. And Eyemouth wanted to support Ma.

Aunt M was visibly impressed. She had only got to know Pa after he stopped fishing. The crowd at the funeral and the warm testimonials gave her a revised opinion.

It was cold around the grave. To his horror, Sid found that he was crying. In theory, his attitude was that he had loved his Pa, greatly respected the hard life he had lived, and only regretted the sad way it had ended. Now we tidy up the loose ends. He dabbed his eyes with his handkerchief, more than once, and hoped the cold wind would be taken as the reason.

Sid did in fact help with a few things about the house. He also, for the first time, looked into Ma's financial arrangements, and did a bit to help there. He set off back to his ship on the last day the train timetable allowed. He hadn't been late back from leave yet. He liked to keep that sort of thing tidy. The railways hadn't fully recovered from the war-time overload and lack of maintenance, but the trains were normally reliable.

On this occasion, they weren't. The locomotive started going slowly before they got to Nottingham, and finally stopped at a small station. The guard walked up to have a talk with the driver, and then back along the train, announcing to each compartment 'All out'. The resulting crowd on the platform was then told that it would be at least an hour before a relief train could be arranged, sorry about the inconvenience, a cup of tea will be available in the waiting room. The locomotive huffed and puffed a bit and then moved slowly backwards from the platform and away out of sight back up the line.

This was serious. It was getting late in the day, and if he missed the last train from London he would be late back. There was nothing he could do about it, except make sure he got on the next southwards-bound train at this station. He availed himself of the tea, and then strolled to the north end of the platform, did a battle turn, and steamed at economy revolutions to the south end. He was in uniform, and he kept his kit bag with him. The station was in a rural setting. Just as he was about to conduct his second 180-degree turn he noticed a small group of men a couple of fields away on his side of the line apparently erecting a mast. With professional interest aroused, he went back to the station entrance and found a narrow road in that direction. It led him to where he could hove-to alongside the mast-raising operation. There was a functional-looking brick building near the entrance, grass around it, and a notice saying 'Government property keep out' but using more bureaucratic language. It didn't say not to lean on the fence and watch.

The first thing he noticed was they were building a tower rather than a mast. Although to his eyes it was too tall and thin to be self-supporting, it had already reached a height of about 70 feet and there were no stays. It had three vertical legs arranged in a triangle with diagonal bracing. At the ground, the three legs were bolted to substantial angle brackets which in turn were bolted down to a concrete base.

His second observation was that the workmen were hoisting a section to add to the structure much the way sailors would sway up a topmast. Instead of a spar they had lashed a thinner but similar lattice section to hold a block high enough.

Two men on the ground were pulling down on the rope. At the top two more men, feet jammed in the bracing, each with an elbow round an upright, were guiding the new section into place. Sid watched with informed interest. They had the process adjusted within fine limits. The new section came up beside the temporary pulley support, just getting to the necessary height. They manoeuvred it into position and bolted it in place. What he would think of as a marlinspike was used through one pair of boltholes to get them aligned so that a bolt could be inserted into an adjacent pair of holes, a washer fitted, and a nut spun on. He noted that they had all bolts in place before tightening the nuts fully, with some shouting from the ground to get the new section vertical.

That was the end of their day. They made all fast aloft and started to come down. The men on the ground secured the end of the rope and tidied up. One of the crew strolled over to Sid, who was happy to discuss what he'd seen, although he checked that he could see the station and would hear any approaching train.

"Hello, sailor. Are we doing it shipshape and Bristol?"

"Much the same as us swaying up a topmast. We would use a spar in place of the metal thing you have the block on."

"That's our gin pole. We use anything strong enough we can lash in place."

"I'd have expected you to have a belay, though. The load you're hoisting would be dangerous if it dropped."

"Well, we normally hold on tight. 'Belay', did you say?"

"It's like having a brake available. The slack end of the rope is taken round something which can give it friction. Something round, preferably. You would need an extra hand. As the hoist goes up, he takes in the slack around the belay. He can take the weight off the hoisters any time they need and can catch it if it falls. The rope is held by friction. Of course, the man managing the belay must know what he's doing. It's easy to get your hand trapped."

The man was tall and obviously fit. He seemed to be thinking about Sid's comments. Sid didn't want to lecture him, so asked about the structure being self-supporting. Was it needed to hold anything heavy or with a large windage?

The man chuckled. "Quite the opposite. All this steel, and there will be another one the other side of the building, and all they hold up is a few copper wires. They don't even need to be very taught. The wind won't have much to catch hold of."

"Sounds like an aerial. Will there be a wire coming down from the middle?"

"I believe there is, but that isn't our affair. There will be some insulators as well."

Sid caught the sound of a train. "Thanks. Fascinating. I must get that train."

"Are you staying in the navy?"

"No, trying to get out."

He pointed to the sign on the lorry door. "We're in Beeston, just to the west of Nottingham. I think we'd find you useful. My name's Guy."

Sid paused. "It's a thought. Thanks. I'm Sid."

"Sailor Sid! That's splendid. Oh, and if you need transport, they're selling ex-WD motorbikes in Nottingham. There's a Triumph model was reliable in France."

"Thanks again." Sid worked up to maximum revolutions and caught his train.

Within the year, Sid was in Guy's construction crew. It had been tedious, back on the ship, waiting for release. He worried the job might go to someone else. However, there were still interesting things to learn. He did his work conscientiously, although not to the extent that it might look as though he wanted to be considered indispensable. He was now looking forward to joining civilian life. In fact, this period in limbo solidly confirmed that decision.

His release came in the summer. He arranged the journey home via Nottingham. While he was there, the news broke of the scuttling of the German fleet. Sid knew it had been moved to Scapa after the procession into the Firth of Forth but hadn't realised German crews were still on their ships. The fleet hadn't surrendered, it was just interred, and still belonged to Germany. The peace talks were dragging on, and the victorious Allies couldn't agree what to do with all those ships.

Sid's sympathies were with the Germans. In effect, they had been prisoners of war on their own ships. For seven months. And in Scapa, of all dreary places. That was no way to treat a defeated foe. These were men who had served their country, like Sid. They'd been brave, and their gunnery excellent. No one seemed to have given them any consideration. Sid remembered his Pa's comment about Eyemouth after the Great Storm: '*We just weren't worth it.*' That's how those German sailors must have felt. The sad event drove any lingering element of militarism from Sid's thinking.

His reception at WIS was business-like. He applied while still in uniform, explaining he was on his way home after demob, and he mentioned his meeting with Guy. He never knew whether either of these made any difference, but he was signed on and told he would have to become proficient in workshop practice before any steel construction. He was happy with this, but it led to some confusion when Guy told him he would be joining his crew straight away. Sid hadn't realised Guy was the officer commanding the crew. It hadn't seemed that way when they met back in January. Maybe Guy had been promoted. He seemed to think he had the right to put Sid straight into his squad. Management sorted it out, and Sid did his workshop practice first.

It didn't take long. Sid proved to be adept at the kind of metalwork going on at WIS. Quite early on he helped with a diesel-powered electrical generator they were installing so they could fit electric motors to some of their machine tools. The chairman of the company apparently took the view that you can do anything yourself if you are prepared to make the effort. So instead of getting a specialist firm to install the generator, they purchased and put it in themselves. Fortunately, Sid was able to tell them sufficiently convincingly that you don't just take wires to whatever motors you want to drive. You take them first to a switchboard. You have isolating switches. You have fuses. Sid also helped them get the engine running, and, what's more, starting reliably.

Once out with Guy and his men on construction work, Sid immediately observed to his quiet satisfaction that Guy had taken up his suggestion about belaying each hoist. Sid further made his mark by getting the ends of all their manila ropes properly whipped. He and Guy then needed to get terminology sorted out. Guy decided it didn't matter if Sid called a pulley a 'block'. The others soon knew what he meant. But he drew the line, with the threat of dismissal back to the workshop, at 'Vast heaving'. Too much chance of misunderstanding. "I don't care if the navy uses it all the time, it doesn't seem to have done the navy much good, has it?" He thereby discovered their sailor's most sensitive point. The sailor in question already knew Guy was ex-army.

It was tense for a while between Guy and Sid. In totally different ways, they were both strong characters. Guy began to be in serious doubt as to whether the same team could accommodate them both. In time, however, they managed to work things out. What settled it most for Guy was how valuable Sid could be aloft. He was as muscular as Guy, but quite a lot lighter, which gave him an advantage in climbing. Sid seemed unaffected by heights and would climb anywhere it was physically possible. He soon became the normal person to go up a gin pole if the rope jammed in the block or needed rigging differently. This would put him above where they had built to at that point. He always inspected how it was fixed for himself, but the tendency of gin poles to wobble didn't seem to bother him. A useful chap to have aloft.

Sid was also intelligent, careful, and conscientious. It was he who suggested they get theodolites so masts could be put up truly vertical from the ground up. The tall thin masts which they increasingly found themselves supplying were only held up by guy ropes, normally of steel and known as stays. Temporary stays were needed during the intermediate stages of building upwards, and previously they had relied on approximate methods to get them true, such as sighting against the corners of buildings, or a spirit level clamped to something to hold it vertical, or even using a spirit level aloft, except they were so easy to drop. Sid had never used a theodolite before, but he knew what they were and was familiar with naval optical equipment. He could see exactly what a theodolite could do for them.

When the chairman, Mr Ingalls, heard the idea, he agreed with enthusiasm. That was just the kind of modern approach he liked. He took the trouble to have a chat with Sid, who regaled him with carefully selected naval anecdotes.

"Were you really at Jutland?"

"Yes, Sir, I was a shot-spotter on HMS *Barham*."

"Were you, by Jove! But there's no need to call me 'Sir' here, you know."

"Yes, Sir, I mean, no Sir. Oh, I'm sorry…"

Will patted him on the shoulder. "You'll get used to it, lad. We're glad to have you on board." Will had arranged this meeting with Sid when Guy wasn't around. He had well-tuned instincts for that sort of thing.

A pair of theodolites was just exactly what was needed for masts to rise truly vertical. Sid showed the ground crew how to set them up and use them. All balancing and tensioning of both temporary and final stays was thereafter directed by the ground crew. They were the ones who did not climb, for various reasons. Their main task up to then had been sorting the sub-assemblies and attaching them to the hoisting ropes, in the right order. It was by no means a trivial occupation, since the sections needed to hang from the correct point and at the required angle from the hoisting rope. Now the theodolites gave the ground crew a new skill to deploy, with pleasingly precise results. Once they were proficient with the new instruments and everyone understood the commands for making the adjustments, the men aloft could continuously build upwards while the men below ensured they were accurately rigged.

Sid quickly settled into the WIS family. His value to their elite construction crew was plain for all to see. This might be why he was allowed a concession on travel. Will had laid down, and it suited everyone else, that your place of work was the WIS site on the edge of Beeston. If you needed to go somewhere for the company, then WIS would arrange and pay to get you there and back. For the construction crews, who mainly worked on customers' premises, this meant the back of a lorry in most cases. If the customer was too far away for daily travel, then the company arranged accommodation and paid for that too. Will considered that he was looking after his staff in a proper manner by doing this, but he was also exercising a degree of control.

Sid, in the first place, was sensitive to being controlled, and in the second place, loved his motorbike. He travelled to work on it, almost anywhere. Occasionally, a job was too far away, and he accepted company transport, but these occasions were few. And he got away with it. It might have been partly the 'Guy' effect. Guy was only rarely overruled on issues to do with his team. But the arrangement also worked. Sid was reliable in his travel. He found the place and arrived in good time. Will was a bit worried at first that other construction men might want to do the same. But time passed, and there was no rush to get cold and wet in rain when you could be at least under a tarpaulin on the back of a lorry.

Thus did Sid find an agreeable harbour after leaving the navy. His habitual expression led some to think of him as moody, but in fact he was usually of equitable temperament. Occasionally, he could be a wit. Maybe a bit odd, but an interesting chap, with a range of useful abilities. In the economically difficult conditions in Britain after the war, he'd made a good landfall.

What Had Been Happening: Francis

It was the afternoon of Friday 23 June 1922, and Detective Inspector Francis Anchorville was in his office talking with Detective Sergeant Graham Bull. The door was closed, and they were speaking quietly. They were in the habit of discussing cases quietly. The day before, around midday, two men had shot and killed Field Marshall Henry Wilson in a London street. Wilson, with an adventurous and distinguished military career, now behind him, had been a security advisor to the Unionist government of Northern Ireland. The Field Marshall had just got back home, in full uniform, after unveiling a war memorial at Liverpool Street station. He died in front of his own house. It was said that he had drawn his sword and charged his assailants even after they had opened fire.

"The one encouraging thing in all this is that the public helped arrest the buggers. That took courage."

"Some of them got hurt."

"All the braver."

"Some of our men were hit."

"Yes. They were doing their job. We expect them to, and they did it well."

D.I. Anchorville could have been a librarian. Somewhat willowy, with a high receding forehead, and a distracted air, he had been a policeman for nearly twenty years. "What I'm concerned about is that these assassins, we might as well say IRA, did not seem to have any escape plan. No getaway vehicle. It is bad enough having a public figure murdered in broad daylight on a busy street, but the killers knew that they stood little chance of escaping. And they know we will hang them."

"It's difficult to protect the public from people like that." The younger of the two, Sgt Bull was built along lines that suggested his surname might be a nickname which had sort of stuck. He normally opened doors before passing through, but you had the impression the door would come off worse if he overlooked this preliminary. He had been a sergeant in the trenches and was now a sergeant in the police. He was a natural sergeant.

"That's my point. When the Irish pick fights over their politics they know they are taking a risk. The guys in the Easter Uprising really were taking a risk.

The army killed many of them, and we hung some of their surviving leaders. But it was risk. A serious risk, but not a certainty. Soldiers everywhere assume getting killed happens to other soldiers. Well, that's what people say. You will know better than I. But you cannot think like that when you take on a suicide mission. When people are willing to be martyrs to their cause it is, as you say, difficult to protect the rest of us."

"Yet these two men were in the trenches. On our side, too. And one of them lost a leg. What's their logic? They fight for Britain in the Great War, then assassinate one of our Field Marshalls. It doesn't make sense."

"No. I don't pretend to understand it. When we apprehend a burglar, his objectives are clear. He wants to get money without doing proper work. At least he is being logical."

They were an efficient pair when it came to solving crime. Sergeant Bull had a natural rapport with what is sometimes termed the man-in-the-street, although it was more likely to be man-in-the-pub. He was respected by most of the professional criminals around London, and he knew many of them by name. They represented opposing sides in a game they both took very seriously, but in most cases stuck to the rules. Play centred around information. Honour amongst thieves did exist, but it was not total. Bull was sensitive not only to the value but also the potential repercussions of a judicious tip-off. He would buy someone a drink, on occasion, and reliably uphold debts of gratitude. But he never let money change hands. Not his hands, anyway.

For his part, Inspector Anchorville used similar methods for solving both crimes and the *Times* crossword.

They got on well and each recognised the complementary role of the other. The sergeant was quite aware that the inspector, in addition to having had longer to work his way up, had started with much better prospects and education. The inspector sometimes envied the sergeant's social life with their main clients. It was horses for courses, and it generally worked.

Sergeant Bull was silent for a while. The implications of this assassination were unpleasant. He tended to be more practical than theoretical. "Where are the guns now?"

"However, maybe it wasn't so much an attack on our leaders. Our masters, you might say. Sort of a shot across our bows. Well, their bows. A serious warning for them. Maybe it was more for the notice of the Unionists and Free-State people. It could lead to outright civil war over there. Things are already on a knife-edge at the Four Courts. Oh, yes, sorry, the guns. The P.M. asked for them. Apparently, he and Churchill talked the matter over with the revolvers on the desk between them."

"That helped, did it? I hope they didn't get any ammunition as well."

"No, the crime-site people swept all that up. However, I would not be surprised if Churchill carries a loaded revolver around with him. Bit of a warmonger, that guy. But there is an interesting aspect attached to the bullets. We recovered the shell cases and unspent rounds, and they were all manufactured by a small outfit in Nottingham. It was one of the companies Lloyd George converted to munitions during the war. All have the same headstamp, made in 1916."

"Pinched from the army, I suppose. Or do you think they were siphoned off from this company?"

"There is no other information at present. I would have thought it more likely that it would be misdirected somewhere between Nottingham and France. Now we are on the subject, it may never have left England. The Irish seem to have no trouble getting guns and ammunition in Ireland, but we try to be more careful over here. If they nick some bullets in Britain, all they need to do is hide them until needed. They would not have to smuggle them in."

"Webleys?"

"Quite so. Thousands of them around. Even outside a combat zone they are less controlled than ammunition. No problem for the IRA to get what they need."

"Should we have a look at this company?"

Francis could see the gleam in the sergeant's eyes. "We have nothing on them. And after, let me see, six years, there is unlikely to be inculpatory evidence lying about. However, I will talk to Nottingham to put them in the picture. No action unless they know something we do not. It's DS Girling up there, isn't it?" It was indeed, and after the operators had arranged the connection, Francis introduced himself.

"Hello, Superintendent Girling. Inspector Anchorville here, at the Met. This is just a background matter. The rounds used in yesterday's assassination were made during the war by a firm in Nottingham with the initials W.I.S. Do you know it?"

"Oh yes, y'know, well-known. Steel company just outside town, what? Chairman Sir William Ingalls. Colourful local character. In the yeomanry during the war. Friend of the PM, y'know. Knighted after the war. Recruiting mainly, for the army. Not exactly a war hero. I mean, medical exemption, what? Highly thought of. Local events. Speeches and giving out prizes, that sort of thing. Should I have a chat with him?"

Francis hoped this representative of the Nottingham constabulary could assemble cases better than he did sentences. "No, please. I want to keep the provenance of the ammunition just between the two of us for now. And, of course, the IRA, or whoever they were, may well have purloined it directly from the army. We know nothing to implicate the company. I wanted you to know just in case you spot something. Could you please give me a ring if anything comes to light which seems connected?"

"Right-ho. I mean, Mum's the word, what?" They hung up.

Hmm. Knighted for recruiting. Friend of Lloyd George, Eh? Yes, what? y'know? Francis went home for the weekend. Despite the assassination, he was not expecting any work until Monday.

He read several Saturday papers, pottered in the garden, played bowls in the afternoon, after which he went home and worried about just how bad things would get in Ireland. The stand-off at the Four Courts seemed unlikely to end in harmony. On Sunday, his wife Joan went to the 8:00 Holy Communion and stayed on afterwards for a cup of tea with some of her pals. He and their three children joined her for the 10:30 Matins. Then they all went to their favourite pub for a roast, and when that had gone down, a walk and some ball games in the nearby park. And then a quiet evening. The business with the ammunition did not spoil his weekend at all. Whatever theft or smuggling had taken place, and whenever it happened, did not seem likely to his experienced mind to be susceptible now to investigation.

Francis greatly valued his home life. Their children had been too young to take part in the war. But they did have an almighty fright. The threat of Zeppelin bombing raids was taken seriously in England, and since Joan had a sister in Scarborough, she and the children relocated there soon after the war started. They rented out their London home and Francis found a small flat much closer to New Scotland Yard.

This is how it was that the four people Francis most cherished were in Scarborough when it was first attacked by German warships. SMS *Derfflinger* and SMS *Von der Tann* spent half an hour during the night shelling Scarborough, unmolested.

Francis was realistic about civilians coming to harm during war. When he heard someone express the opinion that warfare in earlier centuries wasn't so bad since it only involved armies, it demonstrated as far as he was concerned that the speaker hadn't read much history. Nor, for that matter, much of the Bible. Joshua followed God's instructions on what to do with the inhabitants of Jericho after the walls came tumbling down, and that seems to have generally set the tone ever since.

The history of conflict presents, as Francis recognised, a complicated and mixed picture. Not all wars throughout history have been pure savagery. Negotiations have played important roles, and a besieged city could and often did get good terms, particularly if they opened their gates early on. Moreover, a medieval engagement might well be set up by agreement between heralds, rather like a football match. After all, it was an age when both sides viewed battle as a test in which God would show who was in the right. But even then, most of those doing the fighting were not there voluntarily, but serfs who had been told to pick up something sharp and join in. And the code of knightly chivalry applied only between aristocrats. The common people didn't count.

As a churchgoer, Francis was disappointed that, during much of Europe's history, Christianity's attitude towards war diverged so far from its irenic teaching. He was unaware of any divine command telling the Crusaders to kill all Muslim and Jews when they took Jerusalem in 1099, but they did so anyway. Joshua would have taken one look and nodded.

Thus, as far as the safety of his family was concerned, Francis placed no confidence in history. But he had, up to then, trusted the Royal Navy. Britannia was supposed to rule the waves. It now seemed she didn't. Along with the whole country, he was deeply disturbed by both the uncivilised action of the enemy and the ineffectiveness of Britain's defences. After spending enormous sums building dreadnoughts, the navy not only failed to stop but did not even effectively hinder German ships sailing across the North Sea, shelling our east coast, and going home again. And even though it did no more than maintain historical continuity all the way back to Joshua, to his knowledge the bombardment had been the first occasion modern weapons had been deliberately used against a target of no military value. It was depressing.

Francis had been desperate with worry when news of the attack was first made public. He squashed the temptation to take the train immediately to Scarborough because he did not yet know the family's address. Joan was quite able to rent accommodation, and she wanted to make her own choice. To his embarrassment, Francis couldn't even find her sister's address. It would take a while to find them if he went there, and during that time he might miss a telephone call or letter from them. He sat tight and scanned the London papers for names of casualties. Mercifully, his family name did not appear, but absence of news did not reassure him. Then Joan's postcard arrived. They were safe. It had been frightening. They had heard explosions, although none very close to them. Their youngest, a boy, wanted to watch through a window, which Joan properly forbad. Instead, she insisted they huddle under the stairs, which she said would be the safest place in the house.

Importantly, the postcard gave Francis their address. With a few exchanges of letters, they agreed that they should remain together for the rest of the war. Francis had to be in London. Right, they would all live in London. That did not guarantee they would all live or die together, but they felt better about it. Joan and the tribe stayed on in Scarborough to spend Christmas with her sister and family, but early in 1915 came back to London. Francis allowed their tenants to stay on in their previous home, and rented a larger house further out, in Hampstead. For the rest of the war, he tended to use his flat during the week, or when there was a flap on, but joined the family in the new house at weekends, when he could. It had been a fright, but they now considered themselves better situated.

Back in the office on Monday morning, the business with the ammunition caught up with him just as he had decided to give his in-tray a rest and get some lunch. It was Nottingham. "Y'know, what, it doesn't seem connected, I mean, something's happened. That company, Wiz, y'know. One of their men fell off something they were putting up. I mean, he's dead, what d'you know. He was the foreman. I mean, it's strange. We checked up. They've been OK on safety up to now. Nothing serious at all, so far. I mean, look at the docks. Or building skyscrapers. I mean, can be slaughter. Someone cops it all the time. Bit of a coincidence, what?"

Despite their different attitudes to syntax, neither man believed in coincidences. Police tend to be leery of them. However vague, if there is a common factor connecting two close happenings which otherwise don't seem connected, the policeman's philosophy says cause and effect are probably in play. Neither man in this case could see what ammunition made in 1916 and smuggled or stolen some time since had to do with someone from the same manufacturer falling from some structure they were putting up just after assassins used that ammunition elsewhere. But both were policemen.

"What were they putting up?"

"Well, it was a mast. A steel one, y'know. Government research place over at Normanton. Fell more than a 100 foot. I mean, nasty mess."

"Could you conduct an informal investigation by interrogating each of the workmen? No need to make a fuss. Tell them we must observe formalities. And, in fact, press them a bit to see if anyone gets flustered. What do you think?"

"I've got a sergeant who'll enjoy that. Good at it. Makes them angry. I mean, they tend to spill the beans, what? But we need to be careful with Wiz. Will Ingalls is a public figure. Best we don't go beyond regular investigation after an accident, what?"

"No, that's all I want. But if there is some connection with the ammunition or the shooting, we need to know about it. Even if no more than a distant possibility. Please ask these men to cooperate with you just so you get a detailed picture, and perhaps help to avoid such an accident again. Yes, the usual pious hope. But, alright, let your man push them a bit."

"OK. We've got a demarcation issue. Accident at Normanton, y'know. Small place near a three-county border. I know the people in the other forces. Not likely to take much interest. I mean, I'll say we'll look into it 'cos Wiz is on our beat. OK with you?"

"Yes, but still say nothing else, please. And thank you. That sounds good."

Francis made a second attempt to get out for lunch and met Sgt Bull outside his door. "Graham, pop in for a moment. There has been some news."

"Me too."

"Then let us have yours first."

"The chairman of that firm making ammunition in the war has an Irish background."

"Ah! Has he!" Francis had a bloodhound's nose when it came to information.

"The family came over during the 19th century. To get away from the famine, or about that time."

"And he's not been alerted by your investigations?"

"No, the Irish connection is public knowledge."

"What do we know about his political leanings?"

"Nothing. We can't ask his friends what he says about the Irish question. That almost certainly would get back to him. But from what appears in the papers, either he has no politics or keeps them well hidden."

"Hmm. A bit tenuous."

"Yup. What's your news?"

"A construction worker from that company had a fatal fall this morning. He was the foreman of a gang putting up a tower at a government research site."

"The man in charge of a construction job by a company whose ammunition was used to assassinate Wilson then falls to his death a few days later. And their chairman might be an Irish republican. Can't help thinking something could be going on here. What do you think?"

"It adds up to something suspicious. I'm wondering whether to go up to Nottingham. It could be a national issue, so I'm entitled to. Maybe have a chat with this chairman? Perhaps not. Better not to alert him at this stage. Hmm."

After a late lunch, Francis got back to his in-tray. Considering he was, at least theoretically, a constable, he spent an awful amount of his time reading. After a while, he started worrying instead. Was he being sensible to think of going up to Nottingham tomorrow? He was still of two minds about it. He and Graham could be blowing the whole thing out of proportion. He decided to go home and sleep on it. He had a telephone at the flat if there were developments. He could decide in the morning.

On this occasion, he did not even get to his office door. At about 5:30 p.m., a secretary called him to the telephone. It was Girling. "I'm at the accident site. Finished the interrogations, you know. Looks like an accident. I mean, difficult to see how it could be anything else, what? Normal minor variations in their accounts, of course. Nothing suspicious. No sign of foul play. Well, one of their chaps was *really* disgruntled. But normally like that, they said. But, yeah, hey, I mean, something different. It was the foreman killed. His deputy telephoned Wiz. Spoke to their manager. A Mr Adams, you know. Said he would drive over to Normanton. Straight away. That would've been about 12:30. Wouldn't take him more than an hour to get here. Should have arrived before us. But he didn't. Wasn't here when we arrived. Didn't think too much about it. Got on questioning them. We've just finished, y'know. And this Mr Adams still hasn't arrived. What do you think?"

Francis thought about it and did so quickly. "Where are the workmen now?"

"Staying in pubs and lodgings around here. They mainly walk. The grumpy one went off on a motorbike."

"What are they doing in the morning?"

"Coming back here. I mean, I'm still at the institute. Where the accident happened. Another Wiz manager is coming in a lorry. In the morning, y'know. More men and parts. Carry on building. Or take the men back."

"And you are quite certain it wasn't an accident?"

"Seems so, what? This foreman had a fool habit of sliding down a rope. Good at it, y'know. Done it a lot. Bit of a stunt. Sort of an entertainment for onlookers. Probably a right show-off. On this occasion, he fell. All the men say the rope was securely fixed. No one had time, y'know, to fiddle with it. Then get it right again."

"Has there been a police inspection of that rope?"

"Not yet. I mean, no one willing to climb, y'know. There's a man tomorrow who can. Well, he's willing. Far as I can see the rope is solid. Takes my weight, anyway, what!"

Francis asked for descriptions of Mr Adams and the car. Girling had the registration number ready and could report that it was sign-written identifying it with the WIS company. The description of Mr Adams was disappointing. He seemed to be Mr Average. Nothing unusual to make him stand out. Girling had put out an all-stations in his region.

Francis had not worked with Girling before and found it difficult not to wince at his verbal ticks. But when it came to work, he seemed to know what to do. You know.

"Would it be alright if I came up to Nottingham in the morning? I think we need to have a chat."

"Tell our office what train you're on. I mean, someone'll meet you at the station."

Francis decided not to put out an all-ports for anyone answering to Mr Adams's description. He was just too ordinary. But before going home, on a large hunch, he asked the Liverpool police to do an immediate street search for the WIS car. After that, he alerted the New Scotland Yard night duty staff to telephone him at home if certain reports came in, and finally went home, rather late.

The telephone rang about midnight, just as he was going to bed. It was what he had expected. The car had been found in Liverpool, not far from a tram route to the docks. He asked the caller to let Nottingham know the train he intended to catch, set his alarm clock, and despite everything, went to sleep.

At the Nottingham police station, he met Superintendent Girling, who was over-weight and blunt in manner. Francis updated him on the company car and Mr Adams. "Something definitely seems to be going on."

Girling was unhappy. "I mean, Sir William's a popular figure. Must be certain before putting him on a spot. Could stir up a stink, y'know. Wiz hasn't made ammunition since the war. I mean, might just be coincidence?"

Francis wasn't going to be deflected. "There is far too much here to ignore. For all this to happen within a few days of Wilson's assassination, and with the tension in Dublin, we have a duty to check it out. It could have consequences at a national level. I want to visit Sir William's company, please. And I think we should take the construction men into custody for the meanwhile."

Girling leant back and managed to raise his eyebrows and frown at the same time. "That's coming it pretty high, what?"

"It's a precautionary measure. We have had one runner from this outfit. We must do what we can to ensure there are no more. Would you please arrange it?"

It was obvious Girling was having a struggle. For one thing, he was senior in rank. For another, Anchorville was from the Met. Presumably the superintendent was balancing the criticism he would attract if they caused Sir Will embarrassment but then find nothing against him or his company, against the opprobrium coming his way if he obstructs the investigation and it turns out later the inspector's suspicions were justified. He gave in.

Girling placed a telephone call to the Normanton institute and spoke with the local constable. This young policeman had climbed up and inspected the rope. It was securely clamped, and it would not be a quick job to make it slip or otherwise cause a fall. There was still no sign of Mr Adams, but the expected WIS manager had turned up in a lorry.

An assistant came into Girling's office with an extension receiver, and with a thumbs-up from his boss jacked it in so Francis could follow both sides of the rest of the conversation.

Without saying anything about the WIS car being found in Liverpool, Girling asked to speak to the WIS manager. "Mr Baker? Thank you. There are some things we can't speak about just now, Sir. As a consequence, we need to take your workmen into custody."

Oh, thought Francis, he can speak properly when he needs to. Maybe it is only with things a policeman needs to say to the public.

Baker was shocked. "What! I gather you concluded yesterday it was just an accident. What's going on?"

"We just have to take the precaution. Are all the men there?"

"All but Mr Spears. He went home overnight, but I learnt since getting here that he is in the Wiz office this morning."

"You have a lorry there at Normanton, I believe."

"Yes, we've brought some more sections and two extra men. We thought we were free to get on with the job."

"I'm sorry to disrupt your work. I don't think it will be for long. But would you please bring the men here to the central Nottingham police station. I ask you to do this on the basis of cooperating with the police."

"Do you want the two extra men or the ground crew?"

"Only the men who were there yesterday when the accident happened. So please include the ground crew. But we don't need your extra men this morning. And thank you, your cooperation is appreciated."

It was a strange way to arrest men, presumably on suspicion of murder, but Francis had to admit to himself that Girling functioned well enough.

Having dealt with the round-up, Girling instructed the Nottingham desk sergeant to sign-in the crew when they arrived, treat them gently, but don't let any get away.

Francis brought the conversation back to visiting WIS. Girling was still unhappy. "I mean, we mustn't stir things up. Beeston's small place, y'know."

"If I stay out of sight and you made a sort of courtesy, or even sympathy, call on them. Would that seem reasonably normal?"

"Might be, I suppose. I mean, if someone's guilty there they might show it, what?"

"Perhaps."

"Or take their chance as soon as I've gone and disappear too, y'know."

"You've got a missing person reported. Look, can we go to the local station, explain things to a constable, and ask him to follow up on whatever queries have already been made about Mr Adams. Nothing has been said yet publicly about him fleeing to Liverpool and, almost certainly, taken a ferry to Ireland. One of your coppers making a follow-up visit to them at Wiz should seem normal, surely?"

That seemed a good compromise. They took the Beeston constable to just round the corner from WIS, asked him to take a nonchalant stroll to their office to see if they had heard from their missing manager, and was there anything else they can let him know about his habits, etc.

The copper did indeed do a typical beat stroll round to the WIS works but came back after a remarkably short time and at about twice the speed. "Sir William has committed suicide. His wife just telephoned."

Francis started to feel giddy. What was it about this case? "Did you get his address?" Yes, but Girling knew it anyway. He had been to various parties and receptions there. They thanked the Beeston man, left him to continue what wasn't in fact his beat, and went to visit Mrs Ingalls.

Both coppers had experience of talking to newly bereaved people. It wasn't pleasant. You could also seriously mess up an investigation if you weren't careful. Mrs Ingalls had several friends with her, all ladies from her various activities. The news had spread fast. They made a brief show of being defensive but knew the police had to talk to her.

Sir Will's wife had clearly been crying. She was sort of crumpled in an easy chair in the lounge. If anything, her expression was of sad but weary resignation.

The police offices expressed their sympathy. They were surprised, having identified themselves as police officers from Nottingham and London, that she looked up immediately. "My, that was fast. Were you onto him already?"

This was a shock to both men. How much did she know? How long had she known it? She provided answers by handing them Sir William's note. She had found it in the hall when she got back from walking the dog. She hadn't been to see the body. She just telephoned the local police. The note read:

'Darling, I'm awfully sorry about this, but I don't think the old ticker would have kept me going much longer anyroad. I hope you never had any idea about it, but during the war I was compromised by Irish republicans. I helped them get some ammunition. I have never known what to think about them. We have had a much better life in England than if the family hadn't moved, but I felt guilty that we could do so, whereas most couldn't. Also, I assumed that the ammunition would be for them to shoot at each other. And I thought it was all over after the end of the war.

But they've got onto me again. Fighting seems to be brewing. I won't help them this time, but they're vicious sods so it's better I depart. Please forgive me.

Also, no one else in WIS knew about it except Guy. He used it to twist my arm into letting him lead a construction crew. But he's now dead. Tell the police to look around my office. They will soon catch on to what I was doing.

There is no justification for shutting the company down. I was the only guilty person. You will inherit my shares, which makes you the majority owner. Discuss high-level decisions with Lilly. She is the most intelligent person in the company. Leave everything else to Anthony. You'll do fine.

I've always loved you, Dear.

P.S. Wait until the undertakers have tidied me up before you identify the body.'

"This must have been a terrible shock."

The newly made widow just folded up and burst into uncontrolled sobbing. One of her more determined friends must have heard it the other side of the door, since she came straight in and told the two men they must leave immediately. Francis told her that they could leave Mrs Ingalls now, but that they would have to take the suicide note. The widow immediately thrust it at them. And that they would have to search Sir Will's study. "Yes, of course." They quietly withdrew, asked and were told where to find the study, and without seeking further permission, went to have a look.

Will had left manifests out for them. Two stacks of carbon copies, one larger than the other, with paper weights on them. The two men needed somewhere more suitable to inspect them. Francis suggested seeing what the WIS office staff made of them. Yes, it could just be a guilty person pretending to help, but still likely to shed light on the business. They wrapped the two paper stacks in improvised evidence protection and took them to the car. On the way through the hall, they could hear Mrs Ingalls still sobbing, and some ineffective comforting. Both men felt bad. They might be police and used to this kind of situation, but this one still made them feel bad.

Francis was more affected than by anything else he could remember in his police service. Should they search the rest of the study? What about the rest of the house? Strictly they should. But Francis had a strong feeling that they had the explanation in their hands, and he tended to trust his feelings.

For his part, Girling decided it was his crime scene so he must make sure procedures were followed. He told his driver to take Francis to WIS, but then to go to the Nottingham police station and bring back two constables. Francis took something of a punt and suggested that the WIS men could now be released.

At WIS, Francis was met by a neat middle-aged lady sitting at a typewriter in the front office. He explained who he was, and that he had come from Sir William's home, and needed to talk to a company representative. She took him to Mr Baker, the general manager, who had just returned from his trip to Normanton. Mr Baker knew about the suicide. He had also been told by the police that Mr Spears should report to the Nottingham station. Sid had duly gone off on his motorcycle, and a quarter-hour later the station had telephoned to say he had handed himself in, as they put it. "I must admit, I was rather surprised by that."

"Did you think he might run away?"

"No, I don't think he has anything to be afraid of. More likely he would have just gone home. He has a certain attitude."

"Is he a troublemaker?"

"Not at all. He is intelligent and works well. He is particularly good at doing the climbing work. He's an expert at that sort of thing. Knows about engines and electricity. But he is suspicious of authority. We run this company on liberal lines. We've managed to develop an excellent relationship with our staff. They work well for us, and that is good for business. And that means we can pay them well."

"Do you know why he is suspicious of authority?"

"He comes from a poor fishing family just over the border in Scotland. Their village seems to have been picked on by both church and state over the years. I think Sid, Mr Spears, just sort of inherited the local attitude. But another thing, he is disillusioned about the navy, and is very critical of how it performed in the war, particularly at Jutland."

"Do you mean in the sense that most of the country was not impressed?"

"Oh no. He had a ring-side seat. He was spotting shot on one of our dreadnoughts. And he saw a ship he'd served on earlier blow up. Beatty and Jellicoe failed to use the wireless equipment for signalling. Sid knows a bit about it. If Beatty had done the scouting properly and signalled using modern methods, the Germans would have been sunk. That's what Sid says. It's obvious we didn't do very well. But at heart Sid's a good chap. Perhaps he thinks too much."

Francis wondered whether Sid would be happier in the police but switched to explaining the situation. "Sir William's note to his wife said he had been helping Irish republicans get ammunition during the war. He included in his note that we, the police, should look in his study. We found these, carbon copies of what seem to be your ammunition delivery manifests. They were laid out in two stacks beside his typewriter. Could you please look at them and tell me what it all means?"

Mr Baker looked at them. "Can I suggest we show them to Lilly? I expect she typed them."

"Is she the lady...?"

"Yes. With the office being opposite the front door she tends to be the receptionist, although that isn't her job."

"I noticed coming through that you still employ female operatives, as well as typists. Is that the effect of the war?"

He nodded. "Yes, the girls did really well when we were making ammunition, and they rather got used to having a pay packet. Quite a few wanted to stay on. We gave jobs to most of our men coming back after the war, but of course not all came back, and work was growing. And I must say that many of the girls do at least as well as some of the men. But can I mention, before we go to see Lilly, that she is much more than a typist. She is our office manager, and pretty well runs the business side."

"I don't think many husbands have got used to the idea of their wives having their own job." Francis had spotted Lilly's wedding ring. "Is Lilly a war widow?"

Mr Baker replied carefully. "Er, yes. The Boer War. Her husband was a major, Major Loeillet. She prefers us to call her Lilly because we never say it right."

"Was he French or Belgian? There was a composer of that name some time back."

"I never met the Major, but I believe he had British citizenship. I don't think he would have been in our army otherwise. But apparently he was indeed very musical."

"Maybe his family were Huguenots?"

"Lilly hasn't mentioned that name."

Francis decided to close this line of investigation. They went to see Lilly. Her expression changed not an eyelash, but on seeing the carbons she turned to her assistant. "Betty, Dear. Please bring some sandwiches for us, a cup of tea for me, and beers for the men? Oh, two teas and one beer, please. And then take the afternoon off. Thank you. See you tomorrow. Try not to be late."

With logistics organised, they turned to a side table, and Francis put down the two stacks of paper. "May I ask if you recognise these?"

Lilly looked at the thicker stack. "These look like the manifests we prepared to go with ammunition deliveries during the war. I think I typed all of them, and these look like my typing. And since I believe you have come from the farm, I expect they are the carbon copies which Sir William wanted at home."

"Did he say why he wanted them there?"

"He said it was because there were often telephone calls during the evenings or at weekends about priorities for what we should make and where it should go. It also had a bearing on what materials we needed to work with. He said that this often involved people in London."

"Did you think that was normal?"

"This is the only company I have ever worked for, so I didn't think about whether it was normal. He was the chairman, and he wanted carbon copies."

"So did you keep second copies here?" Francis knew about typewriters and carbon paper. And he noted that the typewriter on what seemed to be Lilly's desk was the same Imperial model as in Sir William's study. Francis had the air of an absent-minded professor but was an acute observer.

"Yes. I should have second-carbon copies of all of them in the cabinet there."

Taking the top dozen or so from the larger pile from Will's study and comparing with Lilly's carbons suggested that they were the same set. For matching ammunition deliveries, defined by date and destination, they could see no discrepancies between each pair of copies.

"Good," said Francis, "I think we can assume that we have the first and second carbons here of all the manifests. But," pointing to the smaller pile, "what about these?"

Lilly gave the top few sheets of the other set little more than a glance. "I did not type these."

"How can you tell?"

"This was probably typed by someone using one finger of each hand. Unless you are properly trained you tend to use different pressure with the two hands. And it was probably a left-handed person. The characters from the left side of the keyboard tend to be darker than those from the right. Look at 'Ball' here. The two 'l's are distinctly lighter than the 'a'. And in '303', the zero is lighter than the '3's."

Goodness me, thought Francis, what side did the light come from when he shaved? He liked the Sherlock Holmes stories on account of their delightful improbabilities, but disliked them for making the police look superfluous, at best. But at least he remembered that the handwriting in Sir William's suicide note sloped to the left.

Lilly continued, "I think we ought to see how they match up." She looked at the top of the small stack and leafed down the large stack until she found the manifest for the same date and destination. She carefully placed the sheets she had removed to one side so that the whole could be reassembled in the same order. They placed the corresponding pair side by side. Everything matched except for one small difference. She spotted it immediately, before Francis did. "Look, the quantity here is one box less than on my copy."

Good grief, thought Francis. I'm slipping.

They continued with the comparisons. Every sheet from the smaller stack could be paired with an original manifest typed by Lilly, and each showed at least one reduction in quantity. Francis somewhat recovered his confidence by being the first to comment that the false manifests were all for the same destination. He wondered whether this remarkable woman had in fact already noticed it, but had tactfully allowed him to discover it for himself.

More importantly, Lilly knew what the destination was. "That's the recruits' camp where Guy was one of the trainers."

"The man who fell from the tower they were building?"

"Yes. Mr Beardsley. He had volunteered in the war, and was wounded near Ypres, not long after the second battle there. When nearly better, he was posted to this camp to do rifle instruction. He was good with other men. He had a rough manner, so I am told, but they seemed to like him. It is such a shame."

Things were really clicking together now in Francis' brain. He did not know what to say. Lilly helped him by continuing. "On one of his leaves, he paid us a visit and inquired about our deliveries. He said that their ammunition for training seemed to be of variable quality. It made it more difficult for his recruits to improve their accuracy. He had not previously realised we were making ammunition. He wanted to know whether we made cheaper ammunition for training. We certainly did not, of course. I believe that our ammunition workshops were very tightly controlled. We had a little range too, for testing."

Francis was impressed by Lilly. She really was quite unusual. She hadn't said that she didn't know what things were coming to, nor that she was sure she had never heard of such a thing, not even that this was a respectable company. She had responded to his queries concisely and to the point, and intelligently contributed to the investigation. Some of his detective constables could take lessons from her.

He turned to the general manager, who had observed their investigation without comment. "Mr Baker, could we get Nottingham police on the telephone? I need to speak to Superintendent Girling. If you could, please."

"Do these falsified manifest copies mean you could release our men? Presumably they are under arrest all this time."

"They should have already been released by now. I'll get him to confirm that. But I also need to meet him. He may be still at Sir William's house."

Mr Baker went off to his office to arrange the telephone connection. For just a moment, Mrs Loeillet paused. What was she thinking? This precise and intelligent woman seemed to operate on a perfectly systematic basis, like the tick of a well-made watch. Horology was one of his interests. He wondered fancifully whether she had a Tourbillion within, averaging out external influences. But just at this point the escapement had paused. Lilly seemed wistful. They were sitting at the same table, although not all that close. There was silence for a while. Francis wondered whether these revelations about the company she worked for, and its chairman, was distressing her. But then she continued.

"I showed Guy the last few manifests. The ammunition is described exactly the same for all the delivery points. It was rather strange, for a soldier, that he did not know about the headstamp on the end of each cartridge. On a later leave he said that, since then, he had selected only our ammunition for target practice, and it seemed more consistent. His recruits were finding it easier to get smaller groups. He thought maybe there were small differences between manufacturers."

Francis was starting to wonder whether they should have released the WIS men. Here was yet another coincidence. Sir Will's note had stated that Beardsley knew about the smuggling. It now turns out that he was instructing at the camp from which the republicans must have been stealing the ammunition. It suggested that he was more involved than just being aware of it. Could there have been a reason, following Wilson's assassination, for someone to want him out of the way?

But how could a murder have been arranged? Girling was quite certain it was an accident. The steel rope was too firmly attached to be fiddled with. But Girling could be biased by the local reputation of Sir William. In any case, Beardsley was an experienced steel man. It's most unlikely he could have been caught out by something wrong with the rope's attachment. And institute staff would have seen it being hauled up again. That theory did indeed seem a dead end.

Could someone up the tower have hit Beardsley on the head and thrown him over the rail? It was a chancy plan for faking an accident, and there were five other men up the tower and two on the ground. Is it conceivable they were so intimidated by whoever ordered the killing that no one was willing to report it during interrogation? Or they were all part of the same organisation? Either is far-fetched.

Francis had to conclude, reluctantly, that despite his long history of antagonism towards coincidences, perhaps this one was innocent.

This reflection was interrupted. "War is so wasteful. Why are you men so keen on it?"

"Well…not all men…er…approve."

"No, but many do. Look at the way so many youngsters volunteered."

"Only to start with, when it seemed a glorious cause. Not so many volunteered once reality set in."

There was a further pause. Perhaps unwisely, Francis was tempted to describe what he guessed was the reason.

"But I do think there are basic differences between men and women which could come into it. I'm inclined to accept Mr Darwin's theory. I know they cut across what has been assumed for a long time, and of course many Christians reject the idea. But the fact is we humans *are* animals, at least in terms of biology. There are enormous similarities between us and the other mammals. And we are all specialised for reproduction. In nature, the division of roles varies a lot between species. In our case, humans have a long history of women doing most of the childcare, which needs empathy and protection, and men doing the hunting, which requires aggression and means taking risks. I expect cave men had to compete with sabre-toothed tigers over some kills. Evolution is a slow process, so it seems reasonable that we still have such instincts."

Francis wondered whether this was going too far. She might be religious. She might hate Darwin's ideas.

"Do you know how André, my soldier husband, died? I got a letter from the War Office. 'Died on active service' it said. To begin with I had the notion of his leading a glorious charge. Falling at the head of his men. Then I met Mr Conan Doyle. Did you know he was a doctor? He went out to South Africa to try to help with medical issues. He was concerned that the soldiers were not getting inoculated as they should. He remembered André. André died of typhoid. A lot of civilians died of it too. Mr Doyle was very kind. He brought André's flute back. André said a flute is one of the easiest instruments to look after on active service."

She paused and seemed to be reflecting. Again, Francis was wondered what to say. Would it be better just to wait? He was glad he did, since after a while she continued.

"War is *such* a stupid way to settle arguments. But André was principled about it. He said being in a national army or navy was the most honourable form of public service. When politicians fail, you help sort out the mess. It is uncomfortable and dangerous. You stand a good chance of being wounded and might be killed. And you are not paid much. It's a noble profession. Soldiers do not approve of war, but if it must be done then they do it."

"And you might be right about Mr Darwin. My son never knew his father, but he too has chosen the army. At least, he is intent on joining when he is old enough. André never had a chance to influence Richard, although I suppose he was influenced by the image he would have formed of him. I tried hard not to either encourage or dissuade him about military service. It really is silly. I hate war, but in fact I'm proud of Richard. He's so like his father. But I still say war is stupid. Why cannot we be cleverer?"

She sat there, looking calmly at the manifests, her face giving little away. Almost the same expression as before. Francis was surprised at a sudden feeling of tenderness towards her. He wanted to say something but feared making things worse. She was being rational, and so brave.

"Could it be something about ladies liking to see men in uniform? So people say."

"I think there is a lot in that. Even when in civvies, a man's clothing is much more like a uniform than what women wear. And it is heavier. I have met the suggestion that ladies in history admired men in armour."

Francis nodded sympathetically. Lilly hadn't finished.

"I suppose I must have been trapped by it all. I hated war from my childhood. In my mind, I associated soldiers with it. Then I fall in love with one. Silly, isn't it?"

Her face was creased, with a sad little smile, and Francis was alarmed to see moisture on her cheeks. He did not know how respond. He was grateful, and Lilly probably was too, when Mr Baker came back and picked up the extension telephone.

Back in London the next day, getting to the office mid-morning, Francis dealt with a few 'Immediate' and 'Urgent' missives on his desk, then got Sergeant Bull into his office. They closed the door and settled down for another quiet discussion of the case.

Francis ran through what he had learnt. Although he did so concisely, it took a while. Events had unfolded while he was in Nottingham, and Sir William's note and the conversation with Lilly had provided a great deal of information.

Bull had further news to add to it all. "In the small hours yesterday, there was a shooting near Belfast docks. The victim has been identified as Seamus Adams. He died with one bullet in his head. His height matches Stephen Adams quite well."

Francis, not for the first time, had the feeling this investigation was making progress without his help. In fact, it seemed to be developing in front of him faster than he could keep up.

"If they are the same, and his loyalty is where we would expect, why did he get on a ferry for Belfast? Surely Dublin would be more likely?"

"We know about his loyalty. Seamus was one of the leaders at the Dublin Post Office but escaped before the fighting finished and disappeared. Must have gone into hiding. And if Stephen was the same man, he would probably have taken any ferry to anywhere in Ireland that night. We can assume he was in a hurry. But he was an Ulster man. It was his base. His family is there."

"Do you think he was just unlucky? Someone happened to recognise him?"

"It's possible. There are numerous factions over there, and they're not friendly with each other. I expect many of them go around armed. Presumably it was someone on the Unionist side who fired the shot."

"So, what do we think of the coincidence that the man, Beardsley, who according to Sir William's note knew about the smuggling, was the one who had the fall? Girling is certain it could only be an accident. The steel rope he slid down was solidly anchored. If it was murder, then someone must have pushed him, and that would mean the whole crew were in on it. You could hardly throw a well-built man, as Beardsley was, apparently, off the tower without others knowing about it. And staff at the institute might well have heard the struggle. It seems everyone there remembers Beardsley screaming as he fell. It's difficult to know what to think."

Sgt Bull suggested one thing they could think. "Pure coincidence is feasible. Beardsley, according to the lady you spoke to, discovered the smuggling because he was posted to a camp receiving ammunition from Wiz, and he himself was ex-Wiz. That's a bit of a coincidence, but not itself all that unusual. Can we accept that his fall was indeed an accident?"

"The timing. Four days after Wilson's assassination."

Both men pondered for a while. Then an idea came to Francis.

"Just a moment. What you say about factions has given me an idea. Suppose Beardsley not only knew about the smuggling but had connections with a Unionist group. Let me see. How about this for a scenario. He discovers the smuggling during the war and, on going back to Wiz, blackmails Ingalls to give him a plum job. But he had Unionist friends and he mentions it to them. With the recent business at the Four Courts, they get back to him and ask him to monitor for any further smuggling if the firm went back to making ammunition. They could then intervene. Over the weekend after Wilson's shooting he might have been tipped off by his friends that things were going wrong, which could put him in line for serious repercussions from republicans."

"Oh, yes, they can be nasty, I'm told. A bullet through the knee is one approach."

"A bullet through each knee is another. He had a serious leg injury in the trenches. That is why he was training recruits when he could walk again. He would have known that kneecapping would leave him crippled for life. Perhaps he preferred a quick death if the IRA were coming for him. Could he even have set up this sliding-down-a-rope act as insurance. You could say that it was a perfect way to commit suicide and make it look like an accident."

"Why should he want it to look like an accident?"

Good point. Francis thought for a while. "Maybe to protect his Unionist friends? Perhaps even his family?"

The sergeant pursed his lips and shook his head. "It's rather an extended scenario. Yes, it's possible, but it seems unlikely to me. I find it difficult to believe that someone would behave like that. If I had been Beardsley after getting that plum job at Wiz, I would have told absolutely no one about it. Unionist friends or not."

"But, of course, you are not Beardsley."

"Can't argue with that. But I think I prefer the coincidence interpretation, just for his falling when he did."

They paused, mulling it over. Bull, ever the pragmatist, "So what do we do now?"

"I can only see three people who could be involved, and they are all dead. What else can we do at present?"

"What about that surly one you mentioned? The one with the motorbike?"

"Sailor Sid. At first, Girling thought he must have run away like Mr Adams, but he just got fed up with the questioning and went home. He turned up at the Wiz works the next day. He went off and handed himself in at the police station when told to. Apparently, he arrived just in time to be released. Incidentally, the detention of the Wiz men was not what you could criticise as too severe. Girling was worried about bad publicity for this local company. I expect they can paint it as a tragedy rather than crime."

"Does that mean we're not going to take it further?"

"Not unless new evidence comes to light. Can you see any more we can do?"

Francis waited while Bull thought about it. He had a good police brain. But nothing came up this time. With a small shake of the head: "No."

"Right. I'll finish the report and recommend the case is closed. For that matter, I'm not certain it has even been formally opened. Whatever, I'll tidy it away. I think we've gone as far as we can on this one."

My Story: How It Finished

I stayed on with WIS. As everyone assumed, I took over as leader of Guy's crew. Despite the accident, we finished the job at the Meteorological Institute on time and within budget. It was different from anything we'd done before. They wanted observation platforms at different heights with unobstructed views in all directions, so we provided walkways around the outside of the four legs. The scientists wanted to use theodolites to look at fixed objects at various distances out to the limits of visibility, such as the top of a church spire or a water tower. Something to do with an effect of the atmosphere, and apparently the east of England was a good place for it.

The difficult bit was they also wanted the observation platforms to be as steady as the ground. There were lengthy discussions about this between them and our designers. Making a steel platform several hundred feet above ground as stable as the ground is not practicable. They reached a compromise in time, but to get the steadiness they wanted we made the whole thing like a smaller version of the Eiffel Tower. We asked them why they didn't make their measurements from the actual Eiffel Tower, but that was no good. *'All those visitors clumping up and down. Far too much vibration. Anyway, it's in the wrong country.'*

Once that job was finished, I started to introduce some variations in how we managed construction. Just to start with I launched the revolutionary concept of speaking politely. It didn't seem to upset anyone. They still worked well. On a rather different level, and in consultation with Anthony, I started moving people around the crews. Some of our experienced members joined other crews, in some cases becoming foremen when the incumbent retired. We brought some less experienced men into our team. Basically, I wanted all our crews to work to the same consistent and high standards. No one's pay was reduced, but we let the previous non-elite construction pay catch up. The elite concept was bad psychology. No announcement was made, but as the changes took effect the situation became healthier. At least, Anthony and I were happy with the results.

I also introduced a terminology policy. Guy's men had coped with a few naval terms from Sid, but confused discussions sometimes took place on tricky assembly issues because not everyone appreciated some important structural distinctions. When you are hanging onto steelwork high above ground and a new sub-assembly is coming up on a rope, it's no time to ask, 'What do you mean?' So I established and enforced terms that we all must understand in the same way. Such as the difference between a beam and a cantilever. Diagonal bracing became a working concept, distinguished from corner stiffening plates. The men might not be able to calculate whether a particular bit of steel is under compression or tension, but they must know what these words mean. They must also be able to see whether bending forces are involved. Most of it is common sense. The important thing was an agreed set of words. Something like the army's insistence on naming of parts.

Also, we took a less casual attitude to safety. Everyone on construction work, whether aloft or not, had to read, and to sign that they had both read and would comply with, a Construction Safety Policy. It wasn't unduly prescriptive. It accepted that it was impracticable, and possibly too complicated, to require that everyone working above ground must be secured by a harness at all times. Harnesses were made available, since there are circumstances where they make a lot of sense and are much stronger than an elbow round something. In general, however, we preferred just sensible precautions aloft. One of these was that every hand tool must always be secured to the user by a lanyard. Dropped tools were recognised as one of the main hazards, particularly by the ground crews. You can't have nuts and bolts secured by lanyards, but they must be raised and secured in special canvas sacks designed for the purpose. And, specifically, the practice of sliding down any kind of rope was totally banned.

Several of Sid's innovations were retained, particularly the safety belay when hoisting, which was made compulsory. But Sid himself left the company a few years after Guy's fall. Said he wanted to live closer to relatives further north. We gave him a good send-off party organised by Val at what was now her farm. She and Lilly pretty much made all the business decisions after Will's suicide, and I think they both enjoyed it. And strange to say, I had the impression that Val liked continuing the tradition which Will started of having special company events at the farm. I wondered whether she hoped Will was looking down from a cloud in approval. (He had never been the slightest bit musical. She said she just couldn't imagine him with a harp.) The farm certainly had some useful outdoor space for entertainment, such as football matches between construction, design, and workshop (alphabetic order to avoid bias).

I did wonder about Sid moving away. He said he had family scattered around in the north. But with his motorbike he could easily have continued to work with us and visit them when he wanted. Moreover, he didn't really give the impression of being much of a family man. Compact and self-contained was more his style. Of course, he might well have had a wife and family not far off. Or even several. Sailor could tell some yarns when he was of a mind, but you didn't learn much about his personal life. But I had thought he was happy with us. He was in line to replace one of the construction foremen who would be retiring in a few years. He must have realised he was a candidate. I had almost hinted at it. So why did he leave us?

One possible theory was that Guy's fall had alerted him to the risks in steel construction. Maybe he kept going for a while to prove he hadn't lost his nerve, but then, having demonstrated that point, decided to get away still in one piece. But this scenario seemed unlikely. Guy fell because he was showing off with a stupid trick. Sid had nothing like that in his make-up. What's more, he was a skilful and athletic climber. He mentioned to me once the happiest moments of his life had been out on a yard during his sail training days. "And don't believe that 'One hand for the ship and one for yourself' nonsense. When you are lying over a yard trying to tie a reef knot with the wind yanking the sail around, you need both hands. You just need to be quite certain where your hands can go, quickly, if things go wrong." But, he allowed, the next best thing was being up a lattice mast bolting the next section on and then climbing higher. So, as I asked myself, why did he leave?

Perhaps he felt guilty about the prospect of, sort of, replacing Guy as one of the foremen. They had been frankly competitive at times, with, of course, Guy the boss. Sid had nothing to do with removing him. But would people perhaps view him in that light? I had difficulty imagining him to be that sensitive about what others thought, but then I knew so little of what went on within his stubborn exterior. What, for instance, had his war experience done to him? We all knew the navy had been a disappointment. He would most definitely have commanded the fleet at Jutland differently from either Beatty or Jellicoe. But what had his more personal experiences been like? He had been in an observation cabin, above the ship's superstructure, spotting fall-of-shot. Since their 'fighting top' was not hit by anything, he came down without a scratch. He had his own personal tongue-twister, which he brought out, or possibly made up on the spur of the moment, when Guy started to make fun of his small frame. Was Sailor, Guy would ask, pretending to be a Scottish shot-putter? In response to which the Scot concerned would cheerfully, for Sid, announce to all: 'I'm not a Scottish shot-putter, I'm a Scottish shot-spotter'. What do you learn about him from that?

His ship had taken hits at Jutland, but by the time he had come down from his spotting station, after the battle, the casualties were being cared for and the bodies had been collected. Sid had told me that the worst shock was to learn that the sick berth had been destroyed by a shell. He'd been a sickbay attendant on his previous ship. For that matter, he had seen his previous ship blow up. He commented once that serving on an armoured ship and fighting with big guns gave you the feeling that, if you copped it, you would be like meat in a grinder. But he seemed matter of fact about it. Obviously, you can never truly know what goes on inside another person's mind. But Sid did not give the impression of someone running away from his past. Nor a particularly sensitive soul.

His war had been mechanical. The closest approach to enemy sailors might have been a few miles during the confused night action after the main battle. I compared that with my war. We had been trained to use our bayonets on stuffed sacks. That didn't prepare you adequately for using it on a person. It's hideous. I only did it once. It was also the only time I had to 'go over the top' in the notorious process by which most attacks were launched. By some miracle, we reached the enemy front-line trench with a useful number of us still on our feet. We were behind a creeping barrage, and one of our shells fell short. A great deal too close to us if it had been in front. But it fell on our flank, right on the machine-gun sap which had just started to enfilade us. It was a fluke, because by that time our shells were otherwise falling on the German support trenches, beyond where we were going. And then another fell short, right into our target trench. We heard it coming, and order or no orders, sensibly fell flat, before getting up and following it into the trench.

I happened to land opposite the opening to a dug-out. The Germans made very good ones. A dazed but whole-looking soldier emerged from it, choking from smoke, but holding a rifle with fixed bayonet. It was one of those situations where you don't wait to decide. In a panic of haste, I pushed my bayonet into his body as far as it would go, just before he might have done the same to me. I never knew what his intention was. But instead of conveniently collapsing backwards he dropped to his knees with a shriek, grabbed my rifle with both hands, sunk his head over it, and with panting yelps was trying to keep my blade from moving. It hurt less if he kept it still. For a moment, I was frozen in horror. Then, hearing someone coming up behind me, kicked the man back, twisting the rifle to get it out, as I had been taught, making the wound larger, and then whisked round to nearly hit our sergeant in the face with the butt. This second shock was in some ways worse than the first. Later it made me realise that I was getting carried away. Maybe it was what some people call battle-frenzy. I don't know.

My sergeant was thinking more clearly, and promptly threw a grenade into the dug-out. After that, we all cooled down to assess our situation. We had secured the trench, and the neighbouring bays were also in British hands. We now had to prepare for the inevitable counterattack. Your courage can leak away far too quickly while waiting to be attacked. But for us it didn't last very long, since our creeping barrage, of all things, started creeping back towards us. There must have been a foul-up, by no means unheard of. Bless him, my sergeant was recognised as a brave man, and decorated for it, but he had no time for stupid heroics. After waiting long enough to be certain that our barrage was indeed in reverse, he was incisive. "Come on, boys. Time to beat it."

We got back to our lines while our gunners dropped shells around and into the trench we had just taken and then relinquished. It had been a waste of lives. We had killed a few Germans, but we'd gained no ground and our losses had been much higher.

That was the worst day of my war. I found myself unable to sleep, rerunning it in my head. What could I have done better? It seriously bothered me that killing that German, rather than *vice versa*, was just an accident of split-second timing. And it was similar with my sergeant. If he had been only slightly closer when I swung round, I would probably have at least knocked him out. In the panic, I might have bayoneted him as well for good measure before realising who he was. It was all a matter of just how things happened to turn out. And that was without the short shell on the machine-gun crew that allowed us to get to that trench in the first place, and the snarl-up with our barrage that evicted us from it. Without that we might have had to lie in the trench during a German bombardment and then fought off a counterattack. The unpleasant feature of that day was being subject to so many effectively random events. If I must fight, I'd rather be able to make sensible decisions, not just be tossed about by happenstance.

I was lucky, not only in that action, but with the memories of the horror, because they slowly sank into the back of my mind. By the time I was demobbed I still remembered it all, but it didn't haunt me. Maybe I'm pathologically unimaginative? Cold-hearted? Or just fortunate?

That was a comparison of our two wars, as far as I could make out. Sid's and mine. So different. Sailor had been a popular person in our construction crew, and the two of us got on well together. But how can I have any picture of what the world in his head was like, any more than he mine? And so, he had left what I feel sure was the best job he'd ever had.

Speaking of jobs, during the various readjustments following Guy' accident it became apparent that I was starting to do what Stephen used to. By the time I had started to think I should stop acting as though the Operations Manager, I was promoted to the position anyway. I suppose I was starting to feel my age. It didn't take long to discover that I didn't at all mind spending most of my time at ground level.

With Val and Lilly providing much of the guidance, Val on general principles, and Lilly more with the details, WIS continued to develop in capability and volume of business. Wireless stations still wanted masts and towers, not only for telegraphy, but also for broadcasting. Some thought wireless would be the next big thing in entertainment. Others were sure it would be talking films. It seemed likely to me both would be important, since one would be in homes, and the other in cinemas. Going 'to the flicks' includes a social element along with the entertainment. People like going out to enjoy themselves.

The difference as far as WIS was concerned, we couldn't see why cinemas would want much of our steel, unless for some fire escapes. On the other hand, if wireless starts to bring entertainment into our homes, then more aerials will be needed. That should mean more masts. It could be a useful expansion to our activities.

We weren't greatly affected by the strike in '26. We were too small and too specialised to attract much union attention. A few of the men announced they would join the walk-out. We managers had a special meeting with them. All WIS staff were invited, but it was mostly those who wanted to strike who attended. They acknowledged that WIS treated and paid them well, but they wished to show solidarity with others in less favourable situations. We accepted that this was a fair position and assured them that we would issue individual warnings if their jobs became threatened. No one knew at that stage how long it would all last. Anthony, who had his ears remarkably close to the ground in these areas, said we would also do all we can to prevent victimisation from staff who didn't join the strike. During its first day we held a meeting with all those who turned up for work and explained our strikers wished to show solidarity. We asked everyone to respect them. We'd already asked our strikers to respect our non-strikers. Not everyone was happy, but we felt we had done all we could. As it turned out, all our strikers were back at work within a few days, well before the total of nine days the strike lasted nationally. Personally, I didn't ask, and wasn't told, what they had done during those days. I don't think anyone else asked them.

We continued to maintain our non-unionised position, but that was proving increasingly difficult. In theory, the Act of '27 weakened the unions' powers. In the longer term, it didn't make much difference. It might have increased working-class resentment of employers, even while needing them for jobs and pay. It was disturbing how often industrial disputes appeared in the papers.

In WIS, our main protection from disruption was that Val and Lilly maintained the firm policy Will had set up in the beginning. Our staff were paid and treated better than those in comparable industries. We could afford to do this because, working only on our chosen types of construction, we offered excellent service and competitive prices. We were still small enough such that senior management could at least recognise all our staff, even if not always knowing their name. They liked this sort of family atmosphere, and they also knew that we could treat them well because we knew what we were doing, and we all worked hard. WIS staff served the company enthusiastically because doing so was in their interests.

One rather nice example of where our policies paid off occurred when we were approached by what must have been an inexperienced TUC official who hadn't done his homework. He demanded that union representation be set up in WIS. Anthony counter-demanded that he shows us the terms and conditions on which they would insist for our workers. The TUC man wasn't expecting that and asked for time to prepare the details. We arranged a meeting the following week. He duly turned up and we perused his terms. Anthony, perhaps craftily, made him assure us that the TUC would indeed demand these terms and nothing more for at least the following year. The union chap should have been suspicious by now but gave this undertaking. We then showed him *our* terms and pay scales. He didn't contact us again, but we may have helped with the TUC by providing useful experience for one of their beginners.

We had to defend ourselves in other ways. The main weapon was a written policy on employee under-performance. We laid down the sequence of events, starting with verbal discussion or warning, through written warnings, and if necessary, ending in the sack. Everyone knew about this, and we rarely needed to take the process far. But we could show the policy to any union representative to make it clear we meant business. It held them at bay, at least for the time being.

I started to consider why I so often found myself thinking in anti-union terms. After all, I accept that trade unions are justified for protection of employees from unreasonable conditions, and that workers should have the right to associate. Moreover, I also take the perhaps over-optimistic view that management and unions ought to work co-operatively for the benefit of both employers and employees. The idea of an unregulated labour market might sound fine to a dyed-in-the-wool free trader, on the basis that a man would rather work for a pittance than have no job at all, but unless there's zero unemployment that leaves all the power in the hands of the employer. Working for a pittance is slighter better than having no income at all, but if it isn't a wage you can live on then it's immoral.

Of course, a few industrialists have proved to be enlightened philanthropists in their employment policies, as well as where they make conspicuous donations. Many of these do so on religious grounds. Interestingly, it had always seemed to me that Will had not been motivated by any such philosophical considerations, as genial a person as he had been. His policies on staff conditions were based on a calculated balance between cost and benefit. Treat people well, make everyone feel part of the same enterprise, and they will pull together for the benefit of all. In his normal casual manner, Will had made it work.

So why did I want to keep unions away from WIS? Basically, because I was afraid of them. Horror stories went the rounds, perhaps exaggerated, that once a shop steward is installed, he can claim special facilities and time off for union activities both within the company and at union meetings elsewhere. If the results were generally beneficial this could be worth it, but I had received the impression that it more often led to an anti-management culture amongst the workers, in effect class warfare. That would be a tragedy for WIS. We would lose our tradition of cooperation and might never get it back.

It was also becoming clear that many union officials believe their best path to promotion in their union is to earn a reputation as leader of successful strikes.

So how does a company like ours reap the benefits of organised labour and avoid its dangers? To be candid, I couldn't see a recipe.

Business started to slow down after the crash in '29. Britain wasn't as badly affected as the USA, but we received few orders for a while. Val and Lilly had to stop any further recruitment, but any natural decrease in staff numbers wasn't enough to match the reduction in work. Some people had to be laid off. Nothing like this had happened before. It was a dismal time.

Something else to distress us became apparent in the late '20s. Lilly had stayed in touch with Deidre. They had been on visiting terms soon after Guy rejoined WIS after the war and his young family moved into housing in Beeston. They had two children at the time of the accident. Like Guy, and to some extent Deidre, they were adventurous. Not wicked, but not the sort to behave decorously if it was more fun not to. Guy had probably encouraged them in their more acceptable japes, but he would have maintained firm limits. After his fall, it started to become apparent that Deidre couldn't handle them on her own. They needed Guy's presence, and he wasn't there.

Being around the office more since coming off full-time construction, I got to know Lilly better. She mentioned her concern about Deidre's youngsters. "I am worried what they are going to be like when they get older. I do wish she would find someone else." Lilly's style wasn't normally that of a match maker, but she was talking sense. Poor Deidre had settled in her mind that Guy was the only one for her, and that was that. 'Nonsense' is how Lilly viewed it, although I never had the impression she was looking for a replacement for her André. On the other hand, her soldier son Richard had by that time happily graduated from Sandhurst and was now proudly a Second Lieutenant.

As business started to pick up again, the question of safety standards in the construction industry started to be a concern amongst government, union, and business leaders. These bodies all had different priorities, of course. We became involved, in a minor way, when I attended a conference in Leeds organised by government for industry representatives. I submitted a short paper, and it was assigned to the afternoon of the second day of a two-day event. It was clear where that put us in order of importance, but it suited me fine.

The conference was held in an up-market hotel. I had booked into something more modest. During the first day various government spokespeople expressed concern at the accident rate in construction and suggested various measures to reduce it. Interspersed with these, various industry spokesmen explained why such proposals would be ineffective, impracticable, unaffordable, or various combinations of all these. I did not know any of the speakers, but from their accents and vocabularies the proceedings did convey the impression of being North versus South. I even started to think that my short paper the following day, in which I would describe our written safety policy and explain why it was necessary and realistic, might even inject a small element of common sense. It would at least be delivered in a sort of compromise Midlands accent.

Quite apart from not recognising the speakers, I did not seem to know anyone else among those attending. I had wondered whether our near-neighbour Ericsson's would send someone. I should have checked with them before the event. WIS had done a few small jobs for them in the past, so I knew some of their managers. But presumably they considered making telephones didn't come under the heading 'construction'.

Thus it was that I went to my hotel in the evening by myself. It did not have its own restaurant, so after a rest I went out and found a reasonable looking place not too far away. It was neither suspiciously empty nor noisily crowded, so I took a table and ordered a modest meal. It took a while arriving and wasn't brilliant, but pleasant enough when you've had a tiring day. Why am I more tired sitting down all day listening to speeches than if I had been climbing around steelwork? Over a cup of coffee, I took out my book. I don't have any embarrassment about reading if eating out alone. I was browsing its pages with one hand on the coffee cup, feeling peaceful and happy enough about tomorrow, when I realised a waiter was standing in front of me.

"Oh, fine, thank—" I started to say. It had been no more than adequate, but that's what you say. Then having looked up and adjusted to the sight, my deceitful eloquence was cut short.

"Sid!"

"Hallo, Sir. It's good to see you again."

"And I'm delighted to see you looking well and so resplendent. I had forgotten you spoke about coming to Leeds. You're well established, I gather." He did look well. I had the impression he probably weighed a bit more than when I saw him last.

"Oh, I feel really well settled, Sir. Have a wife and family now. Three kids and another coming."

We chatted for a while. I wanted to say that there was no need to call me 'Sir' until I realised it must be a burnt-in part of his job by now. After saying it to all the officers in the navy and now to all his customers, the men at least, it must be a well-rooted habit. He asked for news about WIS. I asked about his family. He asked was I up here for the conference? So, he kept up with local events. I suppose in the restaurant trade you are always interested in anything bringing visitors to your town. I mentioned that Deidre was finding it difficult without Guy.

He commented that he mustn't spend too much time talking to a customer. We were in the process of saying goodbye, would I come again, and so on, when he paused, glanced briefly around, leant forwards and, quietly, "You do realise, Sir, don't you? I didn't mean to kill him."

"Eh?"

He down, in the chair opposite me, in his waiter's uniform. "You know Guy was getting more and more against me? He saw me as a threat to his position. It got really bad after that job which got stuck on the gantry."

"I remember the job, but I was on holiday."

"It was unusual, and we were hoisting some complicated sub-assemblies. One of them wasn't attached properly. It had to be held too far out during the hoist to make it clear everything. We had it nearly to the gin pole when it slipped and twisted round and bashed against the section we were on. The ground crew scarpered, and it dropped much too far before the belay caught it. The bloke had let it get slack. We had no option but to just keep out of the way. It bent two of its struts and got jammed. We couldn't pull it up or let it down. We were stuck, about 60 feet up, with a section tangled up where we didn't want it.

"I'd seen something like this coming. The hoisting crew were getting careless, and Guy shouldn't have let that lift happen. But up to that point I hadn't interfered. Guy was getting too difficult. But now he was badly stuck. He obviously didn't know what to do. He started to talk about dismantling the hoist and just dropping the bits.

"I thought it could be sorted out much quicker, and repaired where we were, so I volunteered to see what I could do. Guy didn't seem happy about it but told me to go ahead. I think he was in fact pleased to have the problem off his hands. If my solution worked, he could claim some credit, and if it didn't, I could take the blame."

Sid went on to explain that he had another block hoisted, transferred the weight to a different hoist position, and this allowed the assembly to be twisted free and hoisted, slightly damaged but strong enough, into position. The two bent struts were replaced, and the surveyors on the ground confirmed that the alignment was correct.

"It got him out of a hole, but all I got after that was a stream of insults. That's when he started making fun of me about being a shot-putter."

"You were able to respond with your own joke on that."

"Well, maybe, but I was getting more and more fed up with it."

He paused. I wondered where all this could possibly lead.

"That morning," he said.

Yes, I knew what morning he meant.

"I was up the gin pole re-rigging the block when he went down for the midday break. He said his normal piece about leaving everything secure, and then added, 'Y'wee Scot midge'. Well, OK, I was used to that. But then, as I had both hands on the rope and block, *he shook the gin pole!*"

I was genuinely shocked. Up to now I had thought that Sid was just unloading the effect of Guy's insulting manner. But this, if true, was far worse.

Sid continued: "You know we never get the gin pole completely steady? It always flops a bit one way or the other. But when you are up there you can guess from what you're doing how it will move. The wind can make it wobble as well, but you feel that and know what it will do. But this was a deliberate sudden shake. I was only holding on with my legs. I reckon my heart stopped. I thought a lashing had slipped or the rope had broke. I looked down, and there was Guy with two hands still on the bottom end of the gin pole grinning up at me. It was an evil wicked leer. Then he went down to your walkway.

"I came down seething. He could have killed me. And all he could do was grin. As I got down onto the leg and started climbing down, I passed the anchor of his rope, and a bit lower the whole thing sort of exploded in my mind. 'See how *you* like it, you bugger' and I kicked his sodding rope. I kicked it hard. I wanted to frighten him. Then I heard that scream."

We had to stop this. "Sid, I can see how that could happen. I don't blame you. Guy was totally unreasonable towards you, and you're right, shaking the gin pole could easily have made you fall. But how many other people know about this?"

"No one, Sir. But I'm glad I've told you. I knew you'd understand."

"I do. And in a way it helps to know what happened. It *was* an accident, only a very fluky one. But potentially your situation is serious. Would you please never say anything ever about it to anyone else?" I wondered whether he had even though of the possibility of being charged, at least with manslaughter.

"Yes. I mean No. I won't ever mention it again."

"And I won't, either. That's a promise. But I think we have been speaking too long. You have other customers. I really do wish you and your family well. Best wishes to your good lady."

"Thank you, Sir."

It took me a while to get to sleep that night. The next day I had to present a paper explaining how a few simple rules, formally written down and agreed by all, had given us nearly 50 years of steel construction with only one serious accident. And now I knew that it wasn't what everyone might call an accident. There was no question of it being murder. I was totally certain that Sid had no intention whatsoever of killing Guy. Frighten him, oh yes. But Sid wasn't a murderer. And it was entirely understandable that, after Guy's campaign of insults and then his appalling act of shaking the gin pole, Sid should lose his temper. For that matter, Guy hadn't wanted to kill Sid. They were two tough men, both experienced at climbing, who both thought the other knew how to look after themselves well enough for a bit of horseplay. Even on a construction job high above the ground.

What Sid probably didn't know, in fact what few if any knew apart from me, was that Guy's rope was just outside his reach from the 120-foot walkway. Because the four legs of the tower converged upwards, and our walkway went around outside them, the rope, anchored to the inside corner of a leg section above the walkway, was just too far to reach. Guy had to climb over the handrail and lean out from it with that arm straight, the other hand almost reaching the rope, and then he would let go with one hand and grab the rope with the other. With his strength, he could then easily adopt his position for braking before reaching the ground. It was all sheer bravado. He could have used a hook to pull the rope to him. He could have anchored it differently. But he knew he could reliably transfer to the rope, and probably enjoyed that thrilling little moment when he was not securely on either the walkway or the rope. That was our Guy. Sid's kick happened just in that thrilling little moment.

That was the truly accidental element, the timing of the sudden movement of the rope. And as he fell, Guy understood exactly what had happened. That was what his scream had been about.

Next morning, I had it settled. WIS had suffered one serious accident. It certainly had some unusual features to it, but it was just one, and it was an accident. And it was before we had formalised our safety rules. My little presentation was politely received. Some of the few questions afterwards emphasised the small scale and specialised scope of our operations. How do you think your principles would apply to building, for example, the Forth Bridge? Or a skyscraper? I accepted the point, but even if we were on a small scale, simple basic requirements read and signed by the work force seemed a good start. One industry big-wig, more aggressive than the others, asked how many of their labourers did I think could read or sign their name anyway? I thought his attitude might be part of the problem, but left it unsaid.

Back in the office, I dictated a short report on the conference to Lilly. We filed it away with a copy of our paper. Although we were well-known for the attention we paid to staff well-being, we archived all evidence of it. Lilly, who had become knowledgeable about these things, and perhaps therefore cynical, assured us it was more important to have a record of the formalities we had in place than what we did in practice. A bit sad, that, but I think she was right.

I decided not to mention in the office that I had met Sid. I wanted to push his account of the accident to the back of my mind, but it made me think of Deidre. Did we in WIS have any responsibility to help her? Was there any way we could? When Lilly next brought news from her it was so bad that I decided I would at least try to do something. Apparently both Tom and his sister Julie had run away from home. Tom was involved with a gang in Leicester and had been in trouble with the police. Deirdre thought Julie had gone down to London. She didn't know what she was doing there. She thought it might be best not to know. And, reported Lilly, she was desperate with worry. Wasn't there something we could do to help?

That decided me. To start with, rather than ask WIS to get involved as a company, I decided to make some preliminary enquiries on a personal basis. My starting point was the police inspector from London who visited our office after the accident and Will's suicide. He had struck Anthony as a decent and thoughtful chap. His was name was Anchorville. It took a while to work through the people who picked up the telephone in London. They wanted to know why I needed to speak to the inspector. In the end, I got through to a Sergeant Bull who immediately seemed interested and sympathetic.

"Thank you, Sergeant. My name's Tony Butcher. I work for the steel company near Nottingham which your Inspector Anchorville visited some years back following the suicide of our chairman, Will Ingalls."

"I remember."

"I was one of the workmen on that construction job when our Mr Beardsley fell to his death the day before."

"Yes."

"The reason I'm ringing concerns Mr Beardsley's widow. She has two teenage children, and they started to get out of her control after the accident. Now they've both run away from home. The boy, Tom, has been in trouble with the police in Leicester, and the girl, Julie, is thought to be in London. Mrs Beardsley is getting desperate. She says she has no contact with either. I'm asking whether there is anything I can do to help. I'm not related in any way, except for working for the same company as Mr Beardsley."

"Are both the children minors?"

"Yes, I think they must be."

"Has she told the police about them running away? That would be a missing-person report for each of them."

"I don't know, but we could ask her."

"Have the police been in touch with her?"

"Again, I'm sorry, but I don't know that either."

"How do you know the boy has been in trouble with the police in Leicester?"

"That has come from Mrs Beardsley, but I don't know how she knows."

"Hmm. She might have been contacted by the Leicester police, although it could have come to her some other way. The boy may be refusing to give his name and address, or at least, his true details. The police would try to trace his background, but it isn't always possible. I can inquire, but in any case, I'd be restricted in what I could tell you. As for the girl, if she is in London and doing what I rather fear she will be, then she won't be using her actual name, and probably wishes to be left alone. If she hasn't already done so, it really is important for the parent to report any missing child to the local police. However, please let me know if she does hear from either child."

I discussed it with Lilly and Anthony. We wanted to help if possible. Lilly mentioned that Deirdre had a sympathetic and helpful neighbour. We thought the best next step would be for Lilly to ask this neighbour to raise the question of missing-person reports to Deirdre. She may not even have heard of them.

About a week later Lilly was able to report back. The neighbour had asked Deidre about reporting her children's disappearances to the police. Deidre strongly rejected the idea. This seemed so unreasonable that Lilly took it upon herself to pay a visit, with the neighbour, to try to find out why she was so against such an obvious and possibly useful step. Deirdre would not change her mind. Lilly came back with the impression Deirdre was afraid of something, possibly the IRA. She had mentioned the republican movement in a slightly different context during their talk, but it seemed relevant. We all knew there had been speculation about Guy's accident having been arranged by an Irish faction, but I had also stressed what the police had concluded. Guy's rope simply couldn't have been sabotaged.

Now, of course, I knew it wasn't quite so simple, but equally I could be certain that no one had staged an accident to get rid of Guy. Sid's account made total sense, and it fitted the known situation within the crew. I wished I could explain it to the others, but I had assured Sid I wouldn't pass on what he'd told me, and I intended to stick to that promise.

Deirdre's attitude stymied us. It was illogical. I couldn't think of anything further to do, at least then. I wondered whether to report Deidre's apparent feelings to Sergeant Bull but decided not to. However, about a month later he rang me. "I discussed our earlier conversation with Inspector Anchorville. He wonders whether you come to London very often. He doesn't think he can justify us visiting you in Nottingham, but we would like to have a completely informal discussion, both around the accident, and the situation with the Beardsley children. Would that be possible?"

"Certainly. I think it would be helpful. Shall I give you a ring when I have a date?"

We agreed to that and rang off. It so happened I expected to visit London for a chat with the fiends at the Inland Revenue but didn't yet have an appointment. I reported this back in the office when Val was talking to Lilly. It seemed appropriate to let them both know. Val was immediately interested in helping if she could, and she was planning to visit London in connection with the War Graves Commission. I rang Sergeant Bull again and asked whether she would be welcome at our meeting. He thought it would be useful but would quite understand if she later thought it might be too distressing and wished to back out.

And so in due course Val and I found ourselves at New Scotland Yard, in the office of Inspector Anchorville, discussing with him and Sergeant Bull those events ten years earlier. There was a pronounced contrast with the interrogation I had back then. We were in a comfortable office. Val and I had coffee. Pretty good coffee, too. The policemen stuck to tea.

The inspector opened the discussion. "We have no ongoing investigation about the accident. We closed it soon after my visit to Nottingham. But we tend to be suspicious of coincidences, and there were several during those few days. One is that Sir William's note said that Mr Beardsley knew about the ammunition. In view of this, it is natural to wonder whether his fall on the Monday was staged by the people concerned since he had knowledge which could be dangerous to them. This is purely circumstantial. We found no evidence linking the two deaths, Lady Ingalls, but for them to occur on successive days struck us as strange, and still does. On the other topic, yes, we would like to help Mrs Beardsley and her children, but you feel perhaps she is too distressed to cooperate with the authorities?"

Was he hoping to bribe information out of us? 'Tell us a bit more of what you know and maybe we could help with the children'? Perhaps that was being unfair. I was wondering how to respond when Val spoke up.

"Well, she certainly needs help with her children, but she insists she'll have no contact with the police. She might be frightened of you. She may be convinced her husband's fall was an IRA assassination, and if she went to the police, the IRA might find out and act against her. This is pure speculation, and after all this time it seems most unlikely. But we know some people suspected an IRA connection at the time, even though the facts of Mr Beardsley's fall seem to rule it out. So this is no more than a guess. I would be most unhappy if the police approached her while she is thinking like that. I have no idea whether she has any information to throw further light on Guy's accident. I suppose, since I have to accept that Will was helping the IRA, or one of those groups, she might feel under duress to remain silent."

Both policemen nodded, with obvious interest in these comments. I wished we could dispense with the IRA connection once and for all. I tried a different approach. "Is there any official body who could help, other than the police?"

The sergeant took this up. "What's her financial position? Does she have enough for the family?"

"Yes, she has a pension. Not lavish, but they were living decently in a rented house. She is still there."

"Then the Poor Law doesn't apply. There might be a charity able to help, but tracing people is not really what they do. That's our job."

The inspector nodded. "One reason I suggested this discussion bears on what we might be able to do to help her and her children. But there's also the blank in our understanding about the accident, or let us say the unexplained coincidence, if that makes sense. The two might just be connected. Or, at least, one might facilitate the other. At present, none of us is justified in cutting across Mrs Beardsley's position as parent. But if, as you suggest, she is either afraid of the IRA, or has some other involvement with them, it might be an opening. I realise that you think such an investigation is not needed, but it could help both us as police and her as parent."

My heart sank. I desperately wished I could add the recent information from Sid, since it was an entirely feasible cause for Guy's fall. I was withholding relevant information in discussing a death with policemen, and I felt very uncomfortable. But I relaxed as much as I could and put Sid to the back of my mind.

Indicating that he invited either of us to respond, and we hadn't, Anchorville continued. "Since those events, have you formed any further ideas as to whether Mr Beardsley's accident was in any way linked? Or any sense of what was going on. Sir William's note explained the basic issue, and that was corroborated by evidence. But the flight of Stephen Adams, and Mr Beardsley's fall, do not have immediate explanations. I still find the accident theory difficult to believe, although I fully accept the impracticability of sabotaging the rope he was sliding down."

This made me even more uncomfortable. I had some time ago wished Sid hadn't confided in me. But here of all places I must keep my promise. I had already convinced myself that Guy getting over-confident and careless was as feasible a cause of the accident as a row between Sid and Guy. It would not help the police to know which it was. But I was talking to professionals who, however friendly now, were used to talking with people who were withholding information.

But I did think I could contribute something useful. "We did get to hear, at least, the more senior people in our company did, that Stephen might have been an IRA activist in hiding, whose actual name was 'Seamus'. If so, he probably knew what was going on with ammunition during the war."

For Val's sake, I wanted to avoid the word 'smuggling'. But she butted in anyway: "The smuggling."

Anchorville saw the connection. "And Sir William's note told us that the IRA had, apparently, recently made contact with him again. That is, with Sir William."

"So I gather, and presumably Mr Adams, if an IRA man, might well have known about it."

"You're suggesting that a fatal accident made him think that either his own people or another organisation needed to neutralise Mr Beardsley, for whatever reason?"

"Possibly. If his immediate assumption was it must be murder, then he would think things were going seriously wrong. Time to get out. He left before he could have learnt any details beyond that Guy had fallen to his death. So maybe it was the initial report, in fact my ringing the office immediately after Guy fell, was enough to panic him."

Sergeant Bull entered the conversation again. "Do you think the assassination of Henry Wilson the previous week had anything to do with it?"

"Oh, that was—" I started, but Val was speaking.

"Yes, I've thought that for some time. William had gone to a motor-racing meeting the Saturday before. He came back feeling unwell with his heart, and I thought it was either the travel, since he went by train and stayed overnight at a hotel, or maybe was over-excited or even frightened by the racing. Perhaps a combination. It was unusual for a weekend trip to leave him so poorly. He spent the rest of that Sunday resting. We were also holding a small birthday party for him, which in retrospect probably didn't help. However, he seemed better the next day. He rode over to the office late morning and was having lunch nearby when the news came about the accident. I think he probably had a mild heart attack. Apparently, he almost fell off his chair. They brought him back by car in a terrible state. I wanted to send someone to get our doctor, but William insisted it wasn't necessary. I nearly did so behind his back.

"Although this sounds callous, it struck me that he was worried that the company's reputation would be hurt by a fatal accident. Wiz was the most precious thing to him. He must be given credit for it. He had the insights to set it up and make it a success. Guy was a fine worker, but not altogether pleasant as a person. William was not all that fond of him. But the company… Well, I suppose he felt about that just as a mother does about her children.

"Again, he was better in the morning. In fact, almost strangely calm. He insisted he didn't need looking after and that I should go out for my normal Tuesday morning engagements. How I wished now I had stayed with him.

"The shock started to wear off in time, and quite some time later I decided to reread his note. It struck me that his comment about republicans *'they've got onto me again*' could refer to something at the race meeting. It would be a good place, because it was the first time he had gone to that type of event and was just a person in a crowd. Easier to speak to him inconspicuously. That might be why he came home so ill. The Wilson killing not only showed how ruthless the IRA can be, but how powerful they are.

"It seems likely to me that since Guy had known about the smuggling he had blackmailed William into giving him special treatment in his work. Lilly, our office manager, told me once, privately, but I don't think she would mind my saying it, that she thought Guy had made the connection with the falsified manifests. And Guy certainly seemed to be able to bend some of the company rules. So the accident could have seemed to William to be another example of republicans getting rid of a threat. Someone who might reveal their plans. And they could reach into our operations and make a fall look like an accident. These things, all piling up in William's mind, could have been enough to tip him into extreme measures."

Val was a chatty sort of person in the right company, but that must have been an account prepared in advance. The two policemen nodded slowly to each other. There was a thoughtful silence for a while.

Anchorville responded. "We had tried to put two and two together, but what you have said sounds more likely to me." He turned to his sergeant. "Better than my theory, anyway?"

Another nod.

Sergeant Bull spoke up. "Did you know that a Seamus Adams was shot dead as he left Belfast docks coming off a Liverpool ferry late that Monday night?" I looked at Val with eyebrows raised. She nodded. So! She'd been told. I hadn't.

"He was from Ulster, and his family were living in Belfast."

"But does that mean he could have been set up? Was that anything to do with the accident?"

"It could be, but equally someone might just have recognised him in the docks and was suitable equipped to make the hit. There are many different groups in Belfast, and they tend not to love each other. It could have just been opportunism."

It was a lot to think about, but the general picture was starting to make sense, although I couldn't see where any of it would help either the police or Deidre's children. But there was still one aspect about that strange day I couldn't quite understand. As though reading my thoughts, a disturbing idea, the inspector pointed to it.

"Another thing, did you find out that it was Wiz ammunition in the assassination?"

"What, Adams?"

"No, sorry, Wilson."

Val and I looked at each other. No, neither of us had known that.

"I'm glad we managed to keep that under wraps."

"It's rather an unpleasant thought."

"It could have been ammunition stolen directly from the army, and just happened to be yours."

I think the inspector was also trying to avoid any direct reference to Will's smuggling, no doubt to spare Val's feelings. But the same information shed a ray of light in my mind.

"Ah, yes, that explains it."

"Why you were questioned the way you were?"

"It didn't make sense at the time."

"We had tipped off the Nottingham police, just in case anything correlated."

"We were arrested, sort of, on the Tuesday."

"Adams was traced to Liverpool docks during the Monday night. We were certain then that he hadn't got terminally lost between Nottingham and that village you were at."

"Normanton."

There was a pause. Val and I had quite a bit to reflect on. But true to his word, Anchorville brought the meeting around again to Deirdre's children.

"We never had a description from his mother, but we have identified Tom Beardsley. He is due to be released from Borstal fairly soon, and he will then be in considerable trouble with his old gang in Leicester. He needs help, and there are some things we can do, but it is essential that Mrs Beardsley cooperates with the Leicester police. She must be willing to talk to them. Her permission for any steps taken to rehabilitate the boy is essential. And if we can get the boy's cooperation, there is a good chance he could help us find Julie.

"So, many thanks indeed for coming here. This discussion has been most useful. We ask you now please talk to Mrs Beardsley. You can quote the relevant parts of this discussion if it will put her mind at rest. Best wishes to you both, and to Mrs Beardsley. And please give my regards to your Mr Baker as well. He was most helpful."

Sergeant Bull added, "Yes, thank you. We appreciate your concern for the junior Beardsleys."

Val and I took the train back to Nottingham. For much of the journey, we sat with our own thoughts. As we started to recognise the countryside near Nottingham, she said how glad she was to have been present at our talk. "It can't have been easy for you, Val."

"No, but it all happened, and we just have to live with it. In a way, I feel I still have something of William in being involved in the company. The best part of him too, I think."

"It was an achievement, starting from a horse-breeding family. And now you're keeping it going very much like he would."

"Thank you. But I feel so sorry for Deirdre. It's not our fault, but I can't help feeling guilty about her. We simply must find a way to get her involved with rescuing the children."

I was not convinced about the lack of guilt. If Will had been firmer about safety procedures with Guy, there wouldn't have been any sliding down ropes, and Guy would still be alive. But Will didn't risk leaning on Guy because he knew about the smuggling. It was all cause and effect. But at present Val was right, the best we can do is help Deirdre's wayward offspring. That meant she must be willing to talk to the police. Val and I now had some information which we hoped would alleviate her concerns about that.

Just before pulling into Nottingham, Val and I agreed that although Lilly was the closest of us to Deirdre, it would probably take more than a chat just between the two of them for her to overcome her reluctance to talk to the police. Would she agree to a meeting with the three of us—Lilly, Val and me? We could report on the police advice from London which should provide her with a more balanced picture. We thought it best first for Lilly to raise the idea with her. We agreed we should first discuss it with Lilly.

It was a Friday evening. On Monday, there were various things to attend to with the business. Val and I wanted to bring Anthony into the picture as well. He already did think WIS had a responsibility towards Deirdre and her family. Lilly was keen to help. We needed a meeting of the four of us, even if quite brief, to make sure we agreed on our approach. What with this and that, it was Wednesday afternoon before we could arrange our meeting. I started to feel more optimistic. Surely, we could make some progress if we moved carefully, and Deidre supported it.

It was all shattered that morning. Deidre's neighbour came to the office to speak to Lilly. After a few days hearing nothing from next door, she went round to see how she was, and getting no response from the front went round the back. It was not locked, so she went in and found Deidre in the hallway, hanging by the neck from the upstairs Newell post. The noose was made with a slipknot.

I found Lilly sitting at her desk with her head in her hands. I wanted to rage against the heavens. What was this curse on us? Why did the republicans approach Will just after the London assassination? Was it just happenstance, or policy? And the appalling fluke of timing when Sid kicked Guy's rope. A second earlier or later and Guy could have handled it. And now we had been just too slow, by perhaps only a few days, to start mending some of the harm, if only in a small way.

There was a note. The police had taken it, but the neighbour had already jotted it down. Before the neighbour left, Lilly typed it, so we could put a copy in Guy's file.

Deidre seems to have been influenced by what I think may be the truest basis for religion. Believers say their faith gives them comfort and strength, but is it really a sense of the divine, or just the security of being part of a group? Most church people I have known seem to treat it more as a respectable but essentially social club. And, of course, there are some, not many in Britain, but certainly further afield, who derive an intense sense of identity from their religion. Isn't there a better foundation for faith?

My guess is it's the instinct we seem to have, just an inner feeling, that surely, surely, there must be a better place somewhere? Not just a better *place*, but somewhere where *we* are better. Indeed, shouldn't there be a better *me* somewhere? It's a sentiment which can spring unexpectedly to mind at a funeral. Ok, you say to yourself, old so-and-so had a good life, and the cycle of birth and death is natural. And here we are, respectfully sending them on their way. And then we start thinking about what it all means, and before you know it your chin is wobbling and you're sniffing.

I think Deidre may have been influenced by something like this. Her note went to the coroner, who no doubt recorded that she took her own life while the balance of her mind was disturbed. It read:

'I've gone to look for Guy.
He must be somewhere.'

Coming soon…

Manifold

Milton Keynes UK
Ingram Content Group UK Ltd.
UKHW022013091024
449475UK00005B/86

9 781035 866786